W9-DEM-094

NAMED TO KIRKUS REVIEWS' BEST INDIE BOOKS OF 2014

"A word-drunk thickly allusive and poetic novel"

"Shallcross is a brave and witty piece of fiction."
BLUE INK REVIEWS

©2014 Charles Porter

Illustrated by Carol Way Wood, South Dartmouth, MA. Cover art by Gisela Pferdekamper, Loxahatchee FL. Cover design by Dane Wesolko Interior design and formatting by Dawn Von Strolley Grove.

All rights reserved. No part of this publication may be reproduced or transmitted in any form or by any means electronic or mechanical, including photocopy, recording, or any information storage and retrieval system, without permission in writing from both the copyright owner and the publisher.

www.charlesporterauthor.com

Library of Congress Cataloging-in-Publication Data
Porter, Charles

Library of Congress Control Number: 2015906952
Charles Porter, Loxahatchee, Florida

ISBN: 978-09-89-42-56-05

Printed in the United States of America.

SHALLCROSS

A NOVEL

Charles Porter

For Michael, my green-eyed son, my darlin'young one.

And to those people worldwide who belong to the Hearing Voices Network. The network was founded in 1991 under the auspices of Dr. Marius Romme and Sandra Escher of the Netherlands, and others who believe people who hear another voice and are considered schizophrenic should not all be treated as ill, nor are they always distressed.

A famous word palindrome:
You can cage a swallow, can't you,
but you can't swallow a cage, can you?

Glossary Prologue

Carburet or carburet it: A repeated expression used by the main character; to mix air with the fuel of a thought and explode it into comprehension.

Doo lang: Slang that suggests existential gist.

Palindrome: A word, verse, sentence (as "Do geese see god?"), or a number (as 1881) that reads or spells the same way backward or forward.

Pica: Medical term for swallowing unnatural material or objects.

Slip away: From the old R&B song title by Clarence Carter in 1968, meaning just that.

Tater: A neologism. When used as a noun, someone who is self-exalting; as a verb, tatering, or practicing self-exaltation.

Trazodone: Chemical name, Desyrel, approved by the Food and Drug Administration in 1982 to treat insomnia, depression, panic attacks, aggressive behavior, and mania; can cause excessive, colorful dreams.

***True* magazine:** A brand-name reference to the truth used by the main characters, based on the men's periodical published by Fawcett Publications from 1937 to 1974.

Foreword

The diagnosis of mental illness is painful to hear. However, study after study brings new opinions as to its nature and source. A popular paradigm circulating among psychiatric circles suggests the condition of hearing voices is not always pathological, and many high-functioning voice hearers do not come forward, nor do they tell anyone, for fear of being discriminated against or anathematized.

This story is about one of those people. This is *not* a story about paranormal powers, nor is it fantasy or magic realism. This fictional piece is taken from the real world, the scientific world, and the South Florida cultural landscape, except for my theory about the slippers who live on the neuronal roads and vast unknown spandrels of the brain. The reader does not have to believe in slippers…but I do.

All characters in this story are fictional.

Chapter 1

THE BLUE GOOSE

In Miami, a woman gripped the dresser with one hand. In her other, she held the cross at the end of a rosary between her legs while a red-haired man named Carlos stood naked behind her staring at the time and date written in lipstick on her back: 7:30 p.m., August 21, 1986.

Carlos saw a line of heat lightning outside to the north and looked down at the clock on the dresser to time his moment to the moment he thought she was ovulating. When the second hand was twenty away from what it said in the lipstick, he tried harder, bringing him as close to 7:30 as he could. The woman pulled slow on the cross, dragging the rosary bead by bead out of his body as he strained to recite a palindrome, "No, son! Onanism's a gross orgasm sin—a no-no, son."

One hundred miles up the coast, another man, Aubrey Shallcross, leaned over the sink in his bathroom and pulled on something, too—a sliver of meat between his teeth. When he was young with milk teeth, he was teased at swimming lessons over the dark moles on his body, so his devout Catholic grandmother told him a grandmother story to anneal his child confidence. She said the moles were the tops of angels' heads, guardian types, and he was especially lucky because most children have only one angel, but he had many, if you read the moles right.

The boy, Aubrey, chose a peppercorn-looking thing in his left armpit as his first-string seraph and secret friend, then in his mind, changed the mole into a three-inch-tall man in a three-piece suit like the one his father wore to Mass. He named the little man Triple Suiter. Unrelated to this, Aubrey went on to develop what Western society calls schizophrenia.

Now at forty-two, he had become a respectable business man in his small town and had learned to appear normal since grade school when he wanted to, even though he still heard and spoke to Triple Suiter and saw things other people did not. When he didn't want to be normal, he could be more than colorfully crazy around his close friends.

Tonight he'd eaten a sandwich, the kind you brush your grown-up teeth right after—olive loaf, that mess with lowercase green rings in it just one cut above head cheese. "Meatamucil," he called it in the mirror, his brushstrokes going up and down the way the dental lady shows you when you're nine. "You've got to do it right!" she'd say with her stink eye. "Up and down so it cleans between them, no lazy back and forth 'cause you miss the cracks, sonny."

Over time, this would become his onus, this back and forth to miss the cracks that tore down the runway of his hometown heart. Now the dental lady's ghost had him in the bathroom's true glass; toothpaste-spit strings threaded his lip-pop, "What? What?" he asked the mirror.

An hour later, his long blond body sat in The Blue Goose, a bar based on the short-sleeve shirt. On his left arm stood the little man, Triple Suiter, his hallucinated friend and slipper. On his right arm was a tattoo in copperplate gothic font, SERENOA REPENS, the binomial name for the scrub palmetto surrounding his town.

"Aubrey Shallcross!" a big man hollered from across the bar room on his way over to the table. Aubrey disconnected himself from Triple Suiter's hallucination on his arm, and the little man disappeared into his armpit.

"Looka here, The Junior," he hollered back. "Where you been, boy? Sit."

The Junior kicked out a chair, then leaned forward, mouth open all the way in to his bell tongue.

"What you gonna do now you sold your car binness to that Yankee man, Aubrey? Ain't the same at Shallcross Chrysler, anymore. Maybe you live on the goddamn golf course, or move somewhere a little more shee than this shitscape 'round here? Finished."

Aubrey conjured an imitation—a burlesque overdraft of an

abnormal he'd named Head Wound, who was no stranger to The Junior.

"I have a confounding doo lang my friend. Distemper lately of a pernicious kind. I see myself in a gin dream stalled at a four-way intersection and I be caught in the run out of a powerful slip away. That feeling something is either tryin to fill me out or fuck me over. Some angel there at the four-way stop, begging me to turn left, while a voice from hell says 'go straight on across, boy' for the rest of my recently slowed-down life."

"You drivin on across, crazy man, or you fixin to turn then?" The Junior asked him.

Aubrey swiveled in his chair to face his friend. "Straight over the four-way's the road to stag-damn-nation; turnin right takes me to golf and the brunch of old men. The Head Wound turns left with the angel on that crosspiece, doesn't he? For the gorgeous left pearls. Finished."

They stuck their hands into a plate of cracked conch so they could eat with their fingers. It was Florida-hot outside, and the AC blew cool air over the bar room.

"You know, Aubrey, speakin a crosses, four-ways, you see that bumper sticker on Punky's dump truck, 'Jesus Paid for Our Sins, Now Let's Get Our Money's Worth'? Awful thing to say 'bout C. Jay, ain't it?"

The Junior's face was as flat as a tollbooth worker's. Aubrey tried not to laugh, took a sip of his gin, jerked, and pushed the Bombay through his nose, head out, to miss his pants.

"Try 'n carburet that, The Junior," he said as he wiped his mouth. "Look at Punky over there. He's pressed zips through that bar stool for the record since the low eighties, so I'm not sure he's getting his money's worth for what Jesus did for him."

Only Aubrey, who loved the *The*, and a few childhood friends on the level of Punky and The Junior's family referred to him as "The Junior," but never in front of anyone outside the clutch. It was some honorific piece of inbred or well-bred custom from past generations separating The Juniors from The Seniors in old societies. The Junior was strict about everyone else calling him just Junior, especially girlfriends, and even if others knew about the pet article, they were afraid to chance it. He had a stop-sign face and was six-three, two-hundred-and-thirty-five pounds of fuck-you-runnin-white-boy if he needed to call on it.

Aubrey grew up on the south side of the St. Lucie River in the little town of Stuart, thirty miles north of Palm Beach, where a lot of the palmetto closer to the coast is bluish in color. The Junior came from the west side of the river, the county's ranch area, where only the pure-green palmetto grows. Aubrey had been to boarding school and a Catholic college, and liked to wander between redneck and the King's English. The Junior went to public school and Vietnam. Aubrey regretted never being in a war so he couldn't cross it off his jockstrap life list.

When they were kids, Aubrey would go home with The Junior and fell in love with the Florida cowboy life out in the west county's cattle country. When The Junior stayed in town at his friend's, they'd run the beach road called A1A with their blue-palmetto buddies and look for good surf and trouble. Florida can be styled that way with its coastal land—one day in the backcountry, working cattle in snap-button shirts; the next day fishing the Gulf Stream in a cotton tee with a bull dolphin stamped on the front. Bicameral worlds, bicameral minds for these children of the blue-and-green *Serenoa repens*, the palmetto god fronds that rule the woods there like saguaro cactus in Arizona.

"So what's work for you lately, The Junior?"

"I'm still in Indiantown with ole man Zarnitz. He's switchin over gradually from cattle to oranges like a lotta ranchers for the money bump, and I don't like it. But wait, that's the workin woes; here come the workin wonder. See that longhaired dime piece talking to those people by the bar? She's my new split-tail. She's ten womens rolled into one, and you better believe I'm the man-child what rolls into her in the still of the night doo lang slip away and all that other old music shit you like to listen to, Aubrey. Finished."

"Not anywhere near Punky, is she? I don't wanna look at him." Aubrey started to laugh again.

"C'mon, stop it." The Junior checked once more on his woman.

"Her could make me switch from cattle to goddamn oranges resta my life. She get any cow hunter to prowl fuckin fruit trees for a better livin. I shake when I touch that satchel. Know you know 'bout that, cooter man."

They were staring at the young woman's hair draped back when she wheeled around like a mental. The Junior waved, and Aubrey turned back to his glass of Bombay.

"Who is that?"

"Marla Sadacca," The Junior said reverently.

"I know the look. She's what a Frenchman might call a femme fatale. So run for your life and the lopsided limp."

"What's that mean, Frenchy?"

"Heartworms!" Aubrey smiled.

"Fuck you, and she ain't French. They Port-a-gees, or at least her folks are. But I see ya tryin to bird-dog my trim after all these years! Wondering how you could be her sledgehammer, 'stead a me."

"No, I don't sledge anymore. My age…gotta look out for thumper. She's some kinda horsehead, right?"

"Yeah, whole family is, but not cow horses like we grew up on, Aubrey."

"So what are they, shaky tails?"

"What's that?"

"Those five-gaited horses they used to ride to church in the old days, like drivin a Porsche when you wanted to make an impression."

"No, Aubrey," he said over the loud juke. "They kinda like those white horses, those Lip…Lip Panzos or—"

"Lipizzans! Bug fucker."

"Yeah, that's right. And another thing, Head Wound—her people wear those tight pants when they ride. You wear those pants into Indiantown or Okeechobee, a pickup load a numb nuts'd peg you for a funny boy, and run you bare ass all the way to Tampa. Finished."

"Funny boy?"

"You know what I mean, needle dick."

They got quiet. A drifty set their faces, and they stared over the

5

table at the old wood floor. Stiff drinks brought back what this floor meant to them. Dade County pine the local people called it, because Miami was the county seat here until 1909. The stuff was as hard as Rinker's concrete, taken from old-growth timber that flourished on the high ground among the wetlands and sloughs. Their parents and grandparents had danced on this floor, bending the two-by-ten stringers beneath the weight of the crowd as it shifted from clotted groups to single couples, flexing the joist so low it chased scorpions, brown recluses, and sting-back grampuses into ground holes while the music shot blood into everyone's face. Aubrey often heard The Junior announce, after a few vodkas, to the tourists and locals alike that he was conceived in the parking lot.

Stuck in that stare, bare feet spread over the spot each man had drawn a bead on, together their eyes rose slow, tracing the righteous skin and hyacinth blue dress to the rest of The Junior's dime piece, Marla Sadacca. She placed her shoes on the table next to Aubrey.

She knew they were talking about her. As he would come to know her, he'd realize these socio-dramas were part of a grave gestalt she wore—an oversized caste dot some adored her for, some criticized her for. The room always sundered into one of those categories when she made an entrance. Then there was the worldwide third category, the people who didn't move their eyes, lips, or haunches; they didn't sniff at anything much, even her, because they didn't give a shit, like Punky.

The Junior straight-armed a chair to the table. "Aubrey Shallcross, I'd like you to meet Marla Sadacca."

She remained standing. A tall blue water bird of some kind.

"My pleasure, Ms. Sadacca." A practiced radio voice had replaced his country English.

"I met you before with my ex-husband, Mr. Shallcross. We bought a truck from your Chrysler dealership. He's Tom Phillips."

"Well, he's the Anti-Chrysler now. He sold the place," The Junior said.

"I remember, Ms. Sadacca. It was a couple of years ago." Aubrey picked up her shoes and passed them under his nose, switching to his best forgery of Elvis. "I also remember your essence, and it's right in here emanatin from your itty-bitty sooties."

"What the hell's an itty-bitty sootie?" The Junior roared.

"Actually, they are what Elvis affectionately called his mother's small feet, The Junior. Now isn't that peculiar, boy...peculiarity," he said in a perfect radio voice again.

"Really, Mr. Shallcross?" breathed Marla.

"Yes, I read when he approached his mother's open casket at her funeral, he remarked through tears to one of his bodyguards, 'Oh, look at her itty-bitty sooties.'"

"Aw, come on, that's just you Head Wound talking again, Shallcross." The Junior shook his own head.

"No, that's correct information, son, right out of the handable, standable *True* magazine. Finished."

Marla raised an eyebrow and her left foot for Aubrey to place the shoe on her own long-toed sootie. He obliged with slow, sensitive hands, and held out the other shoe, but she took it and handed it to The Junior, then lifted a defined leg onto the table and hiked her blue dress to mid-thigh. Everyone in the bar fell into one of the two aforementioned categories, and the minor third—the don't-see-it, don't-give-a-shit led by Punky, who really wasn't leading because he didn't give a shit about leading anything, either. Aubrey smiled at how well she worked two men, not to mention the rest of the room. She took her place at the table, and The Junior went to the bar to retrieve her drink.

"My friend Junior tells me you ride horses, Marla."

"All my life I have spent with horses. I was taught by the best," she said, like you couldn't touch that.

"What exactly do you do with them?"

"I can do anything with my horses, but my true passion is the European art of dressage. Have you heard of it, Mr. Shallcross?"

"I must say I haven't." *Calling me Mister?*

"My parents are having a small family get-together this weekend. Why don't you join Junior and me, and I'll show you what I do with my horses. And here's my Junior now. Mr. Shallcross will join us this Saturday. Won't that be fun?"

The Junior nodded, and with that, she announced she had to drive to West Palm Beach in the morning and should leave. "Shall we pick you up around ten on Saturday? Junior's told me so much about your unique house."

"Okay, ten o'clock. Night, Junior. Good see'n ya."

Marla headed for the door. The Junior hesitated. "Don't be gettin any ideas bout bird-doggin me outta this lady, Aubrey. That's my splittail, my full-grown baby doll. I'd go to the groves for her, so you watch you ass."

"Yes, your baby doll."

"What the hell? I'm same age as you. She twenty-five or six."

"Well, you're a better cowboy than me in your forties, Scooter. Carburet it?"

"That's right, I carburet it, Anti-Chrysler. See ya Saturday."

Aubrey grinned and caught Marla's tall shape—a Great Blue Heroness walking slow in the water through the room in her Blue Heron dress, milking it for all the aforementioned categories.

Back in his seat, he nursed his Bombay Sapphire with tonic support and a dollop of Cointreau, his usual, unless he was feeling mental, and then he'd drink sidecars, a brandy-based cocktail. A few people said hello to him as they passed his table. Most in the town liked him, not easy for a car dealer.

The bar, an old Florida saloon, was one of his favorites. His Anglo eyes moved across the pecky cypress down the wall to gator hides and taxidermy: raccoons, sailfish, foxes, birds, rattlesnakes, and a single bobcat. Eight-by-ten, black-and-white photos from the Fifties were on another wall, everyone wearing Eisenhower khakis and Hawaiian shirts. Some manling at the next table reached up and stuck his bird finger in the anus of a gator hide while his cutie flailed her napkin and giggled into her Singapore sling.

The town was called Jensen Beach—an old shrine still intact on the Indian River after the land booms. It sat on the mainland across the water from Hutchinson Island, a barrier island with a well-known surf break called Hibiscus Beach, or just High Beach to the surfers, tokers, and working blue-palmetto crowd riding the breeze off the Gulf Stream in their cheap chairs after five with whatever it took in their hand to slip away.

A commotion swerved the sound in the room. A man apparently had choked, and someone was attempting what they could remember of the Heimlich maneuver. Aubrey felt nausea and a familiar chill, then heard his private alarm go off in its single line, Red's wrong! Flame vine!

He headed for the door as the Hamilton Beach screamed into another batch of icky-sweet tourist drinks. When he looked back, the clogged-up man was twitching on the floor.

The hostess nodded him out into the black, brackish night.

He walked in the direction of his truck along the seawall. The snook were balling the mullet between the wall and the jetty—water wolves, the locals called them, rocketing into the bait like depth charges swallowing fish. He knew he wasn't going to get away with this. It was still thirty yards to the truck. The parking lot started to stick to his feet, and the choking man was conjuring something Aubrey thought he was free of years ago.

A streetlight split and broke loose in his eyes; he felt himself starting to crater.

"Nothin's there, Nell Kitching," a voice said.

The evil thing had left its house with Aubrey's head, blown off by a long-story bullet. A rogue slipper, a bad passenger called the Slim Hand, who lived in Aubrey's mind, was choking him to death on a copy of the Hamilton Beach blender.

He tried to support himself on the seawall and still heard the blender in the bar, loud as the slaughter of mullet out in the water. He saw an X-ray of the steel mixer stuck in his esophagus, telling him his old pica had returned—the imagined objects, the crazy boluses sometimes as big as a sink or bathtub, shirt-bursting, psycho-generated terrors caught in his chest after the evil Slim Hand had shoved them down his throat below his glottal stop. And even though any one of them was too large and absurd to be there in real time, or any time, they were very real to Aubrey on bad time.

The little man, Triple Suiter, his hallucinated friend and slipper, jumped out of Aubrey's armpit and screamed, "Look out! He's coming!"

Aubrey's body jerked down the seawall on its way to catatonia. Flank-muscle curtains slid open behind his eyes, and a florid show of terrifying trope lit up the big room inside his skull. Red men shoved hooks on wires through the bones of his hands and hoisted him into the air, arms out, like one of the last looks at Jesus. Red's wrong and he knew it, as he rose to the top of his skull in the deltoid hell of the gymnast's cross.

In the shape of all skin-jacket agony, he hung there like A Man Called Horse in a place he called the Blind Spot Cathedral. Above him was a door of spooling keloid scar turning like the gas from one of Punky's farts through the bar stool, augering its way out to a starry universe Aubrey couldn't see since he had staged a walkout years ago on the God who fathered his old Christ.

Where were the secular people and their search parties, the triage for Christians who had recently dispossessed themselves of religion, and why weren't they looking for him, this blue-coastal palmetto boy caught in the Slim Hand's guerilla theater tonight? "Because the fit is bullshit!" he screamed inside his head.

Triple Suiter wore his meanest face and started chanting their sacred rhyme from Aubrey's childhood at the Slim Hand:

WHEN YOU CAN'T SEE, TAKE A STRAIGHT SHOT

RIGHT THROUGH THE HEART OF THE BLIND SPOT.

TRUE MAGAZINE KNOWS THE TRUTH.

RIGHTY-TIGHTY, LEFTY-LOOSE!

The seizure soon lost its *Pentothal.* Silver foil things flipped around beside him. Two mullet had jackknifed over the jetty to escape the killing snook, heaving their gills like drowners, getting right in his face.

"More suffocates," he mumbled.

Triple Suiter flew out of Aubrey's armpit down to the forearm—

they both dripped from the struggle and heat. Red lights on an ambulance spun near the Blue Goose, and Aubrey thought they were there for him, but a stretcher appeared with a large mound under a sheet and a hysterical woman running behind. He remembered now: the other choker in the bar.

They sat quiet. He and Trip had lived a long time with this and always pushed away outside help that might intrude on their world. But he was beginning to wonder if Heimlich himself, the man who could pop the chock out of anyone, shouldn't crack his back and shoot him through the keloid scar out to the lone universe or the supernal heaven he was raised on, whichever turned out to be the truth.

He rose from a squat and breathed deeply to stabilize his blood pressure, then walked the rest of the way to his truck. Nobody saw it—one of his biggest concerns. There had been a girlfriend who was epileptic; she could deal with it, so why couldn't he? Yet a brutal psycho sore it was, worse than an obvious broken body part that drew sympathy every day, and he felt butchered that this old coinage of his brain had shown again after all these years.

He cranked his truck and eased through town onto U.S. 1 toward his place.

The tiny Triple Suiter slid back out onto Aubrey's arm to talk. "Good lord, Mrs. Calabash, how did that hangnail show up? But you, you have to help me with this tetanus of yours, Head Wound, this snuff skit you conjure. The brain in here where I'm from is as large as your whole world out there, and you can't expect me to find this Slim Hand son of a bitch and kill him without your assistance. You need some balance back in your life, Aubrey, some gravitas. Or you do something major on your own about this throatlatch crap. I'm serious."

"It was that choker in the Blue Goose, goddammit, Trip."

"No, it's this cold front you're running. No preoccupation with work to distract you, irrational fears I've tried to talk you out of for years with my best Cartesian tools. That saprophytic slipper waits for these moments when you're stressed on dead time and the cosmoramic doo lang you ponder. 'Nothin's there, Nell Kitching,'" Trip said sarcastically. "I heard the Slim Hand say that to you right before you went down. Some of your favorite fettles on the God thing have jacked their boxes again, and the slipper's even using poor Nell now."

"Maybe. Aw, shit, what's this?'

Cop lights. He slowed to join the car line, trying to see the wreck ahead. When it was his turn, he saw a dump truck had run in and out of the ditch, then flipped into the pines on the other side. They stopped the traffic for a moment, and two belly-up words on the truck's bumper were readable: *Jesus* and *Paid*. He pulled onto the shoulder and walked back.

"Is that who I think it is, Morgan?" he asked the deputy.

"Yeah, it's Punky. Got thrown out of the truck. Damn thing rolled on him. Killed him."

"God a mighty. That him under the tarp?"

"Shame, ain't it? He got kids, right?"

"Uh, he does…did."

"I know 'im since I was a boy like you, Aubrey."

"Yes. Hope he got his money's worth."

"What?"

"Nothing. Nothing."

On the way back to his truck, his eyes started to water, and he was sick to his stomach. He turned to the woods where the ten-wheeler lay on its side. The tow workers' floodlights were bleeding out into palmettos and myrtles, and there they both were in a grand hallucination, Punky and Jesus, standing chest high in the scrub. Punky was smiling and reenacting the rollover with his hands to show Jesus how it started, then he threw his arms out to demonstrate getting thrown from the truck. Jesus was jumping up and down like a Masai in a blood dance, his head tilted back with a wrong-looking grin. Punky grabbed his chest over what seemed like his heart's last beat and sank into the scrub. Jesus looked down, still smiling and jumping.

"Oh, yeah, he got his money's worth, and so did I," Aubrey heard Jesus say. Then a loud, "Times up!" from the only child they call "the truth and the light" echoed through the woods.

Had to get home, and he was upstairs in ten minutes, sitting on the side of the bed, trying to make himself cry again—give it something more than he thought it deserved. He took two trazodones for sleep and spoke to the bedroom wall and the homunculus creature in his armpit, blowing on the rage of a hemorrhagic rant.

"What a fuckin beauty, Trip—rollin the thing over on him. Who got his money's worth out there tonight? Your Jesus, right? Bought that ticket to see Punky go under that hunk o' shit to get his own goddamn money's worth, didn't he? Same Jesus who got flush with the flesh and the old man, then cleared the check Abraham wrote. Paid 'em all off—Abe, Punky, and the maggots—to get back upstairs to the good seats. Unholy motherfucker!" Trip blanched inside the armpit, but kept quiet.

"Fourth quarter for me, son, my own slip away," Aubrey quipped.

"Fourth quarter? Did I say that? Run for your life, you bubba piece a— I'm not some save-the-tiger dickhead. I'm not like The Junior, tryin to be as young as the woman he feels, or some spleeny old man, am I, Trip?" He stared hard at the dry wall to make it atomize and chewed on the inside of his cheek to distract his pounding head.

"'Paid for Our Sins, Now Let's Get Our Money's Worth'? What the hell is it supposed to mean? The long party? The warning? Pay for your sins so Jesus gets his money's worth—that's on C. Jay's truck so he can sell tickets! That God kid ran up that hill with that crosspiece on his back to get out of this murder factory...chicken shit suicide!"

"No, not suicide! Not chicken shit! And what's got you coming on so Jesus since you think he was just another swinging dick, anyway, Aubrey?" The vocabular natty dresser, Triple Suiter, was out of the armpit again, down the bicep to Aubrey's forearm, in a baseball slide with his signature stand-up stop. "And here we go again with this Jesus smoke of yours because you want to decoct that bumper sticker. And here we go, after years with no swallow spook around until the Goose parking lot tonight. You've gotten too slim on me, Head Wound. You go hunting upstairs in the house of yours alone in bad company, like your hero, Ambrose Bierce. Finished. No! Not finished!

"Look, it's not so much the absolved sin thing, Aubrey, this crucifixion. He just wanted to set an example for you to follow your conscience like he did and die for that conscience, if you have to, but with a warning: You better not violate whatever the decision turns out to be, even if you pick the Rosicrucians and dance at their chemical wedding. He doesn't care if you choose that to save your soul and butt, instead of him, if your heart is in it. He just doesn't want it to be some stupid, conjured nihilism like you get into, and neither do I."

Aubrey didn't answer. Stared harder at the dead air space behind the drywall, the place he wanted to hide when the bad slipper with the blackout dome gear came to suit him up for the next flying snuff skit. Hammocked in there, safe between the wood studs and sheetrock, drawing a tollbooth-worker blank like The Junior when he drifts off to God-knows-redneck where.

"Better not deny it, Aubrey, 'cause it can get spooky out here without your old God or something else you've chosen to give you a high colonic when the whittle monster gets too close to your air puck," Trip scolded.

"Air puck?"

"Yeah, air puck, Aubrey, and don't think I don't find it interesting to be part of your life. I mean, brother, you're a short-listed, pyro stump-jumper." Trip managed a grin. "And I'd love to stay up and overwhelm you with my confutations on this doo lang you brood over, but I'm going to bed, and so should you. I'm falling off my hanger from the Hamilton Beach thing tonight. I want you to quit obsessing about this fourth-quarter stuff. Don't you know everybody who's getting old has to go through it?"

"Oh, right. Easy for you to say, midget fuckin immortal!"

Trip walked up Aubrey's arm muscle, turned halfway, and waved in the spotlight Aubrey always threw on him. Then the voice and visage so dear to his psyche slipped through the skin crease to the armpit and his second home outside Aubrey's brain. There, Trip called on his own slipper, the tiny Amper Sand, who lived in Trip's sternum and didn't speak. To communicate, Amper Sand typed backward letters on Trip's chest in a version of the same Copperplate Gothic font tattooed on Aubrey's arm to be read in a mirror.

Trip stood before his reflection, shirt open. His tiny slipper sat cross-legged inside the bone bowl of his chest with an old Underwood on his lap. The metal-lettered type arms transcribed themselves onto Trip's hide with a pleasant sting:

THE HEAD WOUND IS A MOODY CHILD
A GIFT OF TONGUES, HIS FACE IS WILD
RED MEN SCREAM, HOLD 'EM BACK;
REDHEADED THUGS...MANIACS.
THE ONES THEY SAVE
ARE THE ONES THAT PAY. TICKETS!
FINISHED. &

"I know, Amp, always for tickets!" Trip said.

"&?" Amper Sand typed.

"And I might bring it up again later. The bumper sticker's going to put me back to work with the Catholics and the Slim Hand again, just when things had smoothed out. But maybe it's good so I don't get too slim myself."

Amper Sand had seen something written on a clothes dryer, and he hit the keys again in a Jerry Lee Lewis flurry:

CAREFUL! BE SURE THE UNIT HAS
STOPPED SPINNING BEFORE REACHING
IN.

"Yes, I will. Promise, Amp." Trip flicked off his light.

In another bedroom across town, The Junior and Marla undressed.

"You know, honey, when we pick up Aubrey on Saturday, I just wanna tell you, the boy ain't exactly right." The Junior shook his head. "I mean that place a-his weirds people plenty, and so does he when he turns his head around backward and gets to talkin.""

"Can't wait," she said.

The Junior poured himself another drink. He hated competing with Aubrey.

She touched him there when she wanted sex, and now she followed him into the bathroom to watch him stick two safety pins through his scrotum the way a certain hooker in Vietnam had taught him. The Junior liked the burn from those little wounds while he mashed bosoms and broke beds. He positioned two pillows under the siren satchel he had told Aubrey about earlier.

She yelled his name.

Aubrey lay in his own bed thinking about the awful events of the evening, his head turned to the screening. The sliding-glass doors were pushed to one end so he could look out to the southeast night from the second floor. Those doors were always open because he hated air-conditioning.

"Air puck," he mumbled over the pillow and forced a grin, mulling Trip's use of those words. He was kind of sorry he had remarked about Punky's life on the bar stool to The Junior. *Sed libera nos a malo* from his Catholicism puffed out in skywriting. He loathed the chronic Roman doxology he still trucked, but petitioned a Hail Mary for Punky, anyway, and said, "Requiem in pace," because he couldn't help any of it.

Off in the dark sky, past the barrier island, the heat lightning torched the cotton thunderheads over the Gulf Stream, and Aubrey stared at the wonder as if he was witched. The two trazodone pills he took were getting him there.

He moved into his head, where the visuals popped light strikes in his own cotton. One showed Punky and Jesus rolling over and over in the cab of the dump truck, laughing like two cretin mummers. The hollow wall voices came to him from his congenitally split mind, "Pick a film, Aubrey, any film."

"*Two-Lane Black-top*," he whispered, half awake. "James Taylor." This pleased Trip inside the armpit.

"Yes, Aubrey," the voices said.

He slid into a sleep and went down to the Trazodone Lounge, got into that fast Chevy with sweet baby James, and James turned left at the four-way downtown that haunted Aubrey. They drove east in his dream toward the heat lightning out over High Beach. The great waves that only break left from the northeast swells were rolling in— the gorgeous left pearls.

~

In Miami, the red-haired man named Carlos, from the beginning of this story, drove, too—across the Venetian Causeway. He had one more ovulating woman he was paying. He wanted his dead daughter back from the world of spirits the juju way, by bringing her soul into someone else. This man, gone wrong and unredeemable, who believed in that kind of xxx voodoo smack.

Chapter 2

AUBREY'S HOUSE

The Junior's girlfriend, Marla Sadacca, moved here ten years ago with her family to escape the seeping population of Miami, where her father stabled his horses. The little town of Stuart on the St. Lucie River, just south of Jensen Beach, was one whose economy circled slowly around retirees, flower farms, cattle, citrus, and the game fish-loaded Gulf Stream five miles out from the breakers off High Beach. Marla was sixteen and didn't want to leave Miami, but where the family's horses went, she went, because nothing in this world would interfere with the votive obsession she was raised on: riding in the esoteric, moneyed world of elite, competitive dressage.

When she did venture out in the evenings to places like the Blue Goose, the ladysmiths lined up, and she rode that, too, which not only fed her interest in drama and exhibitionism, but a bone-deep detachment and solitude she doctored with her own dental lady in the mirror before bed every night, like Aubrey did.

The bar room always fell into one of the aforementioned categories when she made an entrance. The men on the make, an occasional polo shirt, and unshaven Nick Noltes, not famous, funny, or moneyed, rolled their drinks and coke lines in the bathroom to run their best lip. And Punky used to do his lines, too, staring at the lines of liquor bottles behind the bar until the colors ran together in an abstract light piece that amazed his dump truck eyes, while outside, the night sky moved another inch around his functional dipsomania and big garbage can coons shit palmetto berries on the wood steps behind the bar because they hated the place for making them live off the trash.

As the story goes with most searchers, she soon met a man she thought she was in love with and married. It was either real love, or as someone once said, "It was so cold I almost got married." Only

Marla really did. Her husband's old-school daddy told him it was okay for gentlemen to have paramours as long as they were discreet and respectful of their wives. It was bad advice.

She followed him three months later to a doublewide and caught him doing the walls of a woman. Rumor had it Marla kissed the frightened lover on the lips and thanked her for the light while her legal stuttered a stupid contrition on his knees.

Thunge! went the judge's gavel. "The marriage is irretrievably broken," and the Blue Heroness walked slow from the courtroom, like she did from a bar room, dropped the pain and papers in the trash, then headed home to sit a horse and forget about it.

She met The Junior soon after. He became her hell-raising friend, her loyal friend, and desperately-in-love fuck buddy. They were dangerous valentines together, plenty fresh with handgun tempers. Still, despite her image as warm ice, her heart was a heart: hot chambers, cold chambers, like all of us. She would kill for him in one but not in the other—the one that pumps Freon to lead-lined ambition.

~

A half-mile down the shell-rock road to Aubrey's, the house would show, disappear, then skip like a Forbes balloon through the filigree of Australian pine running with the ditch. The Junior turned into an open field, and there it was, a clear view of the wood landship Aubrey Shallcross considered asylum. A large parallelogram dropped from the sky on one sharp end with pine poles jutting through roof and two and half stories like king post in a triangular wood sandwich. An unplanned look of creation— something psuedopodic from the plant kingdom, made of glass, tin, and plank, staked out not moving, but you thought it could if you turned your back on it. There was a silo tower within the tectonics that reared taller than the house, and a stained-glass eye in its top looked over a hundred acres. A pool and guesthouse were to the right of the main residence.

Aubrey was drinking coffee in his living room when he saw The Junior's truck drive through the gate.

"Hello, Junior! *Bom dia,* Ms. Sadacca!" he hollered the only Portuguese he knew from the porch of his backwoods argosy. "Too bad 'bout Punky getttin rolled on like that." He looked down sad and toed the wood deck. "I saw the bumper sticker when I went by. Remember, Junior? Told you that when I called."

"What bumper sticker?" Marla asked.

"Punky had one on his truck, 'Jesus Paid for Our Sins, Now Let's Get Our Money's Worth.'" Aubrey winked.

She prinked a careful smile. "Oh, is it supposed to be funny or profound? Anyway, who designed this house?"

"He did, but I'm the one named it O'gram, on account of its shape, you know," The Junior said, trying to get a head start on Aubrey. "It's a stood-up-looking parallel o'gram, like from geometry. 'Course that gram thing went over big when everyone was all over the devil's dandruff back then."

The Junior took her hand under the living room's vaulted ceiling and walked to a bank of light switches. The glass walls on the sides of the room lit up like department store windows—beautiful dioramas of displays protecting taxidermy and mannequins—manifestations of Aubrey's mental favorites he called jars, bred into his life by a girl who sat next to him in the seventh grade named Nell Kitching. Nell kept a Ball jar on her desk, and told Aubrey the cricket inside talked to her and helped her make any object she imagined. All day long, she sat with the cricket, convolving strange, munificent shapes until they yanked her out of class to prod and dose, forcing her deeper into what the blood test croakers called juvenile dementia praecox. Aubrey created an imaginary jar after that, and it became his great carburetor of unworldly objects, fantasies, and distally sheared skits he'd take to the big room inside his head to cavort and have his way with.

"What you say, honey? Bet you never saw anything like this before." The Junior squeezed her shoulder.

"Well, no, not in a house, and I never saw a round slide coming down from an upstairs. Looks like the McDonald's slide," she whispered.

SHALLCROSS

"I tell ya, Aubrey used to send me out here with these corporate types. Those folks felt safe at this hideout, smokin rope all horn colic-y with the local girls. Know what my momma used to say? 'Baptists are like cats; they raise hell, but you can't catch 'em at it.'" He laughed at his joke. "And I call Aubrey the Anti-Chrysler, mostly because I thought he never shoulda done that car binness thing with his life. Shoulda been a' art boy, a actor, or didn't I tell you he could sing like Sam Cooke and Jesse Colin Young? But he's crazy as hell. Finished."

"Thanks, Junior. Now Ms. Sadacca is convinced I could be the Anti-Chrysler after your impressions of me hypnotizing customers with dope and women in my little home."

The Junior frowned.

"Oh, come on, Mr. Shallcross. I haven't exactly led a sheltered life. This place of yours, would you give me the tour?"

They walked along the glassed-in displays. A male mannequin wearing a white shirt, white suspender trousers, a large plaster-of-Paris jockstrap on the outside of its pants, and a bowler on its head was in the first window.

The figure sported one heavily made-up eye and eyeball cufflinks.

"I know who this is. Who is this?" Marla asked. But she was twenty-six, and this was 1986.

Aubrey stopped, roboted his arm, and inserted his pointer finger into a small, triangular piece of sheepskin on the wall that looked female. The room shook with Ludwig the German's historic music. He moved his hand back to the V of hair after ten seconds, and the music stopped.

"What is that evil-looking thing?"

"He's the evil in all of us, Ms. Sadacca. That's Little Alex, little *A Clockwork Orange* Alex from Anthony Burgess's book and Kubrick's film. It's from another time in my life, 1972. But I see he's starting to resurface again in the mall, so he might have to get outta this house. I don't need to get camp because he's so big at Spencer's now."

"I remember my sister had the video, and it scared me," Marla said.

"It even scared the grownups. I never got over the country visit he and his droogs paid on the married couple. Haunted me. I was young and recently married, and very protective of her handsome sight. Always checking the locks, afraid he was coming to these woods to violate her in front of me. And at the time, there were killings around here by this guy they called the Tin Snip Killer. I know you've heard of him, Ms. Sadacca. I was fascinated with Alex's character, though. I even wore the outfit on Halloween, but now when I see him there, full of rote larceny and testes, his pop sociopathic mind cooking off some sick reduction, I wonder why I was so taken with him. I think it had to do with sleep deprivation and my own testes at the time."

"What you mean 'taken'?" The Junior asked him.

"I mean he wasn't one hundred percent disgusting, like our Tin Snip Killer was. Anyway, I read those serials sleep well after they've acted out, like murder or rape is their favorite receptacle for anxiety. Truth was, I just wanted the good sleep part; I don't have the stomach for the other two." Aubrey winked at Marla

"My mother says there are two kinds of crazy: the ones who can sleep at night and the ones who can't," Marla said.

"I had another guy stuck in my teeth back then to balance the little Alex thing—Holden Caulfield. Ole catch-em-runnin-through-groin-high-rye-self-exalting Holden. I wanted to save everybody, when I wasn't murdering them; that was the other half of the hormone-machine shop I dealt with in my twenties."

"Well, I would like to see the rest of this place, Mr. Shallcross. Do you have a Holden Caulfield exhibit?"

"No, no, I really wanted one, but you know that new book of Norman Mailer's, *Tough Guys Don't Dance*, even though I bet they're dying, too? Well, tough guys don't have Caulfield exhibits, either. Nobody in the mall with that T-shirt really knows the good shit about *Catcher in the Rye* or what a clockwork orange means."

"What does a clockwork orange mean?"

"Something biological that appears mechanical. And as far as Holden goes, I thought he was just another Tater man. Anyway, that's not who I really wanted to be."

"What's a Tater man?"

"Uh, self-exal Tater, Ms. Sadacca, but the subject is a long layout for now."

"So who did you want to be?"

"This guy." He walked her around the circular slide to another display.

"*Que es esto?*"

"Johnny Yuma. The Rebel!"

"I don't know him."

"Johnny Yumaaah was a rebel," The Junior sang off-key in a low-spirited bass, like Johnny Cash on the old TV show every week.

"Yes, Johnny Yuma, a tragic hero and loner," Aubrey said, getting like The Junior warned he could, a little crazy. "A Shane who drifted around the West on the ABC Pictures movie lot in the fifties."

"What's a Shane?"

"Later, Ms. Sadacca. I respect the fact you're young, and Shane's another long layout for now, like a Tater man."

"Yes, Johnny, Johnny," he said, imitating his man Head Wound again now. "I can still see him on TV, in the museum of my family home. He was the real McCoy in that old Confederate hat he wore, Ms. Sadacca. Not the usual cowboy star, like Gene or Paladin. He always looked ragtag and hangdog, and the light never bounced off the bridle or his face like those other over-tacked macaronis. The night scenes looked all wrong, filmed during the day in black and white, then dimmed to twenty-watt by a technician. And Johnny's face and eyes weren't right; they were dimmer-switch eyes, twenty-watt…pitiful.

"I really wanted to be him when I was a kid, and I wanted to be pitiful. Pitiful to my parents when I needed attention, and pitiful to my girlfriends so I could get something. And I was more pitiful later, in my aggressive thirties, because I wanted to be Michael 'The Godfather' Corleone, but that was an embarrassing pitiful. No, it was Johnny, in my home mirrors, who had me most dressed out in the slim light of the slimerater."

"Slimerater?" Marla frowned.

"Yes, a dimming device that can slim something down to the real of it, Ms. Sadacca. Strip you inside a Ball jar naked as that naked lunch so they can read the tiny numbers on your body parts."

"I see, but there must be more to your hero than looking pitiful."

"Oh sure, he was a certified saver. He would do wonderful things. Save the kids in the sneaky rye before they fell off the cliff into a kitchen disposal, not like that damn Holden, who just nerd-dreamed stuff like that. Tater stuff, you know, and then Johnny would leave town the next day to avoid applause. He knew about self-exaltation and Taters, Ms. Sadacca; ruins every hero, and that's what tatering is: a whooping cough, a virile hubris of inner applause. And who knows? If it ever happened to Johnny, the film crew would make the sun spark off his gleets, and he'd sink in the eyes of the TV audience who knew how to act pitiful in the twenty-watt, so they can get somethin off you. Carburet it? Finished."

"Gleets?"

"Flying spit." He hung his head.

She laughed.

The Junior rested a hand on Aubrey's shoulder like he, too, was a member of some group of damaged people.

"This boy here goes off like a speed reader, don't he, Marla?" The Junior said.

"Oh, I thought it was just the everyday for you guys, *True* magazine, sweetie. Oh, and I carburet it, Junior." She crossed her eyes.

"Hey, you want something to drink? I gotta get out of these people, I do. Here I've just met Ms. Sadacca, and she's thinking she sure would hate to be sitting next to me on a train."

"Yeah, right, boyeh. I'll take me a beer."

"Just a glass of water, please."

In the kitchen, Aubrey thought about running his mouth too much. Trip slid out onto the left bicep from his armpit to go after him.

"Nice show in there. Let me commend you on your allegorical casting of good and evil, using Holden the righteous nerd opposite Little Alex the sociopath. You do the same dance every time to get to the new ones, don't you, Tater man?"

"Oh, you think it was my hen pecker talking in there."

"Well?"

"You're wrong, midget. She's twenty-six; I'm forty-two, and I'm not waking up in the morning with someone who feels too good—as in no osteoarthritis—and looks that much better than me. So leave me the fuck alone."

"One Tater, two Tater, three…" Trip cartwheeled back into Aubrey's armpit.

The Junior and Marla were looking at something much quieter than Little Alex's single billboard eye when Aubrey returned with the drinks: taxidermy.

"This is gorgeous, Mr. Shallcross. Where did you get these animals?"

"He gets 'em from a guy we call the Tax Man, and I don't mean the gov'ment, either, do I, Aubrey?"

"No, he's an artist. Don't look back, you know?"

"What?"

"Nothin. Mostly he considers himself a resurrectionist."

"I carburet that," Marla said.

"Hey, over here, honey. Pair a whooper cranes like we saw on the road comin in."

"These cranes were roadkills, Ms. Sadacca. Happens all the time. The Seminoles believe they are spirits of people who used to live on the ground underneath their flyovers. I might sound like a drama king, but I raise my arms when those majesties go by and bell their eerie cries right back at them, so they'll know I know who they are. Could be the great chief Billy Bowlegs just flew across my place. Leaves me helpless, helpless, helpless." He winked at The Junior.

"Oh, but Mr. Shallcross, I am becoming a great fan of your drama and helplessness."

"Let's go on outside and sit, Aubrey. These drinks gonna sweat out'n on us," The Junior said.

They moved to the deck by the pool. Another blue eye, like the one in the silo at the top of the house, was painted on the bottom of the deep end. The last of the morning air was barely around.

"You know, boyeh, the damn Blue Goose might be jinxed or something," The Junior said.

"What, you mean 'cause of Punky?"

"Well, yeah, and also 'cause of some other guy. This dude choked to death on his food in there same night."

Aubrey sat silent, but wanted to say he saw it, maybe tater and grandstand some more for Marla. He was about to describe the Heimlich stuff and take over the morning again when his stomach rolled and his left arm went numb, so he let The Junior talk.

"That guy had a piece of steak the size of a cigarette pack stuck in his chute 'cordin to Millie, who works the emergency room."

"No way. That big?" Marla yelled.

"Will you excuse me?" Aubrey stood. "I think I left something on."

The nerves were all over him by the time he tripped on the door threshold. Strides stumbled up the stairs to his bathroom mirror, where Trip appeared on his arm in case the Slim Hand tried to show.

"Listen to me, Aubrey," Trip said. "You know what to say to yourself, and it's self-talk that means everything here. Repeat! *Toro feces, veritas, toro feces, veritas.*"

Aubrey mouthed the words.

"That's right, boy," Trip said, turning up the coach. "Bullshit and truth, righty tighty, lefty loose, chicken salad and chicken, you know, the what's what, the great quid, the way of the world. There's only the *True* magazine, then righty tighty and lefty loose. The rest is for tickets and toro feces!"

Aubrey threw cold water on his face.

"You were okay for a minute, Tater boy." Trip was at him now. "Oh, just fine till The Junior mentioned the cigarette pack size of meat in the guy's throat."

"Enough! Can't take any more of your shots now, Tripper. Leave it alone and get off my ass. Fuckin slipper. Jesus twerp."

"Yeah, yeah, you and Jesus again, Aubrey." Trip walked up the arm to the armpit.

Aubrey sat on the end of his bed to calm his breathing, then stepped onto the balcony and looked down at his company. *Gotta blow this off somehow.* He could hear the song, "Smile, though your heart…"

Trip flew back out of the armpit down Aubrey's arm. "Jesus jumping roadkill crosses, not that song. It's so par and maudlin, Aubrey, and not so you with your platinum repertoire!"

"I know, I know, take it back. I want comic relief, the good feeling I had in front of Little Alex in the living room."

He stepped back inside to a closet of clothes and role-play getups from his past. A large papier-mâché crane's head leaned against the wall. He looked up and took down a long pair of celluloid wings, then reached for a gray cape with a short feathered-tail apparatus and white tie-on bib for his chest. On the bib was an illustration of the Hollywood RKO Pictures tower on top of the globe—the same one at the beginning of those old films beaming a pulse out to theaters worldwide, and to him since he was twelve and in love with the movies.

Aubrey put on the costume, slipped the wings on his arms, and pulled the beaked head over his, then exited the closet to the full-length mirror. Once again, he was the RKO Crane Man of Jensen Beach, Florida.

He walked onto the balcony in the sliding stride of the great bird, spreading his fake-feathered fronds and shrieking the famous meta-bleat of the surreal flier. Marla jumped into The Junior's lap. The Junior let out a holler and did the best he could of his own whooper shriek, considering his bass-chord voice.

Aubrey pumped his wing props in big harrier strokes, slow and even, and looked down on them like one of those angels in America.

~

In Miami, in another house, a man shook. The issue was money and what it would cost him for stealing from Carlos. Carlos put a bullet through the man's nose on his way back from the bathroom, then poured the murdered's expensive bourbon and fell asleep on the nice sofa. The sleep Aubrey talked about. The post-homicide sleep. The one the specials considered a great receptacle for anxiety.

Chapter 3

LUNCH AT THE SADACCAS'

The three turned out of Aubrey's onto U.S. 1 on their way to Marla's parents and passed the spot between the mile markers where Punky left his pendant redneck world. The world he thought was paid for by Jesus so he could enjoy life with his family, dump truck, and the bar stool signed by his rectal fitting in the Blue Goose.

Things were night and day to Punky. No ontology grinders or personal beefs blocked the way for his Lord to explode his ticket that night on U.S. 1. No prayers or appeals to delay his country swan song as he was crushed in the dry steel and upholstery of his ten-ton truck. Anything for the Carpenter, carburet it. At least, it's what Aubrey and The Junior thought the bumper sticker might have meant to him. And to make themselves feel better, they decided Punky told C. Jay he felt like he got his money's worth, even though he was on the small tour—he was only forty-two.

Off the shoulder stood a roadkill cross surrounded by wreaths and a sign: "We Miss You, Daddy."

"Kinda cuts a trench through ya, don't it?" The Junior stared. "Hard to imagine Punky's gone, really feenished. You think we may hear the Nineteen Ghost again before we die, Aubrey?"

"No, probably never."

"Who's the Nineteen Ghost?" Marla asked.

"Some trucker we heard talking on Channel Nineteen way back, honey. You know, the CB radio."

"He had an all-South baritone voice," Aubrey said. "And his subjects? I'd say...transcendental trucker stuff, wouldn't you, Junior? He never passed on general information, only road wisdom to the other drivers. I used to wonder if he was just out in the air somewhere, instead of on the actual road. When he got to the end of what he'd say, he'd use the word *finished* or *feenished*. That was his novel property, his way to say 'Stop!' like the old telegrams. I never heard anyone do that, and Junior and I have imitated him ever since."

Asante Sadacca happened to be standing by the farm's wrought-iron gate when the wide-eyed bunch turned into the driveway.

"There's my Papa," Marla said. The Papa flashed a white-toothed grin. His hair was graying in thick strands pulled back from a younger-looking brow, like Gilbert Roland, an actor from the Fifties.

"Hey, it looks like Gilbert." Trip popped his head out of the skin crease.

"Does, Tripper . . . poster Mediterranean man, leader of a band Partisans for whom some fucking bell tolled," Aubrey said with the inner voice then cut away from Trip, leaned forward, and asked Marla how old her father was.

"Sixty-five this month," she answered.

"Good shape, ain't he, Chrysler?" The Junior smiled. "I tell ya what, you better watch out when he shakes your hand. He strong. Hey, *señor!*" The Junior yelled as Asante approached.

"Hello, hello to everybody!" the Papa said. When the reach came into The Junior's right hand, they stared at each other and waited. Asante pulled back just before he clamped down, and The Junior thought it was a polite shake this time. But then Asante slipped to The Junior's relaxed fingers and squeezed the middle joints like a test rack, sending him down on a knee. The old man's close friends called him C. Clamp.

"Papa, this is Mr. Shallcross, and Papa, don't do anything to break his hand and embarrass me, or I'll tell Momma, I promise."

"Okay! Okay! I'm not, sweetheart." He gave Aubrey his boneless handshake. "You want him to think I'm a *puto*."

"Papa!" Marla screamed.

"Okay! Okay!" He leaned into Aubrey. "Her mother and her have me captive here. You must promise to help me escape."

"Be by your gate tonight at midnight. We'll go find the thin-lipped women, the ones who dance all night for the blue goose down by the Indian River," Aubrey whispered.

"You like women with thin lips?" the Papa whispered back.

"Yeah, and those women seem to like the blue goose, or is it the swan?"

"Me, too, my friend! I mean women. I have no interest in loving a goose or a swan." Asante winked and released Aubrey's hand, then narrowed his eyes at this comfortable stranger.

"Come on, Papa. Momma's waiting."

Asante held the door, but Marla said she'd lost an earring and went back to the truck. Aubrey followed to help. He could see down the back of her jeans when she kneeled to look under the seat, and there in all its skin-job splendor, below the L5 vertebra, was a tattoo, a backstreet Rembrandt—a still life some parlor wizard with a camera eye had drawn in blazing chromas of plural color. An intricate floral frame the size of a medium cookie, but the center was blank, with only the sweet corium of a woman in her twenties.

"Look out, Your Shortness of My Head!" Aubrey said to Trip in the inner voice again. "This is no ordinary tramp stamp. That's a very red 'n swollen art piece right there, c'mon. This ink could be a crypto thing. See any messages in the circle?"

Trip stared at the work.

"Or is it supposed to be blank?"

She stood up.

"Find it?" Aubrey asked her.

"Nope. Doesn't matter. I'm starved. How about you?"

"Third world. Hey, Ms. Sadacca, I couldn't help but notice your tattoo. Beautiful work, but why the empty frame?"

"I wasn't sure what to put in it. I thought of pasting a little picture of my husband's mother in there when we started to hate each other. It was his favorite position, you know."

"Oh, clutch the pearls, lady."

When he was introduced to Marla's mother, Solana, her green eyes seemed to search for a seam in his chuck. A severe woman, well-aged and attractive, but a little suspicious of him.

Marla motioned him to a screen porch overlooking an arena.

"You school your horses here then?" he wanted to know.

"Yes, but another, legal-size, dressage ring with mirrors is on the far side of those trees."

"Why the mirrors?"

"I tell you what. After lunch, we'll go down, and I'll show you what I use the mirrors for." She held onto his eyes.

"Here's your daddy with the drinks." The Junior stepped in between them.

They all sat down at the table for lunch.

"Everyone, a toast!" Asante said. "To life, *L'chaim, saluda, prost, vaya con Dios*, and all that shit."

The doorbell put Solana on her feet. "That's my sister. I'll go."

The women walked to the kitchen. "You see, I am truly a prisoner here, surrounded by all these Portuguese women, *muchachos*," Asante said. "But my new friend, Aubrey, has agreed to meet me tonight. I will go with him to find the Anglo women, the ones with thin lips who dance with the blue goose by the Indian River."

All made the sign of the cross for the food, except The Junior, a Southern Baptist, who told them once he'd like to learn it. After lunch, Asante, Marla, and The Junior walked down to the stable.

A semi-conspicuous sign hung at the entrance of Asante's barn: The Problem Is Never the Horse, It Is Always the Rider. Aubrey tried to stretch that for a minute, but didn't want to ask too many questions.

In a twelve-by-twelve wash stall off the center aisle stood a bay horse, tall, tack in place. The groom, a dark-complected young girl of unknown ethnic provenance, but not a Presbyterian, pulled on the bridle. She slipped a thumb into the toothless corner of the mouth looking for the bit space God made. Aubrey went off right there. Had to look at it all in his jar, Nell Kitching's jar, then tumbled into a big drifty.

The girl led the horse to a mounting block. Marla pulled on her gloves and examined the bridle with her eyes, made a minor adjustment, and stepped on.

The men walked to the ring behind her. Aubrey watched her figure spread around the giant rib cage, swinging from right to left in the rhythm of the walk. He was spellbound. Her lower parts slow-danced from the straddle once shut off in history by the required sidesaddle. Same stripe as a woman required to cover her hair before entering a church.

When they got to the ring, he walked away from the men and moved his drifty into the world he saw inside his head, the one used to create magic and stories—not the scary one that rose up in the Blue Goose parking lot the other night. This was his skull-room cyclorama where the RKO movie tower stood in the middle of a cane field, symbolic of the exegesis taken from the miles of movies he'd seen in his life. He took a pull off his imaginary Ball jar progenitor—the powerful apparatus of carburetion that twisted canon forms into the bent and the beautiful, then moved them back again into the objective world after he'd denatured them. He rose like a gossamer, a cobweb kite, holding on to a rope tied to the tower as he circled above the cane field. The centrifugal force of the orbit around the Eiffel ziggurat pumped the strength needed to deconstruct and reconstruct the woman and the horse in spike after spike of the gorgeously weird.

When he'd had enough of the horse, he pictured Marla with a lover and increased the orbit until it became Wonder Dog him, face up under her bed made out of Plexiglas. He could see through to her naked backside, and inside the empty frame of her ornate tattoo was a picture of him smiling at himself like a dickhead. Her lover moved between her legs like her horse, slow, in the slow swing of the slow walk. Click!

Next image…a Plexiglas exam table, Aubrey underneath, his eyes pinned to the tattoo and what it would show him this time. Marla's lover had vanished, and she lay on the cold, clear clinical piece. Then quickly another face appeared inside the tattoo's frame: Aubrey's beloved mother. Exactly what Marla said she would like to do to her husband while he made love to her from behind. It creeped him. A Catholic punishment. Still, he found the whole tableau beautiful, scary, uncomfortable, erotic, and comical—biological, yet mechanical. A clockwork orange.

He had gone too far. Steamed it too strange and left most of its beauty out on the tower's strong orbit. After seeing his mother in that skin, he couldn't make the design slim enough to do what he wanted: put it through the blades of his jar and swallow the show in an air-sucking synaesthesia of his other pica, his sensual pica, his passionate pica. At least not with the look she was giving him, the dental-lady look that could turn into choking by the Slim Hand. The usual mentation blue balls of failing to slimerate and swallow what he'd created had him gnawing his cheek flesh and flinching Tourette's with his shoulders. He slowly returned to the world of the *True* magazine and the Sadaccas' dressage ring.

"Aubrey, boy!" Trip wasn't allowed to go with him to the big room, but he saw it start on this side with the jar. "Reducing and swelling things in there, were you? Couldn't get all that slim enough to come? To swallow? You broke a sweat, Biggie. I could see it forming before you left me. You're too much, you know, you and that prophylactic Plexiglas you use, and still it scares the shit out of you. I hope you maintained some kind of respectable esthete, because it seemed plenty prurient and misogynous before you disappeared. Now you *really* know why those Victorians made them ride sidesaddle. They were ashamed of their erotic life, and maybe you are, too, you and that Catholic scar tissue churning around in the top hole of your skull. Yep, those Vickies couldn't stand to see the ladies with their legs apart. Made the body fluids too jumpy."

"It wasn't dirty or misogynous, Trip, you little shit. I adore the female form. You know after all these years I'm not ashamed of my erotic life."

"Maybe not, but it's true, isn't it? A lot of sensation marvelation is in your throat, so you'd rather swallow something you've created in your head than ball it."

"Or both." Aubrey smiled with Trip.

Marla walked the horse around the perimeter on a loose rein and began a slow posting trot, rising to the syncopation of the gait with the horse's neck low and deep toward the ground, making his movement more cadenced and cat-like, lifting his back into a bridge that freed his shoulders underneath her. After a short time, she walked him again.

"Is that it?" Aubrey asked, wishing he hadn't.

"No, no, just the first part. She's stretching and making him loose, like you would before you run after those women with thin lips so you don't pull a muscle, *monsieur*. Lorraine!" Asante yelled to the girl in the barn. "Music, *por favor*. I want to hear my Amália Rodrigues sing *fado* while my daughter rides."

Marla brought the horse to a halt. The neck was high as a chess piece, the gelding's face on the vertical perpendicular to the ground. He stood motionless, hind legs squarely underneath him. She moved again into a trot, but now she was sitting the horse. The front end of the big warmblood was elevated like her posture—a bosomed-carved woman on the bow, with the same backbone in a dance to the greatest singer of Portuguese blues alive, a gospel sound that stretched across the property and bled out for miles into the palmetto kingdom.

She left the circle and rode on straight lines around the rectangular perimeter. From deep in a corner, she shot out on a diagonal path forward and sideways at a forty-five-degree angle to the adjacent corner. The horse's legs crossed in wide-sweeping, lateral strokes, flowing to Amália's song. The scene was stunning enough to drive a hyperthymic person like Aubrey to an emotional decision, where he might raise his hand and say to a world-class store clerk, "Gimme all this right here. I don't care what it costs."

"The movement is called a half pass," Asante said. "This a grand prix dressage horse and he can move with ease in any direction you want and with beautiful expression for, how you say, the dessert, *monsieur*! If you are experienced and talented enough to ride him. And do you know what for?"

Aubrey shook his head.

"So he could help the rider get the advantage on another man and kill him."

"Kill him?"

"True. If you know your history, it became a military thing, fighting on horseback. A Greek named Xenophon wrote the first book about it five hundred years before Christ. I have a copy in the English. I show it to you later."

Marla came down to a walk on a long rein, and the music moved into another piece.

"So, this Greek wrote a how-to book, and then what happened?"

"How to, huh, Junior?" Asante shot him a wiseacre look. "This little how-to book, my new friend, saves the Greeks from the Turks, because the Greeks learned to ride and fight better. And then others wrote books, and the dressage, which is simply a French word that means training, was getting better, and armies with the best-trained horses and men were the most feared. They could protect their home or take yours away. Napoleon, the Prussians, they sent their best dressage-trained killers to the battlefields."

Asante looked at The Junior, and they danced around Aubrey like assassins, doing half passes, slicing the air with air swords in canter jumps, laughing and making drinking faces.

"Hey!" Marla yelled. "You're scaring my horse, you bunch of drunks."

She did another sweeping half pass just as beautiful in the other direction.

"Horses, you know, Aubrey, are like us. They are either right- or left-handed. We teach them to be balanced and to bend in both directions like the baseball guy, Mickey Mantle. His father made him use the bat with both hands when he was little, and he cried because he was right-handed. I saw it on TV! Then he became the most famous, how you say, switch-hitter in America. My God, if you were born with the left hand in the old country, they would tie it behind your back because they believed it came from the devil."

Marla reached the other corner. Her reins looked soft and light as she carved through the turn using only the torque in her torso and weight in her inside stirrup, bending the horse's body on the track, making him step more under himself with his inside hind leg to lift his forehand higher and amplify the movement. Then lengthwise across this historical stage on the diagonal, she took a shot at the far end in a huge trot that seemed to barely touch the ground—the horse's front legs extending straight out in front like a prizefighter's synchronized jabs.

"Wow, impressive," Aubrey whispered.

"It's called the extended trot," Asante whispered back. Marla halted the horse and let out the rein to give him a break.

"Very nice, very nice, darling. A little change of cadence in the down transition, but beautiful, very nice. *Deixe ele anda a passo.*"

She nodded, looked away, and took a deep breath.

"What we do in the dressage, Aubrey, is only improve on what the horse does naturally. There is nothing we do with him that he doesn't do when he plays in the pasture without a rider. Marla, do a little piaffe and passage, then put him away, dear. Lorraine! *Ponha a Segovia outra vez!*" he yelled to the barn to change the music.

Marla adjusted the walk to a slow march, the steps closer together, building and holding energy. Her legs said something barely noticeable, and the horse began to trot in place in the piaffe—effortless, active, and graceful.

It was beautiful to Aubrey: the neck arched, her sitting so quiet, the guitar of Segovia's shaking the speakers and mirrors. She moved her legs a little forward, and the horse stepped out of the spot in big, slow elevated strides—a high bolero that celebrated his kind even in the wild. She halted, patted him on the neck, and it was over. And so was a lot of the old Aubrey, more than touched by this beautiful art form he'd never heard of as long as he'd been around horses.

"Very nice, darling, thank you," Asante said. He proudly turned to his guest. "That last movement is called the passage. I taught her all I know, but there is more to learn from others."

Aubrey applauded, and Marla pulled the elastic band out of her hair and tossed the live pile over her head onto the neck of the horse, then spread her arms out like a story. The horse and woman had become one creature again, and he couldn't seem to keep them apart. He wanted them both.

"Au-bree," The Junior called, like his mother when they were kids. "You having one a your driftys? C'mon, we're goin to the house."

"Oh, I see. A drifty. You are a dreamer, Aubrey," Asante said. "That's okay. Me, too. Horses and women. Let's go, monsieur, get another drink and tell some real lies."

They talked into the night on the screen porch about riders, music, love, passion, and crimes. Aubrey asked them many questions about their horses, and in exchange, told them stories of his days as a young man with quarter horses in the cowboy culture.

The South Florida night was its usual living power plant, a running meta-cola of protoplasm and exoskeletons man will never imitate with bio concoctions or cyclotrons. The moon looked like the New Mexico sun logo crosshatched through the fiberglass screening—brown mosquitoes clinging to the outside dreamed of what it would be like to drink the blood of all present. Bats made supersonic passes over the floodlights around the house, chasing insects, and God knows a new species appears every week on this piece of U.S. map four hundred miles out in the ocean some called the Big Sandbar.

"Sante! Marla! Come now. Christaine is on the phone. Aubrey and Junior, please excuse them," Solana, Marla's mother, said and looked at Aubrey with the propositional smile. "That is my other daughter, her older sister." She returned to the living room.

"The big sister? What's she like, boyeh?" Aubrey asked The Junior.

"Lives in Miama."

"Uh-huh. With four kids, right?"

"No, divorced, Aubrey. Had a kid that got killed in some accident, and they don't talk about it. They ain't happy she don't come around much."

They kept drinking. The Junior said something Aubrey couldn't hear after a quiet moment, so he asked him to repeat it.

"L.S.M.F.T.," The Junior said louder.

"What's that? Military?"

"Well, no, it ain't military. It's on every pack of Lucky Strikes at the bottom, or at least it used to be. It stood for 'Lucky Strike Means Fine Tobacco,' accordin to the people who made 'em."

"Oh, thanks. Good to know tonight."

"Yeah, ain't it? I was thinking about Punky and how he smoked those Luckys in the eleventh grade, and that was when nobody was getting laid, but we was all gettin damn close. And Punky used to say L.S.M.F.T. really meant, 'Let's Stop, My Finger's Tired.'"

"God, that's awful, son. It could be a new country porn song."

"Here's a better one." The Junior sat up straighter. "Punky double-dates with me to the prom. We go out to High Beach later with our girls to do a little pressie bod and kissy face, you know. You's off at that private school. The girls get out of the car to go pee, and Punky starts telling me how this girl he's with is a queer. 'What do you mean? She's a dyke?' I said. He says no, a queer, 'cause she's always trying to give him a blow job."

They laughed and coughed.

"So I says, 'Hell, Punky, when those girls come back, you wanna trade?'"

"Jesus, I swear he musta grown up in a house with lead paint. What'd he say?"

"He said nope, that he was going to try and save her from a life of queerin and shame. Finished."

"Shelter me, Nelson." Aubrey pumped his knees up and down. "You shouldn't be talking about the dead like this."

"Aw, come on. I got one more. So then, he's all worried I don't think he's cool after that. So he says, 'You know how to keep from gettin the clap?' I said, 'Yeah, rubbers.' He says, 'No, I know a better way. My old man learned it in the army when he's in France. You put your little finger in your ear and get a bunch of wax on it, then you stick it in her. If she starts to jump around sayin it burns, then look out, 'cause she's got it.'"

"I can't take anymore, Nelson." Aubrey turned red-faced and teary.

"That's 'cause I cain't, either." The Junior pitched forward off the chair like he was throwing up.

Yelling erupted in the next room. Aubrey thought it was the TV until he realized it was the family upbraiding each other in Portuguese. Marla was screaming at her father, and Asante was screaming at both of them.

"Don't worry 'bout that in there," The Junior said. "Goes on all the time. I realized it's just the way these other people are. Hell, they'll all be huggin and kissin by tomorrow. Guarantee."

39

"What do you mean *other* people?"

"Aw, you know, Aubrey, not like us. Can you see Bible Belters carrying on like this? Shit, we'd've bin to our pickups to get the pistol, or fistin already and never speakin again. That's why I think it's kind of healthy what they doin in there, 'cause it never festers or eats at 'em like it does a Southern Baptist."

"A very red and swollen observation, The Junior. Maybe we ought to go in there and flush our tanks, get this Anglo-Saxon muck out we been carrying around for years!" He stood.

"No! Shit, don't! You a little drunk. Sit down." The Junior yanked the voice-hearing choker back into his chair.

Aubrey looked stoned. "Fuck, who are those people? They're great. I wanna be one of them. Hell, they sound like they're in a scene from *Seven Beauties*, and they do all this cool stuff with these horses and had these cool lives and…yeah." He burped and stood again, but The Junior's big arm sent him back to the chair.

"Aubrey, it's gettin late, and I think you had enough of that shark snot you been nursin."

Solana appeared from the living room. "I apologize, but Marla is upset her sister isn't coming up to see us tomorrow, and my sister and Asante are accusing each other of being one of the reasons she doesn't come. Both of you please come to lunch tomorrow. It's Sunday."

"Love to," in unison.

"Where's Marla?" The Junior asked.

"She's in the barn," Asante said as he walked into the kitchen smiling and shaking his head. He shook Aubrey's hand and gave him just a glint of strength to strut the fact he may have a clockwork orange in his forearm.

They drove down to the stable, and The Junior walked into the lighted runway while Aubrey stayed in the truck.

"Umm, Juicy Fruit," a voice said. The small man was back out on the forearm. Trip always said Juicy Fruit after something good happened, because when the big Indian said it to McMurphy in *One Flew over the Cuckoo's Nest*, he thought it broke the film wide open.

40

"Ho ho, mini-stealth, it's Slipper Man. Where you been all evening? Juice indeed, Trip. Good one in there tonight, huh?" Aubrey said, sticking Trip from his drinking.

"Yes, Aubrey, and I was determined to keep quiet because you were having such a time, and God knows you could use a good time, especially as of late, because of that juju monster's four-way stop sign downtown you carbureted into existence to make your pain a little more exquisite."

"And what am I supposed to do about that?"

"How about a swan dive into this Rabelaisian party, Ursa Major! This dressage thing, these new friends." Trip pointed at the barn. "How about doing your music and writing songs again because you're happy, and dancing in the afternoons with Asante Sadacca, waving air swords on your drunken feet—food, horses, family fights, beautiful women, my goodness. Finished." Aubrey could see The Junior and Marla arguing.

She grabbed a saddle pad and threw it. The Junior finally threw something, too—his hands up—and walked back to the truck.

"Ooh-eee! She says I'm a *cara de caralho*, Aubrey. That's the first buncha words I learned in Port-a-gee. It means dickhead. Goddamn, I love a hardheaded woman."

On the way home, there was more talk about Punky and his funeral Monday. Punky's wife, who had waited on Aubrey and the Junior for years at the local diner, wanted them to be pallbearers. It was going to be a sad occasion. The two men decided not to sit next to each other because they might start laughing and crying at the same time about the earwax clap test.

Aubrey asked The Junior to let him out on his road so he could walk the trace to his house. He needed the swamp air so the bed wouldn't spin. He turned around and sang a few bars of "Hard-Headed Woman," and his big friend smiled a cooner and shot him the bird.

"Hey, don't forget we goin back there tomorrow, whooper-crane man. You remember how to get you drunk ass over there?"

"No *problemo*, not that gin stinky." He started walking.

41

The ditches along the roads through Florida's wetlands render enough dirt to get the grades above water. Aubrey stopped on that dirt and pulled in the methane muck scent with his boozy senses to see if he could smell being twelve years old again and taste the brown water he was raised on. One zillion frogs sounded like they had been put through a synthesizer and were loud as a Miami nightclub, their heads thrown back in song from their new album, *The Electronic Frog Pond*.

Aubrey's eyes dilated. He saw tiny houses with balconies stuck to the sides of the ditch filled with singing frogs. A mini-*Fitzcarraldo* floated on the pond, and frogs hung over the guardrails blowing out their throats with air-raid top notes. He blew out his own throat. Trip appeared on his arm with a watermelon grin and mimicked them, too.

He walked down the road in the slow gait of a processional altar boy holding his carburetion jar out in front of him like the solar monstrance he carried for the priest during benediction. Some backwoods spell came over him between the froggy hosannas and the last of the Bombay Sapphire's pleasant lidocaine, and he didn't even feel the gala-whopper mosquitoes filling up their back ends with his hallucinating, ex-Christian blood.

~

In Miami this night, Carlos drove under lutescent lights on Key Biscayne with a corpse, killed so clean not to bleed out on the back seat. He would leave it by the auditorium door for the rat-dance boss to find in the morning. This boss, this snitch, would know, and he would say his name, "Carlos," then leak some urine. Carlos was hungry and tired. He had to take his mother to the doctor in the morning for her headaches. He loved her very much.

A good slipper like Triple Suiter wanted no part of a Carlos; three or four others tried to live in his mind when he was younger and decent. Though a good one stayed on and lived in hiding, a heinous one was working bad stuff. That one cried like an abandoned baby and lured Carlos into the dark to show him what he didn't want to see, much at one with his mother's crucifixion by the mad eye of the fourth-person singular.

Slippers have been with people since their minds were divided by nature into two seats. The corpus callosum was an open hallway between the brain's hemispheres, and most slippers lived peacefully and helped each other. They can move from one person to another through the nose and can form outside a brain like Triple Suiter, or appear as living gods or fairies. But sometimes, when fear strikes a human, a bad slipper might try to crash their eyes as something mistakenly beautiful to assist in their destruction, like the old Irish kelpies.

The brain changed over thousands of years, and the hallway of the mind became narrow, less patent. Though slippers are in everyone, the lion's share never interact with them except in dreams and free associations, and here they are discounted as dreams or a muse unless a stressful time brings them out as an audible voice on this side. Mankind for the most part put aside the notion of slippers. The encephalon's two Camelots moved into a more singular seat run by a lone ego, but those with the gift could still hear and speak to their slippers through the hallway, like Aubrey. Today, these people are called schizophrenics, or split minds, and are thought to be crazy.

Even though some people don't believe in other voices, strangely enough, they believe in vampires and wizards. There are no such things. A slipper can make one for you, but it would be out of smoke and just fuel more deluded tatering on a false power to get you through a Monday, or past your dental lady in the mirror at night. If you are lonely or scared, you should summon a good slipper, a great whittler. The hallway is still there. One will come, and you can slip away. *True* magazine.

Chapter 4

CHRISTAINE

The next morning, Aubrey stepped up in his truck and drove his usual backed-off rate down the shell-rock road. He stopped when he reached the middle of a wetland the grade bisected like a causeway. Surrounded by water on both sides, it felt like he was in a boat every time he drove across, or the guy on Punky's bumper sticker when he walked across. The swamp there supported acres of hypericum, a variety of St. John's wort thirty inches tall that looks like bonsai trees forested a couple feet apart. It makes you adjust the scale, as if you were with Redford and Meryl in that plane flying over the Serengeti in *Out of Africa*.

Parked on the road, he would conjure his Ball jar and summon a flight above the savanna to be entranced like Meryl, looking down from his Dodge truck at what he called the knee-high Serengeti.

"We'll fly it like they did," he'd say to Trip, and all he had to do was call on the most cherished thing of being kin to the bonobos: possession of the neural jewel of plasticity and time travel. Then up over the Florida lowland they'd shoot into the pellucid sky of the surreal slip away.

Anchored between the stunted worts were thousands of spider webs beaded with morning dew. The matinal sun lit the reticulations like fiber optics on a bughouse flyway of spider spit and death. After circling a few times, he landed his steampunked truck back on the shell-rock road, then stored the jar in his mind's foyer and drove to a diner Trip called The Catheter Café in clogged-heart speak.

"Hi, Aubrey, want your usual?"

"Thank you, Janet. Same."

People's brains are slow in the mornings, before they drink the drink to step up to the door. Aubrey always waited an hour before coffee. He liked that morning largo, that backwoods tai chi to a soft boondocks drag around his bedroom while thoughts streamed in like too much phone service. Stuff would appear in his staging area, talk the trope, jack around, change clothes, leave. Sometimes just a single word would audition, or a sentence would letter itself in an atramentous line of **Show Card Gothic font**.

He owned a photographic and audiographic mind, one that designed words, run-on sentences, himself, tree lines, highway art, still life, and torn skin—all in a cranial ring of benign madness with his sacred sidecar and consigliere, Triple Suiter. His head was a builder, a wild whittlewright and comic bettersmith, and his two-story house, O'gram, was the wood-frame manifestation of what he really was up the stairs: an unencumbered freebaser of the calcium toadstone rock that bore down on his red-means-wrong senses every day, slimming things to take down his throat as an honest-to-God practitioner of that marvelation of sensation and derangement. He would throw the gas on anything and light it, this rainstorm inside a flipped car, this connoisseur of the psycho-generated souvenir who also had a powerful fear, because with carburetion like that, you easily could be unhorsed and chased through the doors of your own rectum when the wrong whittle monster got loose.

This morning in the café, he thought about a group from the '50s, Frankie Lymon and the Teenagers. A mini jukebox in the booth triggered memories of two famous songs by the bygone tenor—"Why Do Fools Fall in Love?" and "I Want You to Be My Girl." But those songs were not on that jukebox, nor were other songs by Frankie, who was dead in the pine box, kicked in the heart by a China White horse at an age too young to die.

Aubrey conjured his Ball jar, then went to his head room and found Frankie on Alan Freed's TV show, *The Big Beat*. He wanted to fly it around the RKO tower on top of the world…stretch it out just for the love of it. How innocent the chocolate singer looked holding on to his microphone and smile; the boyish featherweight must have made an angelic corpse for the grieving doo-wops and acappellas who filed past his coffin to get a last look at the kid with the golden throat. Shame he wasn't given the stardust Elvis and Morrison got for their chemical exits, but in Frankie's day, moral society rejected the hypodermic sword of the peaceful warrior; rock n' roll was wrong for the children of the frozen pelvic people, though *Rolling Stone* beatified him in the end for dying in the ring with Hendrix.

Aubrey turned his jar up to drink the whole scene. A hole the size of a quarter spun in the top like the knives of the Hamilton Beach. He covered the opening with his mouth and swallowed all of the ethereal stage show, shivered once, and was sated.

"Aw, it's just too bad you shot that dope, Frankie. Your ten-carat tenor influenced some of the greats...The Temptations, Smokey Robinson, The Beach Boys..."

"Talkin to youself again, Aubrey Shallcross?"

Janet the waitress had arrived with coffee.

"Caught me, Janet. As I get older, I do it more and more."

"What my husband says. Charlie says he's always lookin around to see if anybody saw him. He dud'n want anyone to think he's one of those weirdoes got an imaginary friend, know what I mean?"

She marched away on the terrazzo.

"Whoa, good one, Anti-Chrysler." Trip was out on the arm. "I think she's truly worried about her other set of bones being a twerper. Could be a slipper Charlie's hanging with lately. Could be. Weirdos, she called us."

"Not to worry, sock puppet. Your secret's safe with me. I don't want you and I to get thrown in the sana-tater-house. Then again, it might be worth it if Nell Kitching's there and we got to see her again."

"Well, that's different."

"Maybe we'd get to meet other people with sidecars, too—even the great Kaw-Liga, that tower of a wooden Indian standing by the door. Pack a Juicy Fruit in his mouth, c'mon." Aubrey squinted to follow a trail on the Formica marble tabletop. "I think about Nell a lot lately, me and Arquette Orlander watching her in school. Straight-A Nell, all the conjures we saw, her talkin to the cricket in the jar. She pretended she had ten sets of clothes for that fish bait—strip it down, dress it back up with her straight-A eyes. Maybe the cricket was a slipper screwin around with his morph...doing shapes in there like you and me. She put those wheelworks on me forever."

"What were you doing in the big room just now, Aubrey?"

"Resurrecting Frankie Lymon. You changing the subject?"

"Not on purpose."

"Then let me finish. Nell kinda went nuts after the jar thing, right? Didn't show for school anymore."

"Christ, Aubrey, the sheriff found her mother's cut-up body in an abandoned refrigerator out in the woods, the work of that so-called Tin Snip killer. Nell didn't show, Aubrey, because she was sana-tatered, as you like to say, or institutionalized. They convinced her folks she was a genuine schizophrenic headed for full blown. You never got into that kind of trouble because I told you to keep your mouth shut, considering its stigma in this culture. In the Amazon, they'd consider you a certified mystic, but not here. When you were a child, you thought any bad voice was the devil's and the good voice was me, your guardian angel, remember? The church was telling you that. The church has blamed bad, intrusive thoughts on the devil for centuries to make people feel better, and it works. Today, the doctors say it's rotten neurochemistry so they can get your money, same as the church.

"Of course, back then you thought the Huge, your old God, was driving the bike around with you in the sidecar. You didn't look at yourself as a schizophrenic; I made sure of that by pushing the catechetical-style Rome religion at you. You're driving the bike now instead of your old God, Aubrey, and I'm in the sidecar. Nell's family wasn't religious. She couldn't piggyback the voice she heard on a religion like you could. The doctors got hold of her and convinced her parents she was really apeshit. They said the cricket was driving the bike and she was in the sidecar."

"I know, Trip. MD's for 'Money, dammit.'"

"And these same people are the ones who use soliloquy to talk to the oldest, most famous slipper of all, Aubrey—God—and they think he talks back to them, carburet it. They're selling tickets, son. Stay away from those medicos. Promise me. Now how about we do some Frankie Lymon?"

Trip was a fool for Frankie and could reproduce the surface of any hi-fi thingamajig in the electric house. He imitated the sound of the forty-five drop with a few crackles from the needle and launched into the song until Janet interrupted him during one of the *ooh wahs.*

"Here you go, Aubrey." She was there with the food. "Adam and Eve on their itty-bitty raft. And don't you be talkin to either one of 'em. Oh, it might be all right if you talk to Eve. You still single?"

"That's me. Last of the reservation loners."

"You cowboy holdouts never change."

He considered what she said. There he sat: just him, Trip, and Adam and Eve on their raft, which is diner speak for two eggs poached on a piece of toast. And when the thought of being all alone started to knock the glow off the Frankie Lymon concert, the big grin of Asante Sadacca appeared in his camera blue eye. He'd be at Asante's place in five hours for lunch, and it made him grin, too. He returned to his jar and invented some killer handshakes.

On his way out the door, he ran into an old friend and confidant, John Chrome, who taught English at the high school. They met surfing off High Beach twenty years ago and drank together at the Blue Goose to get mental and trade drifties with their friend, Arquette. Chrome was always stoned immaculate in those days and knew about Trip, and Aubrey insisted Chrome was an ally. He needed that kind of ear to share his more distally sheared skits.

John Chrome was the opposite of Aubrey as a male specimen, a serious surfer in the wrong body—a padded endomorph with upholstered-looking skin. His bald head could bounce light and break the wind. Not an athletic sight, but a magazine major on a surfboard: a graceful bear out of physical context and a bishop of the beach, whose ex-cathedra moves on a wave left all the young Tommys slack-dicked when he worked what the ocean sent him. His high school students called him Chrome Top.

This morning, a hurricane named Eileen was three hundred miles off shore. Chrome said he was going to the beach after breakfast and told Aubrey to meet him there in an hour.

Aubrey looked again at the knee-high Serengeti on his way out, but didn't stop to fly it. Instead, he checked a fence line espaliered with flame vine at a house on the main street of Jensen Beach to make sure there were no blooms. He was superstitious about the glowing flowers that looked like burning embers with the sun behind them right before they fell to the ground. He would not surf when they bloomed; they had brought him tragedy once.

He crossed the Indian River causeway, turned to Hibiscus Beach, and there it was: big waves breaking left—left pearls, banging the beach from behind and pulling on its sea-grape hair.

Chrome was outside the break, but disappeared in a trough. When Aubrey saw him rise again, Chrome sat up, spun like Johnny Yuma with a gun, and took four strokes into the wave, carving its face like a knife fight—tearing open the hydrol wall sent to him by a disturbed barometric woman south of Bermuda.

The next wave rose and curled over into a hollow tube. Out of sight inside that trochal grommet of other worldly space was the English teacher and his Ancient Mariner, celebrating a place surfers talk about like Fatima—something they call the green room or birth canal of the ocean, where few in the family of man have ever been and almost all will never go.

Chrome walked out of the water and sat down on the sand next to Aubrey. He was a man of gnomic emotion. They watched another set roll over the reef and didn't speak for thirty seconds until Chrome broke it with two words from Clarence Carter's famous song in 1968, "Slip Away."

Aubrey drove to the Blue Goose. Fred, the owner, bagged up seven pounds of stone crab claws for him to take to the Sadaccas for lunch. Ten miles later, he pulled through the farm gates and saw a parked van; the dealership name was from Miami. *Must be the missing sister whose no-show habits caused all the welter in the living room last night.*

Asante was there with his searchlight smile.

"They down in the stable fooling with some horse-shit thing, Aubrey. Tell them to come back to the house to eat this feast you have brought."

Outside, he lifted his chest, chewed the inside of his cheek, and watched the small vitreous floaters on his eyeballs like cats do when you *think* they're looking at you, instead of looking at you. *Marla's sister could be in that barn. Wonder if she looks like...*

"Hi." The Junior and Marla were fiddling with a piece of tack.

Aubrey didn't see anyone else.

"Yikes a mighty! It's the Anti-Chrysler, the Second Comin, for lunch," The Junior said.

"Very funny, boyeh."

"Hi, Aubrey." Marla smiled and cocked her head.

"Whoa! What happened to the Mr. Shallcross?" The Junior asked them.

"Oh, we decided to drop it last night when you went into your little office off the kitchen with the toilet," she said.

"Uh-huh." The Junior came at Aubrey with the mean face. "You know what I told you 'bout these bird dogs 'round here," hands out like a gunfighter.

Aubrey pulled a riding crop from the wall and assumed the position of the foilsman, the Beau Sabreur of the palmetto kingdom, and grabbed a second crop to make threatening gestures. The Junior drew his human hand pistol and shot him dead.

Down to the floor, crops crossed his chest in a military-casket pose, his dead eyes wide open. He didn't notice the two figures standing behind him. If he had seen Solana and her daughter, Christaine, he would have been sucking air for the big chest like an asshole again instead of this embarrassing shit.

He was staring at the rafters when a hand reached down as if to help him up or shake. On the third finger was a ring, a piece of ivory carved into a replica of an old Underwood typewriter. Then the hand spoke.

"Hello, I'm Christaine Sadacca."

He sensed the hand just wanted to shake, so he did.

"Aubrey Shallcross at your feet, ma'am."

"Yes, yes, you are."

"Aubrey! You cannot stay there on that cold floor," Solana ordered like his mother. "Junior! Tell him to get up."

He jumped to his height. Christaine stood in front of him, her brown eyes, big as an infant's, fixed on his. They were so large that he couldn't see the rest of her. The floods traveled to his left behind him. She brushed off his back and came around to the front again.

"Well, that was a good show, Aubrey. Wasn't that in *Raiders of the Lost Ark*?" her lips, with three small scars on the upper left side, asked.

They were Tuesday Weld lips, classic Tuesday in their porn-flower shape, but those scars made them more than unique—they were her lips. He thought to defend his barn skit, but he was too distracted by the ambrosial mouth and those Keane child eyes.

"Yeah, I saw that in *Raiders*, but, uh, Junior and I were doing the act in the seventies before that."

"Then I think Indiana owes you some money," said the small breasts under her white pima tank top with *Tell the Truth and Run* written across the front.

"Well, maybe he does," Aubrey said. "Oh, uh, Asante asked me to have everyone come to the house to eat."

The five-foot-eight, split-lipped, *Tell-the-Truth-and-Run* woman simpered a smile.

Everyone walked in a kind of procession: Solana arm in arm with her beloved daughter, Christaine, The Junior with Marla, and Aubrey, who wasn't entirely alone because he had Triple Suiter on his arm looking embarrassed about his stammer in the barn. Trip wanted more than anything for Aubrey to be happy with a woman, but the car lot king of High Beach had jammed. It wasn't fair. He got caught silly in front of this beautiful, smooth-talking daughter of Eve, and the spontaneous part of him so good at shooting from the top of his femur gun stand stuck on something.

The conversations at lunch were side-barred into pockets of overlapping English and Portuguese. Aubrey noticed Solana and Christaine turning to look at him as if wondering, *Who was that tongue-tied Jute laying there in the barn?* But he'd never know what they were thinking, and he became uncomfortable for caring.

Did everybody do the quantity of skits per hour he did in his upper stove? Did they do all that dialogue and guest appearances, those dramaturgies of Wonder Dog them, jumping rope in a room of impressed women and jealous men? Those indoor cross talks with invented human builds covering the pertinent amounts of existential doo lang out there that kick in the serotonin medicos talk about? Only the medicos call it a syndrome when the serotonin quits and say things like George Carlin, "Oh, shit, man! Your serotonin quit," and then some doctor is selling you a wolf ticket to his own self-exaltation show to become the king of your disconsolate taproot and Rexall habits for the rest of your wing-dragging life.

The old question does mill: Was it possible to think of doing anything without the self-exal Tater behind it, especially with those other Taters watching you? Aubrey knew about this thorn apple in the human head, this jimsonweed he called certified Tater stuff, and he had such a nose for it because he caught himself doing it all the time in his private conjures and hero-baked skits. He divided self-exaltaters into two categories: the sight Tater and the blind Tater. The sight Tater knew he did it, but the blind Tater was pitifully deluded and could go on that way until he died or figured it out because none of his delusional shit ever came true.

So there he sat down from Christaine—nervous—needing the serotonin to kick in, wondering how he looked, and designing an essay to make him seem interesting, because his blood jerked when he first saw her. It was ligature love—sweet lakes of those eyes, and he heard the CB transcendental trucker he worshipped say, "Aubrey, I think you feenished."

Everyone was up from the table thanking him again and again for the crab feast. Christaine walked toward him.

"So, Aubrey, how are you feeling since you were gunned down by your friend, Junior, in the barn?"

"Truthfully, I feel remarkably good, considering," in his straight radio voice. "I've been dying like that since I was a child. I was famous in my neighborhood for dying—the best killed-in-action player in town at twelve. I staged dramatic falls and roll-overs, held my breath like a corpse, and never was I without my favorite photo of a man shot in midair by a lucky bullet during the Spanish Civil War."

"You mean Robert Capa's?"

Shit, she knows it. Keep moving.

"Uh, yes, that one. But guess what the best part was. I used to relish the idea of just getting to lie down and rest after all the running around the neighborhood. And I hoped it would feel like that when I grew up and lay dying, like when you first go down after being on your feet for hours, that take-a-load-off feeling. Only now in my years do I know dying probably hurts like hell."

She laughed, and it was his tiny grip—the even chance to reveal to her in a straight truth and with a bit of tatering, he might be one red and swollen master of the backyard story.

"As I lay there dying and resting, I would hear music. 'The Battle Hymn of the Republic,' from our Civil War, would rise out of the sandspurs because my Victorian grandmother played it in her house. Yes, it was Rebels and Yankees to us local kids and our winter friends. We never played it in the summer, because nobody local wanted to be a Yankee after the Yankee kids went back North."

She seemed to search his face for artifice and looked satisfied there was none. This was honest stuff, wasn't it? The true story of his life as a boy, no hotshot male dance.

He began to sing "The Battle Hymn."

"Mine eyes have seen the glory of the coming of the Lord: He is trampling out the vintage where the grapes of wrath are stored."

Everyone turned and looked at them. She started to sing with him, "He hath loosed the fateful lightning of his terrible swift sword. His truth is marching on."

With Aubrey leading, they folded their bodies to the carpet in stages from their battle wounds so they could relish the feel-good part of dying just to take a load off. Down on the floor, quiet as nerve-gassed sheep on a military test range, their singing softened until their lips stopped moving from the gas. When death came, angels took them aloft because they were Confederate soldiers fighting for states' rights. Aubrey's grandmother, a member of the United Daughters of the Confederacy, had told him angels didn't take the souls of damn Yankees to heaven, that only the Confederates got to go up, even though the "Battle Hymn of the Republic" was written by a Yankee. So he got to be Johnny Yuma at twelve, way before Johnny was even cool.

They turned to each other with quarter-moon smiles, as if they had worked the part for a long time. Aubrey heard a loud crack in his head; the wishbone had snapped off longer on his side.

Everyone was silent. Asante and Solana stood arm in arm smiling like a couple in a baby ward, and then they all applauded.

"Are you thinkin what I'm thinkin?" Aubrey heard The Junior say to Marla.

"Uh-huh," she answered.

"Jesus, honey, it's the Anti-Chrysler and your sister, Christ." Or as Aubrey later learned, the family preferred to pronounce the sobriquet, Christ, so it rhymed with wrist. However, Marla and Christaine's close friends called her the hangman's Christ, but never in front of the Catholic family.

"Want to do a double?" Aubrey asked.

"Like what?" she said. He loved how her lips moved—all torpid and Montgomery Clift.

"You tell me a story from your life when you were a kid, like I just did, but first I would like to ask you a personal question, and if it's too forward…"

She nodded.

"I was wondering how you got those beautiful scars on your lips."

He saw her try him on again with the prehensile look, as if suspecting he thinks he's pretty wide or something. She held up her hand and glanced at her ivory carved typewriter ring.

"Oh, that's a story, but I might start acting it out in front of the family, so let's move to the screen porch so I can smoke and be comfortable."

She lit one and began.

"The name of this story is The Burdines Jesus. When I was thirteen, I had my first crush on a boy in our parish church. He was a young altar boy, a long-haired, blond teeny who could've played a teeny Jesus in one of those B flicks." She took a drag. "I sometimes would go to two Masses on Sunday, once with my parents and again with my Aunt Cosa, so I could see him twice. My parents thought I might have a vocation for the convent and were very pleased with my worship routine. Of course, they didn't know I was fantasizing about lying next to the altar boy while we said our rosaries together. You wouldn't be Catholic, by chance, would you, Aubrey?"

"Yes, I am. Was."

She took another drag and spaced a little, gathering more wool.

"Well, then, you know the rosary has five decades to coincide with events in the life of Christ. The first part of his life is called the Five Joyful Mysteries: the Annunciation, the Visitation, the Nativity, the Presentation of Jesus, and the Finding of the Child Jesus in the Temple, all important to me because I would announce the name of each mystery but not see our Lord when I prayed. Instead, I'd see the altar boy, especially in the Finding of the Child Jesus and in the Visitation, where Mary tells her cousin, Elizabeth, she's pregnant."

Aubrey looked at her stomach. "How do you remember the names of those mysteries? I can't."

"Oh, I was zealous about attending Catechism to double my chances of stealing his altar-boy suit. I wanted it. I believe it's called a cassock and a surplice. Am I right?"

"Right. I was an altar boy."

"Really?" Her kalamata-olive eyes looked like his answer had sex-stroked her.

"So, did you get it? The suit."

"Yes, I went back after class one day, walked into the sacristy, and took it." She shrugged.

She paused each time as if about to stop the story, same stripe when a woman is necking, works a tease, stalls, maybe to create more moisture in her body…or a morality play is coming, or perhaps she's a control freak. Aubrey fidgeted in his man's part and prayed she wasn't going to play the morality. She seemed to love it.

"I took the church clothes to the tree house my father helped me build in this large banyan and hid them. You have to remember, Marla was in kindergarten. I'm eight years older—thirty-four, in fact—so I had the place to myself."

"I had a tree house," Aubrey said. "So what did you do with the cassock and surplice?"

"I laid it on the floor of my hut in the shape of the altar-boy's body. I'd lie beside it and say the five mysteries. When I got to the second mystery, the Visitation, where the Virgin Mary visits her cousin, Saint Elizabeth, and knows she has conceived the little white Jesus, I would feel these strange, low-down urges because I was on the precipice of puberty. I would press against the pitiful air pocks of thin cloth and robes, which made the actual nudge and nearness with a palpable form impossible." She pulled on her cigarette again. "In other words, it was some kind of juvenile air fuck, I guess."

A shock shot to gauge his reaction. His eyes widened enough to lose his lids. She exhaled her smoke and looked pleased. A wonderful, dangerous woman. He could see she knew it excited him, and he worried he might get an altar boy himself. So he ironically started to do what he always did since he was thirteen to stop it: say machine-gun Hail Marys in his head.

She lit another cigarette. An embarrassed Triple Suiter, who had been enjoying her story from the deltoid mole hole, retreated to the armpit when Aubrey's area attempted to summit. Trip stood at his mirror and opened his shirt, disgusted.

"What's this he's doing now, Amp?"

The typeset from Amper Sand's Underwood flew down Trip's chest:

RED AND SWOLLEN, LOVE THAT MAN

TRIP SHOULD LAUGH WITH AMPER SAND.

CHICA LOCA! &

Trip decided to go back.

"Well, should I continue?" Christaine asked.

Aubrey nodded stiffly and moved closer.

"My mother had a friend who worked in the women's apparel section of Burdines. Mother liked to make a lot of her clothes, so the friend gave her two full-size mannequins the store was throwing out. She used one and put the other one in a shed behind the barn. I took it to my hideout in the banyan tree."

Aubrey picked up the Hail Marys again because he knew, or at least hoped, this was going where he thought it was. Now a mannequin was involved, one of his favorite things on Earth, and he was going into the spin, the one the clothes-dryer lid warned about sticking your hands into before it stopped spinning. She looked down at her feet as if a balk was coming.

"Oh, no!" he said. "Don't stop. It's okay. I mean, if you're shy about any of it, of course I would understand."

She shook her head and looked past him. "No, I probably need to tell this story in case I'm repressing anything. It could fester, don't you think?" She rolled her eyes and smiled. "Mental health stuff, right, and it's a good story, yeah? I'm not inhibited. It's my turn, right? You don't think my frank is inappropriate, do you?"

"No, no, 'course not. I love it. It's very red and swollen, yeah." *Did she look at my pants?* "That, that, means something's cool, that swollen-and-red slang thing I say all the time with Junior."

"Well, good, thought that's what it meant." She tilted her head back and widened her neck like confidence. "I dressed the mannequin in the cassock and surplice, and even though it looked like a bald woman, I didn't mind because now my altar boy and junior Jesus felt like the shape and parts of a real person. No more air boy, a real boy, exciting or swollen, like you said. I just never looked at his Burdines's face much. Now, I'm only going to pause to take a sip of my drink, so don't get that worried look.

"My hut leaked, and I would have to leave the boy made out of American plaster while I was at school. Moisture and mildew started to deteriorate the indoor form his father in heaven had chosen for him to walk among us at Burdines, but I thought it was something else making him deteriorate. I thought it was God making him take on my sins of thought, word, and deed, as Jesus had, too, and that his body would rot all the way out like ours, and if I didn't help him, well, he would be just become another dissipating homo sap instead of a Highlander or vampire and live forever, the way he was supposed to in his story. I thought he was going to lose his soul like a mortal mutt for my sins and miss his resurrection at the passion play over in Lake Wales. You know, the one close to Tampa."

Aubrey laughed. She sipped her drink again, but he didn't worry this time.

"I decided to take my weathering Lord and love to an abandoned shell-pit lake in the woods behind our farm, where I was forbidden to go because Miami kids drown in those deep-water mines." She pulled out another European no-filter and snapped open a Zippo with the one-hand fire trick.

"Christaine!" her mother shouted from the living room. "Not around the house, please. Your father's asthma."

She shut the lighter. "I decided the shell pit would be his Lourdes, and I would bathe him in the healing waters and pray to Saint Agnes. Don't ask me why I picked her. I always liked that saint because her name sounded like agony—what religion really is—and then a funny thing happened."

"What?" his lips let go.

"I walked out in the water with him in my arms and pressed against him so hard because I knew he was leaving, and I felt this little flutter in my belly and my femininity. It felt so good and non-Catholic that I couldn't stop pulling him into me till it was over. Then I was sure I made the Burdines Jesus do something wrong, something so sinful I wanted to hide him from God the large Father in the shell pit so I could save his clothes-rack ass. That way, I wouldn't have access to him for his sake. Protect him from fornicating little me and his old man's famous temper. My embarrassment and guilt wouldn't allow me to look at his peeled face again, so I pushed him underwater and watched him sink, smaller and smaller, thinking maybe his papa would grant him absolution for what I made him do if he stayed under Miami for a while and got clean.

"I ran crazy from the shell pit through the woods with my eyes closed out of fear, waiting for the archangel to strike me down for my corporeal transgressions and then…he did."

"Did what?" Aubrey stretched his neck out.

"Struck me down. Well, not really. I ran into the banyan tree because my eyes were still closed. It knocked me out and split my upper lip. The angel left these three marks to remind me of my sin with the Burdines Jesus. The wrath of the Trinity?" She double-blinked a coy kind. "As I grew older, I was able to turn the incident from a mortal into a venial sin because I figured I should be tried as a minor for that sex offense. Don't you agree?" She picked up her purse and looked desirous at the cigarettes. "You know, I remained fascinated with what my little woman's body did in the water that day, and I get the same stir to this day as I pass those abandoned shell pits along the turnpike to see my family, and, well…The End!

"So! I've got to get going because I want to beat the traffic from the weekend people," she said.

Aubrey was still in the water with the mannequin, but managed to say, "Thank you for the visitation to your childhood, man." Which came out stupid and straight, not to mention he said man like a Sixties dork. What he wanted her to know was he considered it a touching, erotic, coming-of-age piece, along with his tumid semi-hard-on.

"You know, you're an interesting man, Aubrey."

"Well, thank you. So are you, a woman."

She gave him the Ellen Barkin squint and the toothless stretch smile with those lips, then started to walk. Aubrey was half behind her and drifted into a corner while she said her goodbyes to the family.

"What a hidden Venus she is, Trip. Burned me down! Were you here for all this?"

"I saw it. I heard it!" Trip said, excited as Aubrey.

"I'm just in cutlets. Tribe marks on those lips like some witch doc threw bad girls into banyan trees for jackin off on something. Can you carbur-fuckin-rate it?"

Christaine hugged her parents. Aubrey walked out and opened the gate.

"Well, I hope I'll see you again soon," he said when she idled the van next to him.

"Maybe you will. I'm planning to come more often. My parents aren't getting any younger, and Marla misses me, too, I think."

"So what do you do in Miami?"

"I'm a writer. I write fiction, like that story I told you tonight."

"No!"

"Well, maybe not." She shifted the van into gear, pointed at Tell the Truth and Run on her T-shirt, and was gone.

On the way home, his top-load crush was suspended as he crossed over the Florida Turnpike. He turned on his CB radio to tell an eighteen-wheeler in front of him that his taillights were out, and another voice in the night heading north or south underneath him came out of the speakers in a clear southern-bass burr.

"She crocheted herself right to me at first, then a year later took that crochet hook and pulled my asshole right out through my mouth. Heart 'n all come with it. Feenished."

It was him! He said *finished*. The Tennessee Ernie baritone The Junior and he heard years ago in South Carolina, the Ghost of Channel Nineteen.

"Yeah, I heard that, c'mon," another driver answered him as they moved farther out of range. And for some reason, maybe a run of thin air or his truck was elevated on an overpass, he said *feenished* again into the mic. Aubrey slammed the brakes off to the side of the road.

"What are the odds, Trip? The odds I'd hear the Nineteen again or run into a woman like Christaine Sadacca—and on the same day! It's a sign. Horses, new people, like some silver weather front rolled in. One way or another, I'm gonna get hold of that splendiferous split-lip woman, you watch me. **Not finished? Hear me, Trip? Hear me, Nineteen? Not feenished!**" he yelled at his radio.

"Yes, Your Huge! I think the whole turnpike heard you."

In twenty minutes, he was upstairs dropping his clothes, staring at his bed. His hands were shaking. The headboard was an ornate fireplace mantelpiece with carved vertical posts. He had hung a neon sign that read FLORIST behind the pillows in the opening for the absent fireplace. Fake flowers were inserted between the sign's tubular lettering, and the usual Plexiglas protected it. You could see a small crack where his head had hit the glass after he plunged too purposely forward with a woman years ago.

He continued to stare at the festooned sleep arrangement until he lay down naked and looked out the screen doors at the Florida night. The heat lightning lamped on and off through the coulees and high draws of thunderheads out over High Beach. Refulgent bursts dazzled marlin and barracudas in the Gulf Stream and anyone else that might look away from another face to watch the adipose boils of glowing cumulus. He flipped the switch on the FLORIST sign, and the room changed from a molecular dark to the blue-and-rose hue of the gas in the glass. An aureole formed around him as he lay slathered in the treatment still as a stamp—a colored person.

He thought about Christaine and her story. "Hey, Trip, you awake?" He got up and took two trazodones instead of a single pill, the dream inducer that brought streams of aubergine.

"I'm glad you took that extra pill, Aubrey. You certainly are excited by this woman and her story, and of course, the God of Big Truck Radios tonight."

"Hope I didn't sound too juvenile to her. I mean when I was playing kiddy war, she was simulating with a plaster knockoff of Jesus. Slam dunk me, Julius Erving."

"Well, if you're worried about appearing juvenile, then I suggest you don't mention you like to put everything in a jar, take it inside your head, smoke a toadstone bone, then spin around a tower or whatever you do in there, and try to swallow it. She'll think you're Peter Crackhead Pan."

"Yeah, better keep off that one. Not goin there. So good night, yeah, good night, Trip. I mean it."

"Good night, Aubrey, and I'm glad you had a good day. You need more of those."

Trip walked up the arm and slipped through the skin crease to his apartment. He opened his shirt to the mirror, ready to read what Amper Sand would type on his chest.

CHICA LOCA

SHE DANCED WITH THE NUNS

SHE DANCED WITH THE PRIESTS

SHE DANCED WITH THE BANYAN, TOO

BUT THE FINEST DANCE WAS THE ONE

WITH THE MANNEQUIN

HUMPED IN THE SHELL-PIT POOL

HE WANTS A SIGN TO SHOW HIS KIND

IN THE NIGHT WITH THE CB MAN

HE THINKS THERE'S A TIME

WHEN IT STOPS ON A DIME

BUT IT DON'T 'CAUSE OF AMPER SAND. &

"I know, Amp," Trip said. "Never feenished, none of us, no matter what the Channel Nineteen man says, we are always left with you. Nothing stays the same, and nothing is ever over. Just when we think it might be, there you sit over the number seven on our typewriters."

Aubrey began to fall asleep. The cinema voices came as always, unimpeachable. "Pick a film, Aubrey, any film, any film, any film…"

"Oh, I want Tuesday Weld. Tuesday in *The Cincinnati Kid* with McQueen," he slurred, and Trip smiled inside the armpit.

"Yes, Aubrey," the voices said and untied a knot in the heat lightning out over High Beach so he could wander into *Cincinnati*.

~

In Miami, Carlos watched Christaine go to work the next day at *The Herald.* The coffee was down in front of him with the famous *huevos* and bread. Where did she go this weekend? He'll follow her next time, this woman he married and fathered a child with—a child who died in the street years ago. Carlos still loved this woman, but it wasn't human love.

Chapter 5

GIRL FIGHT

Marla and The Junior took themselves out the next evening. They headed west toward Indiantown and Lake Okeechobee to do a certain cowboy hangout and some dancing. The Johnny Jumper Inn offered a lot of such, named after a Seminole who hunted the cypress swamps there in the early 1920s. Marla hadn't been to the inn, but had heard story after story about the place from The Junior.

When they pushed through the old-style saloon doors, the whole room turned around, and half the people, especially the cowboys, hollered because they knew the big Junior Nelson.

Marla did her Blue Heroness in front of him over to a corner of the bar while the patrons fell into one of the three aforementioned categories. She ran her hand under her hair over the back of her neck, making categories one and two very concerned; the third category, which belonged to Punky, couldn't give a shit.

"Hey, Junior man, what'll it be for you and the lady?" the bartender asked.

"A beer for me, and a dry Beefeater martini for her, straight up with an olive, please, Biggie."

"So, this is the famous Johnny Jumper." Marla took in the high pine ceiling and slow-moving Hunter fans.

"Yeah, this is it. The upstairs used to be a whorehouse in the old days. It's kinda like the western part of the county's Blue Goose, as far as a juke joint goes, but the Blue Goose didn't have an upstairs, so it had whore cottages 'cross the street."

"That's *grande mi caballero*, whore cottages." She smiled approval.

"Here you go, folks." The bartender put down the drinks, and The Junior introduced him.

"Marla, this is an old friend of mine from way back, a famous drag racer. Give a big hand to Cabbage Pinley."

"Nice to meet you, Mr. uh—"

"Cabbage, ma'am, and I don't know how an ugly ole boy like Junior could have the favor of a good-lookin woman like you."

"Why, thank you, Mr. Pinley. What a nice compliment, but he has qualities and powers that you would—"

"Yes, ma'am. I'm listening." His mouth cracked like it was a genetic thing.

She sang it. "He gotta heat-seeking missile that can make me whistle, a rocket in his pocket that can make me smile."

Cabbage blushed. He looked at The Junior and roared hisses and adenoidal snorts.

"If I was a man, I would rather be nicknamed Zucchini, Mr. Pinley." She slowly inserted the olive from the martini.

Cabbage stomped his feet. "Ah-hah-hah, boy, I tell ya, she got some riot in her. Ah-ha-ha, this girl ain't one who's ever gonna walk behind her man," he announced to the whole house.

"That's fine with me," The Junior said back to the house. "At least she don't suffer from one of them deadly sins. She ain't boring!"

"Excuse me, sir, but boring is not one of the seven deadly sins," said a well-dressed man in an English accent as he rose from his table. He looked to be in his late forties.

The crowd fell silent. The dandy stepped forward from the table where two other sport coats were seated.

"The seven deadly sins are pride, envy, gluttony, lust, anger, greed, and sloth. But boring is not, although I think it definitely should be. So my compliments to you, sir, on your observation and praise of this lovely woman."

"Now who's this motherfucker?" The Junior mumbled and stepped toward him.

But Marla stepped in front of him. "Don't. He just paid you a compliment," she whispered.

"He did?"

The dandy acknowledged him with a bow. "Would you and your charming lady care to join us for a drink?"

"Say yes," Marla said under her breath.

"Wonderful!" the man said and pulled over two chairs while she Blue Heroned in front of her cowboy again over to the group.

"How do you do? I'm Walter Doggett."

"And I'm Marla Sadacca, Mr. Doggett."

"It is my pleasure to meet a woman with such brio and spark."

"Well, sometimes that gets me in a lot of trouble, Mr. Doggett."

"I can imagine it would if they are people who suffer that serious iniquity we all agreed on tonight, the eighth deadly sin, which is certainly *ennui, mademoiselle*."

"This is Junior, Mr. Doggett."

"Sir!" Doggett shouted and clicked his heels together. "Bartender! Another round for all here, please."

"So where, might I ask, are you from, even though it is a perfunctory pub-house question," Doggett asked.

Marla hit The Junior's knee with hers.

"Well, yes, I'm from this county, and so is Marla, and uh—well, yeah, that's it."

"And what a wonderful county it is. I come here to your great Lake Okeechobee to fish for your large-mouth bass."

Cabbage came over with a tray of drinks and scratched his bird finger behind his ear at The Junior.

"And now I've told you what my friends and I are doing, what do you do here, Junior?"

"I work on a ranch 'bout five miles away."

"Junior is a cowboy at large, Mr. Doggett," Marla said.

"A cowboy! How adventurous that must be, and please call me Walter."

"Yeah, you know what all the bumper stickers say around here, Walter." The Junior smirked. "'If You Ain't Country, You Ain't Shit.' And, oh yeah, 'Cowgirls Got It, Cowboys Want It.'"

"What does that mean, exactly, Junior? That last one?"

The Junior squinted, then told Marla to stand up and turn around. He pushed a finger into her tight butt. "That's what cowboys want, Walter. Venus in blue jeans right here, son, but there ain't no more around like this."

"And you, Marla, dear, what are your favorite things to do with your time?"

"My time during the day, Walter," the English all leaned forward, "is spent with my legs spread apart," the English leaned more, "to receive the backs of any one of six horses I school every morning."

"On the ranch?" Walter's face lamped up.

"*Nein, mein leibchen*, in a twenty-by-sixty-meter ring on a fifteen-hundred pound German warmblood doing movements."

"My God, it's dressage!" Walter cried out. "And it's right here in the Indiantown. But that's fabulous." This time, he wagged his male head pretty Nancy.

"Hey!" a big man yelled and parted the swinging louvers. "Anybody wanna struggle?"

"Oh, Lord, it's Roland Mitchell," The Junior said.

"What's he mean, Junior? Struggle?" Walter asked.

"Fight, Walter. He wants to fight somebody."

Roland was from the huge Mitchell Ranch on the north side of the lake. Right behind him, strutting like another Heroness, was his infamous, hell-raising older girlfriend, Sugarcane Valdez, so nicknamed because her father was the *Los Patrones* of the sugar industry around Belle Glade on the southeast side of the lake.

"I said, anybody wanna struggle?"

"Not in here, Roland; you either, Sugarcane," Cabbage shot back from behind his polished bar.

"Well, I wanna struggle right here, dammit." Roland laughed.

"Yeah, Roland don't like the parking lot tonight because it's raining," Sugarcane said. "So, come on, Roland, these people don't wanna mess with you. Let's go, because we are going to be late to the party." She wrapped a leg around him, shook her mamarano gigandos, and stuck out her tongue at Cabbage.

The Junior stood up and looked Roland in the eye.

"Not you, Junior. I don't mean you." He grinned and held up a hand. "Me and you is too good a friends, and I ain't messin with no friends tonight. Besides, you too damn strong for you age."

Laughter rose from the crowd.

"Oh, me, either, Roland. I's just going to the little boy's room."

"Would you look at the hair she's running," Marla said to Walter, who was breathing through his mouth now. "So where's the party?" Marla called out.

"Well, well, who is this Miss Curious with the bad manners to ask someone where their party is?" Sugar turned.

Marla stood up. "This is Marla Sadacca, faithful daughter of Asante Sadacca, the horse master from Portugal, Miss Curious Bad Manners yourself."

"Oh, you one of those pure-blood jobs who think the rest of us brown people are from the barrios. Well, I think your last name is a name I have heard before, and they were Moors, stinking Arabs, Miss Port-a-gee holier than thou."

"Oh, yes, and proud of it, you foul-mouth, sloppy *puta*."

The two were of the same athletic height and build, the pro-beach volleyball look, except Sugarcane had a large front porch. Sugar detached from Roland and stepped into the middle of the room. "*Tu quieres chingazos tu pinche pendejo*, bitch."

Marla came to the floor and walked a half circle, then turned to face the tough hen. "Don't we have a rest-area commode mouth on us? A public toilet that needs someone like me to flush it."

Sitcom laughter erupted from the crowd again.

"No, stupid, it is you who has the toilet stuck, and I will be your plunger." She went after Marla's throat with both hands.

Marla swept them aside like a trained move, ducked down behind her and latched onto her hair, then pulled her backward until she could knee her lumbar. Sugarcane bent. It made her pick one leg off the floor, so Marla hooked her leg around it and slammed her to the pine surface. The Junior looked at Roland, who laughed like a man who was living with a bitch and liked seeing her get her ass handed to her, as long as it wasn't him getting a visit from her father's bodyguards.

"Hey, Roland, what do you think 'bout my woman?" The Junior hollered.

"I don't think nothin yet, 'cause mine's just gettin started."

Marla moved on top of her and pinned her to the floor. She slipped her left hand off Sugar's right shoulder, and it looked like she was searching for something in Sugar's thick hair. Sugar got a hand free and shoved it under Marla's armpit to roll her off. They both jumped to their feet. Roland looked at The Junior and beat his chest. The Junior nodded his head in approval as everyone watched the first and only round unfold. Walter blotted his lips even more Nancy with a white handkerchief.

Sugar breathed hard through her mouth, and her gigandos heaved on her frame. Marla still breathed through her nose—riding six horses a day put her in the shape of a runner. She knew she could outlast the cane-stalk heiress.

"So you think you are hot shit for getting lucky on that one, you dirty—" Sugar panted.

"Luck? I'd say I'm just better than you, you pole-humping, big-tit *pachuco*."

"Ooh!" The crowd responded to that invective like it was keeping score as the two rushed each other again in a storm of fists and fingernails. They punched, scraped, and traded headlocks easily slipped out of because of their thick, conditioned hair. Then Marla maneuvered behind her and got a chokehold, freeing her other hand to feel in Sugar's hair again until Sugarcane bit her arm and Marla had to let go, sending Sugar coughing and gasping forward. Marla stood her ground, rubbing the bite.

The chokehold enraged Sugar. Her eyes weren't there—rolled back with that swallowed-tongue look that operates only from the midbrain, and anger flattened her lips to nothing. She came on again, charging and scrambling. Marla stood motionless, feet together like *El Cordobés* to show her nerve. Then Sugar abruptly stopped. Her eyes reappeared, and she reached behind her neck into her hair. The Junior and Roland jumped up; they knew what she was after and weren't going to let it come to this. But time won, and Sugar found the four-inch-long, old-fashioned hatpin Marla had been searching for when she pinned her on the floor. It was a favorite martial spine of tough Hispanic women, and Marla knew she probably had one.

"Don't you do that, Sugarcane!" The Junior warned and moved toward her with Roland behind him, shouting, "No, honey, no, no, honey!"

She rushed Marla anyway, but Marla cut to the left like a cat at the last second and sent the banshee into a table of people, stabbing an older man in the left thigh.

"I been cut! I been cut!" the man hollered.

Roland grabbed Sugar. The hatpin stuck out of the old guy's leg while some people tried to help him. Roland pulled out a money clip and fished three or four hundreds off it, then threw it at the downed senior.

"Here, get somebody to take a look at that. It was an accident."

He picked up Sugarcane, who looked deaf and detached, and turned to smile at The Junior containing Marla. Then he carried his trounced fighter out through the swinging doors.

"You gonna pay for this, you rich brats sons-a-bitches! Just wait'll I tell your daddies, both a-you!" Cabbage screamed.

Marla held the older man's hand and apologized three times.

"Bullshit." He smiled and pulled out the pin. "Hell, just an old hat pin, like my mother used to have. I used to stitch *myself* up when I was cut back on the farm in Michigan." The crowd laughed and he ordered another drink, which put Cabbage at ease, considering lawsuits and bad press.

Walter was beaming when they returned to the table.

"Hear, hear!" Walter toasted. "To Ms. Marla Sadacca, a woman to be taken seriously. I haven't seen anything like that since I lived in Marseilles, but that was just a skirmish compared to this vitriolic confrontation."

The Junior looked at Marla and draped his arm around her. She was crying inside, one of those chin-up headwork cries, mouth closed. The fight had stirred certain machinations and designs she lived with every day. She was determined to reap a private satisfaction over something unrelated to tonight's fight any way she could. Some existential loggerhead she needed to step through in the way of recognition and public approval from another world outside this bar room, and it was about becoming famous in the dressage ring. She wanted to win, as she won tonight, at the Johnny Jumper Inn, in front of everyone.

The Junior leaned over. "Now you know we're having a good time, tears and all, but we got to leave, honey, before that she-devil comes back drunk with a piece."

"Just one more drink, Junior, please."

"This ain't smart, but all right." The Junior went to the bar—ordered, paid, and walked the drinks back to the table. "Here y'all are, more kickapoo juice from the Johnny Jumper Inn made by that famous drag racer hisself, Cabbage Pinley." He cupped his hand over his heart.

Another "Hear, hear!" rose from the English.

"Tell me more about Mr. Pinley's drag what?" Walter asked him, and waved an effeminate hand.

It all went by The Junior.

The highway was dark as a cypress swamp on the way home from the Johnny Jumper that night. Marla lay across the front seat with her head on The Junior's lap. One of those rains fell like it was raining all over the world.

"Honey, I wanna know two things." He rubbed her stomach. "Do you really love me?"

"Si, mucho."

"And the other thing: Where was your hat pin tonight?"

Marla slid her hand to her belt and gripped what looked like a decorative silver rivet, then pulled the pin with two fingers halfway out of its hideout between the layers of leather. In The Junior's mind, he saw a Telstar shot of the biggest river on mainland America snaking its dangling delta out into the Gulf between the legs of Florida and southeast Texas. Anytime her hand touched her belt, that same river would swell in his body because so many times that belt was being undone for him. He knew how much he loved her, even when the river was down, and he wondered how all this would play out one day at his age, living hand to mouth in these cowboy clothes.

"I want you to do me from behind, baby, because my ribs are

hurting," she said when they got to his house. "And while we look in the mirror into each other's eyes."

The Junior poured himself a neat double vodka and was feeling comical. Usually, it was him in bar fights, not his woman. He needed a bigger mark than she had from the battle to get his head right and to make her laugh. He pulled the hatpin out of her belt on the chair and looked back at her. She was a tall nude placing a dressing mirror at the foot of his bed so they could see each other's faces while they made love in the ancient position.

"Watch me touch myself, baby. Watch me in the mirror," she said to him.

He knew she was controlling things, and he loved it, but he was determined to outdo her. He told her she wasn't going to be the only one who got to bleed tonight, and instead of piercing his ball sack with the usual two safety pins before sex, he stitched the long hatpin through the top of his scrotum in four places without making a face while she cringed and smiled in disbelief. "Now I get to bleed for my woman like she did for me." He snapped his big grin and sucked a little blood off his fingers. He looked down at her woman place. "God, I love that dime piece a-yours, baby."

~

Carlos genuinely hadn't loved anything genuinely since his mother's milk chest, except his dead daughter and Christaine. He was so sure he could get his child back from the world of souls by impregnating someone as he rubbed chicken blood on the woman he was with—the one he asked to push the olive oil-coated rosary inside him while the same rain fell outside that fell on The Junior and Marla, and yes, all over the world.

Chapter 6

The Toadstone Ring

A week passed. Aubrey hit the Catheter Café, had his Adam and Eve on a raft, and headed to the Sadaccas' for his first dressage lesson with Asante.

Asante spoke five languages and was a master of the baroque and competitive styles of riding, though his favorite was the old style, with its levades and caprioles. But levades were in his past now; the competitive style dominated the business if you had to make a living and weren't wealthy or a trustafarian.

"I know you know about the quarter horse, Aubrey, but these European horses are of a little different, how you say, recipe. We call this horse a warmblood, a mixture of the hotter, more nervous breeds such as thoroughbreds, Trakehner, and Arab, and the more quiet, cold-blooded draft horse they used to work on the farm in Europe. So it's just like you do with water, you take a little hot, a little cold, and mix them the right way, then you get a horse with the warm blood, *comprendo*?"

"I carburet it. Yes, sir."

"Carbo what?"

"Nothing."

"The idea, you see, was to get the right body, a little bigger bone, and the right, what's that…temperament, not too crazy, but still much energy and quick movement. So a little cold in with the fire, the whiskey, you know, to give the horse less *que*? Sting? Crazy? But they get a good animal to fight on, yes?"

"There it is again, the fighting. You told me about that, Asante, when I first met you."

"But, *monsieur*, are you surprised? They used go to town with them, too, and show off on Saturday for the women, passaging up and down the street like a Mexican kid with one of those bouncing cars. Same thing, capiche? Now these horses, they are for show. They are for a master to demonstrate the horse's skills and his, too, and do it like the old days, by signals with the leg and seat so they could hold a pistol in one hand and a sword in the other. And, oh yeah, the reins in their teeth like the movies." He laughed.

"*True* magazine?"

"What *True* magazine, Aubrey?"

"I used to read *True* magazine as a kid. You don't see it anymore. It was the real man's tabloid in the Fifties, you know, Hemingway, Louis L'Amour. Junior and I still say the name to swear oaths at the end of things we talk about."

"Oh, I see. Well, I don't know about the reins in the teeth, but yes, *monsieur*, in Napoleon's time the cavalry horses were like their airplanes to fight with. The army who had the best-trained horses and men destroyed the other. "*True* magazine!"

"So when do I ride, Asante?"

"Not so fast. Go out to the paddock and bring the bay horse into the barn, then I give you some more silver from Europe to mix with your cowboy *credos.*"

Asante handed him a currycomb and brush. "Here you are, *monsieur*. Clean him up. Let me see how you cowboys do it. You must lean over and bang the comb on the floor at least ten times while you work around him. When I was a boy, I had to have those places on the floor with the dirt and the hair from the horse for my parents."

Aubrey worked. The older man talked.

"You know, it is not easy to become a dressage rider. All of these rich people out there saying, 'Oh, look at these dressage people. That looks easy. I think I try that and ride in the grand prix.' They are idiots! What do they think? They buy a Steinway, they play better than people with those cheap pianos? Most of the great riders come from the hard life, you know, Aubrey. They start as grooms or in the barns. Of course, there are rich people who can ride and work hard, too, like you. That's okay. If you have some natural ability, then maybe you will get somewhere if the luck comes to you. The dressage trainers are the best horsemen in the world. Of course, I am a little bit, how you say, prejudice, because that's what I do."

"No, I promise to do the job, Asante, and you will be my sensei."

"Your what?"

"An Asian word for teacher."

"Okay, and you will call me professor."

"Okay."

"No, no, I'm joking. You call me Sante. After your lessons, when you leave here, you can call me that old bastard, but not to my face."

In the afternoon, hungry, Aubrey walked out of his kitchen with a sandwich and ran his eyes across the cathedral ceiling paneled with *Paraná* pine from Brazil. No one had a ceiling out of that species of wood—purple and red streaked with yellows the length of the boards—blowfly colors bollixed in queer whorls with Amazon faces staring at you if you crossed your eyes hard enough. It occurred to him they were the only other faces in his house besides his own and the ones in the displays, and they had no blood in them. It started to overdo his awareness of being alone like in the diner every morning. It didn't feel the same in this room anymore. Too much house and no work to get him out.

He called the high school and asked John Chrome if he was going. Chrome said he'd see him in an hour at high tide.

Aubrey was there first and sat on the sand in the cincture of the beach. The white noise from the waves locked his eyes in a low-lux snow that even canceled his wondering. When he quit it, Chrome was squatting beside him, staring at the horizon.

"What ya think?" Chrome asked.

"I think something's going on with me."

"Umm." Chrome nodded.

They walked down to the shore trough and paddled through a small run-out beyond the break. They were back on the sand in forty-five minutes, ascendant from what the physical makes of it.

"Is it still going on?" Chrome asked him.

"Still."

"A woman, isn't it?"

"That's right, you clairvoyant fuck."

"Did you talk to Trip about it?"

"Yeah. I mean, some. He's actually pitching it to me."

Chrome knew the clout of Aubrey's other voice. He was counter sunk into such things.

"So you gonna say anything about her or not?" Chrome lifted an alopecic eyebrow.

"Yeah, all right. You remember when we still were sniffing bike seats? You used to say, 'Hey, Shallcross, let's go out tonight and hunt for some thin-lipped women.'"

"Oh, dear. She's a thin-lipper."

"No, this one has Tuesday Weld's lips."

"And?"

"She's got three little scars on the right side of the upper one, as in the classic split lip."

"Good one." Chrome ran his finger across his own. "Like a Helnwein child she is then."

"Yep, one of Gottfried's."

"Goddamn, where do you find these people, Shallcross?"

"Accidents. She's Junior's girlfriend Marla Sadacca's older sister and all of thirty-four, so don't look at me funny, son."

"What's with The Junior and The Marla anyway?"

"He's slaughtered. So kegeled in that cockpit of hers, she skywrites instructions on the backside of his eyes. She's probably thinking, 'Better an old man's darling than a young man's slave.'"

Chrome nodded.

"I don't know, Chromie, this big sister could be critical. Great storyteller about dry-humpin a mannequin she kept in a tree house when she was young, if you're ready for that."

"Festered. Outstanding."

"Yeah, said she'd be back, and I'd rather hear one of her stories than eat cracked conch with you at the Blue Goose till I puke. Nothing personal."

"Talk about The Junior. You may as well walk down in the water with Virginia Woolf."

"Hey, maybe I'll never see those lips again?"

Chrome stood with the surfboard under his arm and smiled, shook his head, and left.

The next day, more currying and brushing horses. It was getting old, but he was determined to stick it out as an apprentice of the elite horseman, this master *écuyère* from the Ecole de Cavalerie, who lived right here in the county. Sometimes he would stay to watch the old man coach his daughter while the Portuguese *fado* played out over the property. It wet him in a way music did everything in his life. On his knees, he was lately over this, this new gambol, this sudden rumspringa that had flown out of a box into his life.

One night, after telling an old lover not to come over, he sat in a small building behind his house used as a studio when he had his band together. "Just an old guitar shrine," he called it when his friends saw the place.

He started picking tunes and thinking about Christaine. In a half hour, he plaited some lyrics into the single verse of a simple song.

She takes you upstairs to the room
She lets her clothes down and perfume
She tells you she has done the moon
Right there inside her dark bedroom
Clothes on...clothes off
Clothes on...clothes off.

Trip slid down to the forearm and began singing high parallel harmony when Aubrey sang it again. At the end, they headed upstairs to lie under the FLORIST sign and watch the stars through the screen while the cyan blue and rose of the neon crayoned a ground fog over his beach-skin body.

In the morning, he flew his brain-born truck, steampunked to the gills over the zillions of spider webs hooked to the St. John's wort flooring the knee-high Serengeti, then headed to Janet and breakfast at the Catheter Café. He stared at the baby jukebox in the booth. Who would it be this morning? He had had plenty of Frankie Lymon and the Teenagers.

"How about the greatest white boy ever to sing falsetto, 1963, the man from Pittsburgh himself, Mr. Lou Christie and 'The Gypsy Cried,'" Trip's voice announced from the foyer.

"Ooh, yeah, you do it, T. I haven't had my breakfast."

Trip began with the vinyl drop and soon had the Gypsy on the floor in tears.

"You bobbing your head to some music again." Janet placed the eggs in front of him.

Aubrey got them down his dangerous throat in one minute and left. On the way to Asante's, he stopped for some rare banana mangos. The tree belonged to Coker Barnes, an old cracker man he'd known forever. Coker was a widower. His deceased wife, Reve, or dream, came from out-of-town heritage: a true Roma, a Gypsy from Quebec. She was a large influence on Aubrey growing up.

When Coker was young, he managed permission to marry her after saving her father from a rattlesnake bite by forcing him to eat a can of alum as he drifted in and out of consciousness along the St. Lucie River for days. God only knows what the alum did—maybe clarify the blood—but it had powers in Coker's mind, even though no doctors agreed. The father charged him for his daughter, anyway, and told Coker that was his first lesson in becoming a Gypsy: making money off the women.

As a kid, Aubrey would run the top of the seawall to Coker's and listen to Reve's stories. She had seen him speaking to the air, and knew he was not alone. Aubrey told her about Triple Suiter and asked why others did not hear what he hears. Reve said she was like this, too, and that her mother was this way and had told her about the small lights called slippers that slip through your brain from their side to the your side where they can speak to you, and you can speak to them if you have the gift. She said slippers are in everyone, and inhabit animals close to humans like dogs and horses, but those without the gift can only see and hear them speak in certain dreams. In these dreams, normal people do not know them as slippers, only dream people. Dreams, she said, are very important to the Gypsies, and this is why her mother named her Reve.

When Aubrey was twelve, she told him about the great land toads that lived in the shade. "Dey have a hard stone like a pebble een they skulls. Eet is a magical stone." She showed him her toadstone ring—a small albescent, round bone from the creature's meagerly staffed brain cupped in a bursa of silver. The ring had been hand wrought by her mother when Reve was Aubrey's age to protect her from hags, kelpies, moochibonereens, the gas-oline-painted skink, and any other wet-toothed malefic ghoul. She said it would change colors if she was in danger or someone was lying to her, but it also would predict if something good was about to happen.

The day Aubrey turned thirteen, Coker and Reve lit a fire on the riverbank for the ritual to make him a ring. It would take thirty days, or one full cycle of the moon—their secret to keep from his Catholic father and grandmother.

They searched with flashlights under the philodendron until they found a large bulbous creature. The toad was killed and placed on a bed of fire ants to strip it of every wet cell; in one day, it looked like a wood-frame house before the siding goes on. That night, Reve told Aubrey to take the skull from the ants and shake it. It rattled like the Roman dice said to be in the bleached backbone of a Florida catfish, the one with a crucified Jesus painted on it sought after by tourists for two dollars and ninety-five cents out on U.S. 1.

They split the toad's skull, and a calcium pellet the size of a .32-caliber bullet's lead fell out. A fuel stone—the future bone smoke of Aubrey's adult imagination, the objective world version of the rock he used for creation inside his etherealized Ball jar, ready to be pagan-consecrated in a campfire church by a Romani priestess and her Catholic altar boy only a hot asphalt street away from the afterlife-loving Christians in the little town of Stuart.

They wrapped the anomalous jewel in plain linen and buried it in a copper bowl filled with earth until the moon ran from new to full. Then Aubrey and Reve retrieved the brain piece. She mounted it in a silver setting like her own and taught him about its elan vital and what the different colors meant: rose for danger, blue for sorrow, green for clean, pale for all is well, and red is wrong, son, run like hell! The sagacious jewel would see farther than beyond, she said, and it would stay pale as his English skin when he was on a peaceful path.

The ring became one of his most sacred experiences and possessions. And in case he might lose Reve's gift, he conjured a copy of the stone for his jar, making it the spectral cowalker of the ring's real stone worn out on his finger in the plain-speaking air of the objective world. Days later, the bishop of the diocese slapped his face as required during his Holy Confirmation, and it seemed prosaic and dumb compared to this Pagan ritual by the river.

He was eying the banana mangos when a noise behind him ended his retrospect.

"Morning, Coker."

"Hey, looka here. It's Aubrey, the king pin of the county."

"Oh, now don't go say'n that, Coker. I'm not king-pinning anymore. I sold the car place."

"I don't say then. So how are you, son?"

"I'm good, sir. Hope you are."

"Oh, hell, yeah, s'ept I got Arthur in my knees."

"You takin anything for it?"

"A little smidgen of alum every day." He winked.

"Yeah, that's good. That always did the trick, didn't it, Coker?" He could see the codger's rheumy eyes watering from his presence. He knew how much he missed Reve.

"All right if I take some mangos?"

"You know it is, boy. Go right ahead. I gotta just watch these Yankees sneaking in here at night and takin em."

"Thanks, Coker, I have to go. Sorry, I'm runnin a little late for where I'm supposed to be."

"Nice to see ya, Aubrey. You marry again?"

"No. I'll come by next week and we'll sit 'n talk."

"Anybody ever figure out what became of your friend, Arquette

Orlander?"

"Nope."

The old man grinned, cleared his throat, and spit on the ground as he walked away. Aubrey stepped off the porch and looked down at the spit. There was blood in it.

He drove through town and crossed the south fork of the river to the Sadaccas' farm. Asante met him at the entrance to the barn.

"*Bonjour, monsieur, ça va bien?*"

"*Bien, merci.* Here, Asante, I brought these for you, hoping they would buy my way on a horse today. I think you'll be surprised."

Asante peeled one with his pocketknife and bit into the flesh. "Okay, does anyone know about this tree besides you and me?"

"Yes, some do. It tastes like a cross between a banana and a peach, doesn't it? It's the only tree in the county. My grandmother used to call it the Raintree, like in the movie with Liz Taylor and Montgomery Clift."

"Oh, yeah. My wife, she saw every movie of Elizabeth Taylor, even *National Velvet*, which I liked very much."

"Doesn't sound like you."

"No, but every woman in America wanted to buy a horse after that." He swallowed more mango. "I sold horses I brought in from Portugal on a ship. I think I even named a few of them Velvet." He chewed his grin. "And for today I have one of those horses right here, a Lusitano from Portugal. His name is Rigoletto, like the opera, a nice white stallion a woman brought last night. An older horse I trained to the grand prix level for her years ago, a good schoolmaster for you. She will leave him until she is better from her hip operation."

"A horse that can teach me flying changes and piaffe passage?"

"Not so fast, *monsieur*. It would not take long for you to harm all this work I have done. You can ride him a little every day, but I will have to get on him at the end and say, 'Patch up everything Mr. Aubrey has destroyed.'"

In the ring, Aubrey walked on a loose rein and came to a halt.

"When his jaw releases, you have to feel it in your hand, in your fingers, Aubrey. He will show you by chewing the bit a little. This is what the French call *mise au main*, or you put the mouth in your hand."

Asante moved in front of the horse and held each bit ring with a facile dexterity. Rigoletto lowered his head, chewed twice, and relaxed his jaw. Each time Asante slightly flexed him to the right and to the left, the crest of the neck rolled over from one side to the other like a breaking wave. Then Aubrey tried, and it took him several times to get the feel of it—he was elated when it happened. A breakthrough.

"Okay, Aubrey! Okay! You did it. Now he will be more willing to swing through his back in the trot because he has relaxed. It all starts in the jaw and poll of the horse, and believe it or not, with people, too, or they have to sleep with that rubber thing in their mouth. What is that thing?"

"Bite plate. Okay, got it, Asante."

"Oh, you got it. *Madre de Dios.* Like if I told you how to fly an airplane, then you gonna sit in the airplane seat and fly it. That Cleveland Clinic cannot teach you how to make love, my friend, or ride horses. You got to figure these things out with time and a lot of wet saddle pads and beds." He winked.

Aubrey drove out the gate for home grinning. At the streetlight on the corner, he looked at his face in the rearview. When the light changed, he jammed down the big truck's accelerator and said under his breath, "I am the Great Tater. The monster carburetor!"

The next day, Asante wanted to teach his cowboy about lunging horses with no rider. He held a flat woven line while he and Aubrey stood in the middle of a round pen with a horse in a trot at the end of the line.

"And I have a question for you, Aubrey. Are you a good dancer?"

"I think I am. I mean, I used to dance a lot."

"That is what it is like; you dance with your horse, like a man who can ask his guitar or his drum to dance or sing with him, or even piaffe and passage with him."

"What do you mean 'like a man,' Asante?"

"Like a man, but a special kind of man—sensitive and gentle.

83

You lead the dance with your partner, and you let your partner lead you, and it becomes a beautiful thing. Some of these people, they ride these horses and the horse leads everything, or they try to lead everything. It must be an even trade back and forth. Come on. Let's dance, sweetheart."

The horseman dropped the lunge line, grabbed Aubrey, and hummed a loud tune. "Go ahead, Aubrey!" he yelled. "Show me you can dance! All the men dance with each other in the old country. You be the man and I'll be the woman, and you show me. Then you must let a woman show you how to be a great dancer, a great lover." Asante blew him a kiss. "Because the dance and the riding are just like making love standing up, *monsieur*."

Aubrey and his sensei spun and kicked in the middle of the pen. The loose horse circled them, snorting, the line dragging in the dirt. A wild sight: one running horse and two men whirling over the sand like Zorba and the Englishman on the beach that day in Greece.

"That's right, Aubreee!" Asante yelled at the sun. "You've got to hear the music, because those who don't hear the music think the dancers are all crazy."

Chapter 7

CARLISLE

The Miami hurricane center was advising South Florida residents August 29 that a mid-Atlantic storm named Carlisle had torn a hole in its eye to stare at the state's coastline.

High Beach was a scene of activity; the entire high school was on its knees waxing boards for the huge swells sent ahead so Carlisle could taste his party. The sky was ambush clear, the sun bigger than a regulation grow light, while five hundred miles out the hurricane marched its power slow toward the west and the Indian River Lagoon like a German panzer division.

Aubrey met Chrome after school. They did the usual sit-on-the-beach and compress it all into tacit one-liners.

"Well, look at all the kiddies."

"Um," Chrome hummed, "half the school was empty; all it takes is a wave maker."

"Yeah, at least they're not sniffing glue behind the hardware store, don't you know."

"Seen any more of that split-lip Helnwein woman you love?"

"Nope. I take riding lessons from her father, so I'm over there."

They stood up and paddled out in the water. After the beach, they went to the Blue Goose to drink.

"Haven't heard a slimerater story or anything about your pica in a long time. You still do that?" Chrome said.

"Not only...I'm still good at it, too. The slimerator part, I mean. I don't wanna talk about the pica."

"Remember our old debates? What sensation was tallest in the body? And you would out-argue my sex theory with your swallowing one. You said it goes on with the food all day, and nobody could ever fuck that much."

~

Aubrey sat on a horse. He bounced too hard at the end of the lunge line, his sensei in the center of the round pen calling out instructions to improve his seat—dressage was very different from western riding.

"Sit, Aubrey, and keep your chest up so your body will follow the movement. Relax your stomach muscles and pelvis. Let your legs hang. Don't try to follow with any effort, just breathe, and sit down *in* him, not on him. Keep your chest up, I said! So you feel like the rest of you is hanging under that and is part of the horse, okay? This is what you have to learn first on the lunge line, then I give you the reins. *Voce lida a danca*, we say in Portuguese! You will lead the dance soon!"

They hosed the gelding with cool water before heading to the house. Solana greeted him with a nervous hello and asked where her husband was.

"He's in his office," Aubrey joked and pointed at the bathroom off the kitchen.

"I'm so worried, Aubrey. You didn't hear about the hurricane?"

"Sure, Solana, but that is way offshore yet."

Asante stood there as the toilet refilled behind him. "Oh, here we go again. Every year she does this."

"Sante! What if we get a big storm and have to go somewhere else?" The lampshades shook. "Oh, why do you worry so much? You know!" Then he lowered his voice and looked at her, sympathetic. "The wind from my chest will destroy it, Solana. I will blow the bastard off the road if it comes this way."

"You see, Aubrey, what I get? They all tease me about this."

"Odds are we won't get it."

"Aubrey is right, Solana. Why don't you prime the espresso machine and let's have some of your delicious cappuccino?"

~

By Sunday, Carlisle was crossing Grand Turk Island, one of the markers in the gun sight of what's called the Florida hurricane trail.

The old-timers said it was the semaphore to start filling your bathtubs for drinking water. Talk was Miami or north of there might take the leading wall and the sun-filled eye, the dead Ted Bundy eye, the one you see before it finishes beating you and the landscape to death. Aubrey had told someone once that hurricanes are attracted to Florida because Ted was waiting to die there in the electric chair—a kind of evil pilgrimage to visit a brother and blow down Raiford prison so Teddy could run.

He saw Christaine's blue van when he pulled into the Sadaccas' to ride. *If it takes a hurricane, so be it.* He was going to ask Marla for her number, anyway. He drove down to the barn to begin the coveted daily lesson.

After the last horse, they walked to the house where he knew the woman called Christ Jesus by her friends was. He had the gorilla chest thing going again, but decided to stroll in composed, bird shit stain on hat and all.

Solana didn't even say hello. "Aubrey, what are we going to do about this storm?"

"Nothing yet, Solana, until we see where it is tomorrow."

"But I am so worried, and the horses, what about them?"

Christaine shook her head at him and looked back at her mother.

"Not now, Solana." Asante stroked her face. "*Amor por favor relaxa.*"

She started to cry. Christaine stood up and kissed her, then walked to the kitchen sink for a glass of water. Aubrey followed.

"Ug, iron water," she said in the sotto voice that killed him. "I always forget the water up here has that taste."

"Yeah, I was raised on the stuff. Takes some getting used to."

"So what do you think about all this, Aubrey?"

"I think you should have dinner with me tonight, and I'll tell ya what I think, and a hurricane's not involved." He pinned her eyes.

"They're probably going to want me to eat here."

"Tough," he said with the *I-mean-it* face.

Yes, she said with her prehensile eyes—the ones he saw when he closed his own now.

On the way home, Trip hopped up and down on Aubrey's arm. "So where are you taking her? Maybe you could cook for her at the farm, yeah, your house!"

"No, that's too much. She'll think I'm trying to impress her, or maybe she'd hate the place. My decorations, not for everybody, carburet it."

"I doubt that, A.C. That girl's no Suzy Creamcheese; that girl's a Leonardo Leda, like your old strangle, Leda, and with a very large imagination. You could be the swan again, her Zeus boy slim, Leonardo, Leonardo, c'mon. She's all over mannequins, stealing, acting out, and who knows what else you might be crimped in together."

"Slam dunk me, Dr. J!" Aubrey yelled at the red light.

The people in the next car looked over.

When it dropped to the green glass, he punched his truck and screamed, "I am truly the great tater, the monster carburetor!" Back at home, he sat on the front porch conjuring the evening for an adoring audience in his jar. The scene was all him, trying on slick dialogue for a balcony of people looking down, loving and envious of the Tater and his beautiful woman—a magical thinker's Candy Land—the result of his years as an accomplished auteur of the third-eye pie and grandstand master of the two-way soliloquy.

"Yes, I am one marshal, meat-eating, son of a bitch!" he yelled at the pinewoods. "Better put a valve on this self-aggrandized smoke. Love to toke my brain-bone stone, my brain-bone jones." He streamed it into his head, excited to explode and drink her as he whirled around the tower. But he stopped. *Not with her.* Too precious today. Too much throttle right now. Yes, he did love people who were truly alive, but the ones, "who longed to be burned to death," like Goethe said, he didn't love anymore. He'd had enough of that better-to-burn-out-than-fade-away religion in his forties. It just hurt too much. This dance had to be a slow lanyard they'd braid together. Swallow her? No. He wouldn't. He had tried with his ex-wife, Leda, but couldn't get her slim enough. She was too abundant, too toothsome.

Leda had leveled him, disarmed him, almost effeminized him. Did she really run away with his old friend, Arquette Orlander? She was like Scheherazade, the woman in *One Thousand and One Nights*, who told a serial story each day to her husband, King Shahryar. The king refused to have her killed like his other brides because she'd never finish the story. Leda could do that—plait and whittle a piece, then splay you with her hand-over-hand stall. A dangerous woman, with stacked stories like this one with broken lips. He had loved her rare earth, and now had a chance to play on the same stage again with someone who had that kind of candlepower.

Or should you become so mix-mastered? What about the wolf in his stomach—the lefty-too-damn-loose that had nothing to do with Christaine? An outsider wouldn't understand his pica and how much it excited him to swallow the great furniture of the world; it would disgust them. He knew he wasn't the only cane-field flyer around, but he might be the only one with a slim-erating jar that shot shapes, word pies, and ganglion thought through spandrel after spandrel of his brain matter. Serial love, yes! A good way to love.

He rolled out of the big room, tatered more on this side of the blood barrier, and changed the place for dinner from a slick restaurant to the Blue Goose.

"Shit, Trip. I'll just sling it, you know? Side arms, hip shots, 'stead of this complicated blocking I do. Take her to the Goose or somewhere else I'm more comfortable."

"Oh, and one other thing, Aubrey." Trip changed himself into Head Wound. "Remember the cardinal idea I had about the hurricane? The serendipity of this barometer-bashing miscreant churning over the Turks toward the great coffers of the largest underwriting thieves in America?"

"Yep, know where you're going with this, Ambrose."

"But of course, you do, Mr. Bierce. Bring the family inside the walls of your Dali cracker compound, complete with concrete horse barn, you ole backyard word slinger. You'll get no time in purgatory for that one, soul in my charge, because it's all in the name of love and the ostensible Samaritan. Finished."

Aubrey made a good face. "I really am the Tater King. Me and Jim M., shit, we can do anything."

He stood for a moment while getting dressed, reverent, then opened a wood panel on the wall of the bathroom. A beat-up silver chalice was inside. He probed two fingers into the dirt it contained and found the felt bag with catgut drawstring. He opened the bag, and a single item clinked onto the bathroom counter.

It was the toadstone ring.

What the beautiful split-lip woman would mean to his future he did not know. All he had for prophecy was his own gut strings and the colors of the ring. When he put it on, it turned gray as it always did, then pale-bone white when it reached his body temperature. He dressed in a blue linen shirt, strung a leather tie belt through the loops of his Levis, and tied the intricate knot in front taught to him by the man who made it.

With the next-to-last look in the mirror, he rocked his head up to make his neck look bigger, turned away, and did a backspin to the glass like Joe Buck in *Midnight Cowboy*'s opening scene.

Excited, he spread his lats and flew the Dodge across the knee-high Serengeti to U.S. 1. Trip railed against believing the toadstone ring really changed colors or meant rat shit about anything. He was jealous of it. "Toro *feces*," he blurted every two miles.

At 7:05, he was in the Sadaccas' yard and out again on the street with her in minutes.

A first-date silence loomed until they got to the stop sign. He looked at Christaine with the strong male smile. "Where would you like to go?"

She looked back, same strong. "It's your town."

"How about the end of the road?"

An approaching exhale made her peerless lips form the letters okay after a quick bite on the lower one.

Aubrey changed his mind yet again and headed to another food joint based on the short-sleeved shirt called The End of the Road.

~

In Miami, Carlos nursed a bad mood while watching the news and hoped the approaching hurricane would "blow the fucking place away." He planned to go inland with a friend to the Big Cypress Swamp and sit it out with some Miccosukees he was tight with from the drug trade. He knew where she had gone: Stuart, the new family home.

And she better come back.

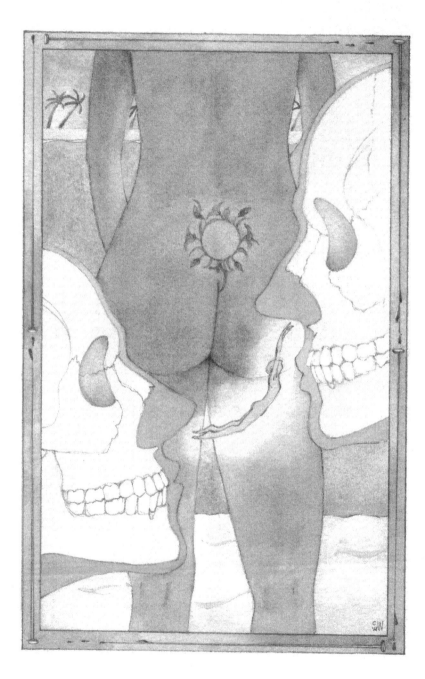

Chapter 8

TRANSITIONS

SIX MONTHS LATER

The loggerhead turtles knew. They laid their eggs high on the dunes that year. Hurricane Carlisle slammed into High Beach at one hundred-thirty miles per hour as a Category 3, and everyone in town still was cleaning up.

Christaine had slammed into Aubrey, and they were cleaning up. Marla slammed The Junior with the news she was going to Europe and he hadn't been able to clean up. He was drinking and trying to be the hard pine stump everyone expected him to be, yet was like a man walking a rope he was feeding out in front of him over a sinkhole. His sense of south even was gone.

Marla assured him she would be back in six months, but he was not that small town and knew an attractive woman in Europe leading the horse high life was fresh stuff for the bird dogs on duty there. He couldn't go; the expenses were titanic, and a court hearing was coming for his assault on a Yankee who touched Marla's ass at the Johnny Jumper Inn two days before. The Junior had thrown the guy from the bar to the porch, then hung him by his shirt on a coat hook and beat the looting snake with his belt. The other lawyer was trying to enter the belt as a deadly weapon. The big man could feel himself stagger in the mid-afternoon from the thought of the rest of the day. He was inconsolable.

~

Things had gone the way of movie magic with Aubrey and Christaine that first night at dinner. Aubrey's toadstone ring remained bone pale—etiolated as a cameo brooch, an indication the summons could be right. Was Reve watching this seat of the realm from another place and offering her *nihil obstat* on the match?

Carlisle had driven Christaine into Aubrey's heart as if it had two-by-fours through street signs. The family, their horses, and The Junior stayed at O'gram during the hurricane's assault. When the blue grotto of the calm eye moved over them, the Tater King coaxed her into the main house while the others played cards across the pool deck in the fortified guest cottage. He held her hand and spoke about his head and heart in a nervous dulcet melody, watching the sky's black horribilis return for the second half of its wind-styled hell. The toadstone ring turned red when the benign nucleus moved inland past the coast and brought an explosion of its other wall.

He began to seduce her, the best of the storm ramming the farm. Dumping rain like gravel. Dragging its fingernails in long galling screeches across O'gram's metal roof. Wailing like the old Telstar as it burned itself alive back to Earth because it had nothing left to live on up there. Carlisle was leaving the ocean, yes, leaving the ocean—nothing left for him to live on, either. Africa had sent him all this way to be destroyed when he hooked north through the cliffs of the Appalachians. This assault on the coast would be his last curtain.

Aubrey made love to her, wild. The hard pine poles wrenched inside the bedroom, breaking glass, wood siding, and skin. At times, it seemed it was them making O'gram bend and moan, instead of Carlisle, who was as passionate about carrying away the lower parts of Florida as Aubrey was. Their bodies then thinned into soft waves until they lay inhumanly still.

And so it was, Christ and the Anti-Chrysler. He repressed certain types of impedimenta from his rogue conjures and slimeration obsession, but had a brave and good heart. And she was a strong Christ lady, except when her powers were overcome in his arms; then she couldn't help it—she'd drop like a ball.

They got on with each other famously, way beyond the bone-on-bone stuff. It was only six months into the relationship, but it was working, sending those vines from foot to foot when they mixed in bed and into bloodlines when their hearts touched through their skin.

They agreed if it felt like this, they really could go to the end of the road.

Trip Suiter loved this for Aubrey, even though he knew the road didn't end, because just when you thought it did, there stood his man, the Amper Sand. Life: always remarkably unfinished.

Christaine wrote in the morning and late afternoon when her second cup of coffee worked till seven. After dinner, they'd walk the shell-rock road and tell each other who they were. It had happened so fast after Carlisle's single asylum eye, the Holy Ghost screaming in Aubrey's ear through the storm, "Eat her body, and drink her blood, boyeh! Christ! Did you catch her name?"

He would leave every morning and ride with her father, who still was recovering from seeing O'gram so close in during the hurricane stay. Out of the blue, Asante would look at him and say in Portuguese, "A sua casa e 'a casa de Salvador Dali."

Aubrey would shake his head. "No, my house is the house of Aubrey Shallcross."

When he returned home in the afternoons, he'd putter around the farm, play guitar, or thumb his way through his books, trying not to stare at her typing on the screened back porch. Trip had warned him about becoming too obsessed or a clinger, because he knew Aubrey was a diehard romantic, like his mother, and prone to that gorge of over affection.

He would take layers of this new life to his head room to revel— things they had said or done together, things he slimmed and sometimes swallowed, but never her and her true élan, only an experience they shared or something they'd seen. The decision not to spin her out around the tower had been made. She was tall magic—beautifully built and mysterious—and he would chase her forever so he could forever stand it.

At night, they auditioned for the same films and plays. They streaked around O'gram, up and down the stairs like mimetic theme-park heads, corkscrewing down the slide to the living room, where he taught her how to dance with him in front of the taxidermy and mannequins, then stand reverently before each diorama.

95

Cognate souls they were. Christ! She was just like him, you see—same tumblers, same cameras, and costumes galore they would pull off the dummies to wear for dinner or in bed. He liked to put on Johnny Yuma's confederate hat, and she would dress as an angel—wings, the works—then stand over him in bed while he lay dying with a cassette of the "Battle Hymn of the Republic" playing on the bedside table. She would drop down and plunge her tongue deep into his mouth—the genuine French test angels perform to see if you are done, then hike up the angel dress, open her knees, and prepare him with up-and-down stokes to be ejected and ejacted from this world into the Land of the Leal, where his grandmother said there were no Yankees, no Protestants, and only one perfect, beat-up Jew boy.

Aubrey gave her an altar boy cassock and surplice he found at an ecclesiastical shop in Miami, and they would reenact her altar-boy fantasy. She would shudder sweetly for him when the moment came, luxuriant now in her grown-up body.

She was not the queen of diamonds; he was becoming more and more convinced, as was Triple Suiter. "Desperado" would drop at least once a day from the capstan of the thirty-three and a third gizmo in Trip's throat, and he'd jump into the iconic Eagles song, frowning over the queen of diamonds part and raising his voice for the queen of hearts as your best friend. It was the winter of '87 in the neighborhood of the Tropic of Cancer, and the weather agreed with all those in the aforementioned categories at the Blue Goose and anyone else who practiced dipsomania with Punky's ghost inside their beloved bar based on the short-sleeved shirt.

~

A Friday night came 'round during high season. Every townie and visitor in Jensen Beach crowded the Goose on Fridays. Aubrey, Christaine, Marla, and The Junior piled into the truck, despite the number of tourists and chicken-neckers in town. The average high was seventy-eight, and the Florida weather was for sale.

A chicken-necker is a tourist who stands on a river dock at night with a Coleman lantern and ties a string to that slaughterhouse part of a bird, then throws the neck in the water to lure the blue crabs into a dip net. Local women refer to a male tourist on the make as a chicken-necker, or a guy who comes in the Blue Goose and throws that cervical section on the bar with a string hooked to his fly, so he can coax a lady to his venereal dip net.

All of them sat around a corner table like old times, and even the whir of the Hamilton Beach didn't bother Aubrey. In fact, there was no hint lately of the Blindspot Cathedral's hairy hawser hauling him lacerated to the top of his skull over the God question. He was on a royal hot fudge cloud since commingling his spirit with the woman called Christ and finding salvation equitation with her father.

Since Marla's Europe news, The Junior's face had ranged from the lugubrious to the forced smile, which really looked more like a twisted scream. He had even stopped singing along with the country stations, especially when the song cried about someone walking out on someone else, and he began to turn white after one jumped the jukebox with Kenny Rogers's classic, "Lucille."

When the last line of the first verse repeated Lucille had picked a fine time to leave, The Junior pulled the Wurlitzer's cord and walked back to the table. A big chicken-necker stood up from the bar next to Punky's reupholstered stool, which the Shallcross rat pack had inspected for its missing fart singe when they arrived.

The necker approached the table. "Suck 'em up," Aubrey said.

"I don't have 'em. You suck 'em up," Christaine said back.

"That was my song you pulled the plug on there, buddy," the man said in an upstate New York accent.

Marla picked a dinner roll from the table basket and threw it at the guy's chest. The Junior didn't say a word. Marla threw another roll, and two out of three of the aforementioned categories were now fixed on the table—even a few people with Punky's chronic dimmer switch were watching. The necker looked bricked; his confrontation with a man had turned to a woman throwing rolls at him and laughing. Aubrey, Christaine, and The Junior's faces were flat.

"Get out of here, chicken-necker!" Marla yelled and threw another.

"I'm not leaving till he plugs that juke back in and I get to hear that song I paid for, lady."

"I don't like the song," The Junior said, and started eating his buffalo wings and licking his fingers.

On the tables of The Blue Goose was a selection of three hot sauces. The Pickapeppa from Jamaica, a mild blend of island spices, mango, tomato, guava, and sugar—the most popular. There was Mr. Mclhenny's all-over-the-place Tabasco. And finally, there was a boiler from San Francisco called Insanity— The Junior's favorite. Only two people in Jensen Beach could stand it, and one was dead: Punky. The Junior used to tell Punky he should use it to check a lady for clap instead of his earwax. The restaurant took it off the tables in the main dining room because children would get into it, and their parents would leave so mad they wouldn't pay the bill. The Junior poured it over his wings and dipped his left hand in it.

"Well, if you don't plug that thing back in, buddy, I'm gonna plug you into that nickelodeon," said the New York man, who looked like a poster boy for the Yankee NASCAR series.

Marla's overhand right hit the man in the chest with another roll.

"Shut up, you tub of guts," The Junior shot back.

"That's his favorite line of Brando's from *One-Eyed Jacks*, only I think Brando said, 'Get up, tub of guts,'" Aubrey said to the table.

"Well, you do have to craft it to the moment, don't you?" Christ said.

"You wanna struggle with me, boy-eh?" The Junior proffered his fool.

"I don't know about that struggle shit, cowboy, but I'm gonna stick that electrical cord up your nose, Bill."

The Junior stood up and Marla grabbed his arm. "Don't do it, Junior. One assault charge is enough."

"Oh, now, honey, I was just gonna put it back in so the man could hear his song." He started to the box but was met with one last wisecrack.

"Oh, you're The Junior, huh?" the necker said. "Well, where is the Senior tonight, sonny?"

Shawmp! came the grouper of all headlocks, the fingers of The Junior's left hand rubbing Insanity sauce into the man's eyes. The man's knees sagged, and he clutched his face like an acid splash. The Junior dragged him moaning across the floor by his feet to the silent Wurlitzer, unbuckled the blinded's belt and pants, and rolled him onto his stomach. The guy's hands were frozen to his eyes. Every one of the patrons, even the two bartenders, backed away because they had missed the upstart and thought The Junior was trying to help this customer's mysterious pain. That is, until The Junior pulled down the man's shorts and exposed a large, nacreous, New York State ass.

Marla and Aubrey jumped up and screamed, "Junior!"

The Junior aimed the electrical cord's three-way grounded plug at the pilgrim's clean-out trap and tried to spread the crack of the man's ass with his free hand.

"I'm gonna plug it back in for this needle dick bug fucker, like he asked!"

"No!" Marla screamed as the two bartenders and Aubrey landed on him like the end of a football play.

The men in the bar howled and stomped their feet. Some of the women turned away from the man's albino melon while the team of three's scrum pushed The Junior through a side door. The manager came out and ordered him off the premises, making him officially eighty-six at the Goose.

Back in the truck, they headed to O'gram with everyone laughing, except The Junior. Aubrey could see his friend in the rear view mirror crying softly. The big one, his heart on bad bearings; his rage, his love, and bulging muscles dragged through the streets of Jensen Beach tonight. She was leaving.

"Gone from me. Tragedy," Aubrey heard him say low while the girls talked.

"Oh, shit." The Junior sat up straighter. "Pull over to that 7-Eleven and let me go wash this damn sauce out of my eyes. Think I nicked myself back there."

Aubrey parked. Marla started to cry when she saw The Junior was crying, so Christ handed her a Kleenex.

"I thought this was going to be hard for him and not so hard for me, but I was wrong. It's hard for me. I don't know if I can leave now," Marla said.

She spoke to Christ in Portuguese. "*Sou melhor do que a maioria neste mundo de equitcao.*" Then she switched to English out of respect for Aubrey.

"It is what I live for—my horses, my riding—but this time, I am cut by my heart's own razor, and so is he. *Que passa?*"

Christ turned around to answer her in their second language. "*Agora escuta, minha irma querida.*"

Then she, too, switched to English. "My loved little sister. You can't blame yourself. The riding is what you've given your life to, like the person who gives his life to the bulls and the *corrida*. You must tell Junior you can love him even more if you are happy. And you will be back soon to prove it."

Marla was silent, head down.

"Do you understand me? I said, *voce me entende?*"

Still silent. Christaine lifted her chin and slapped her. Marla stared straight ahead. Embarrassed, Aubrey looked straight ahead, too, through the largest window in an American's life, the windshield.

"You are a good Sadacca, Marlita. Why do you punish yourself? Your knife cutting *him*, *que passa*? What kind of thinking?" Then she spoke streaks of what Aubrey thought was Portuguese mixed with English, but it slid into something else: Romani. Gypsy. He recognized it from Coker and Reve when he was young. He conjured his toadstone ring in the jar. It was still pale, but flashed a beet red in the middle. Reve!

"Call on mee to help you, Aubree," she told him once. "Watch out for dee sudden storms and dee predator when eet comes. The Roma know more about human nature than anyone. Remember that if the stone is pale white, deep in the middle you will always see a little red shape no larger than a grain of sand. The same one is on the belly of the black widow and between the scales of the skink; it means the predator is never without its host. You are a host. And you are predator. The red mark is on everyone."

Aubrey thought about Christ's T-shirt, *Tell the Truth and Run*. He remembered the other Christ had told the truth, but just stood there for the predators. He didn't run. Soon his hands and feet bled out on the Golgotha Highway, where he became more famous than the Morrison.

Reve told Aubrey that when the Roman soldiers were drinking and rolling dice at the foot of the cross for his garments, a young Gypsy boy reached in and stole the belongings so the executioners of the Son of Man would not get them. Jesus looked down from the cross and said to the Gypsy child, "From this day forward, till the end of the world when I return and break the red hourglass on the belly of the widow, the Gypsies are allowed to steal."

Marla put her hands on each side of Christaine's face and kissed her, then slumped back in the seat. Christaine said one last thing to her in the dying language of the zingaros. Maybe it was something similar to what the hanging Christ said to the Gypsy child to put him at peace for stealing. Aubrey could not know.

The door opened, and his friend got in. They drove to O'gram, and Marla and The Junior headed home.

Later, in bed, The Junior cupped Marla's place in his big hand as if it was a tiny child. Hot on that hand and feeling guilty, she shot her tongue in his mouth, then jumped up and turned on the lights. He blinked at her. She came back with her hatpin and told him to scratch his initials inside her tattoo at the base of her spine. He looked at her like murder, and she could see he was wounded.

"Only while I fuck you from behind, or I won't do it. You just gonna have to take it," he said, mean.

The pain from scratching the letters while he took his andromaniacal pleasure made her feel better—some bent mix of consensual sex and punishment. She swooned and cried a private contrition as he sucked air in a fury for loving and leaving him.

In the dark, with The Junior in a liquored sleep, she said, "Chicken-neckers," and smiled on her pillow at the image of him dragging that Yankee to the jukebox to plug in his ass.

A slipper in the form of a person who spoke German and English came to her in a dream that night and told her all this was meant to be. Marla liked her dreams, but was not a voice hearer.

Chapter 9

RERUNS AND MIRRORS

Sleep came slow and Monday, too, as freight flight 1451 Lufthansa taxied on the Miami tarmac with two hundred thousand pounds of cargo: machinery, automobiles, produce, textiles, and one safe-in-a-stall grand prix dressage horse tucked in the 747's metal belly. Upstairs, in a passenger section, sat the young Blue Heroness from America on her way to Frankfort to pursue her passion for competitive dressage, where even the cab drivers know who the big-time riding stars are.

Things didn't work out for The Junior in the county courthouse that Monday. He had to plea to a lesser charge; they fined him and sent him to jail for two weeks. Aubrey paid the fine and told him to behave in there—no struggling with inmates. He promised to visit because he knew his friend was fragile—muscle, gall, and all.

Christ was waiting on the porch when he came home. "I'm afraid to ask, but how did it go?"

"Jail. He pleaded."

"No! What's wrong with him?"

"I'd say drained. Dumb as a shovel sometimes, that boy is. He smelled of, as a friend of mine used to say, mort…death. Do you know that smell?"

She didn't answer.

Aubrey remembered *For Whom the Bell Tolls*. The woman in the story told Robert Jordan that death smelled like the breath of an old hag with whiskers and no teeth. The one who stops by your house from Mass every morning to kiss you deep in your mouth and exhale her night air into your throat. Aubrey thought he could smell that on his best friend, and he was fingering the angel in front of him who had changed his life and helped quiet the pernicious slipper in his head—that degenerate eater of broken meat he called the Slim Hand.

"Yes, I know about that, Aubrey. I do know about one who is able to smell death."

"I thought you might, my love. Come talk to me. That switch from Portuguese in the truck Friday night sounded like Gypsy."

"How do you know what Gypsy sounds like?" She dragged her fingers through his hair at the foot of the Johnny Yuma display. "Some people don't like the Gypsies."

"I know. Still, I always wanted to be one."

"I could disappoint you. Marla and I are not really. We know only some of the language from our grandmother, who knew lots of Gypsies in the old country. We use strings of it to make a point, like when you say *True* magazine, but not often. My father can speak it."

He searched her face. "That's good enough for me, my love. Now this inbred Anglo child, this refugee with a blue-blood smile, this Caucasian with some busted dreams, has found a woman with more interesting papers than him. She will save him and flush the cold Victorian sump from his mien. She will make his pale-blond soul hot again with her exotic Portuguese blood, and they will love each other until heaven shakes hands with hell."

"You don't seem so hidebound to me, Aubrey Head Wound Shallcross. Just listen to you talk like the crazed prosateur." She started to tear. The scars on her upper lip spread like little pleats. "You sound like the Roma already, only without the white lies, because I don't think you can lie to me. I love you, Aubrey. You are such a wonderful drama king when you color in your book. Now if I ever lose my Gypsy libido, you'll have to build a fire and play that sweet ax of yours to fix me."

"For you, I play it sweet as all cane in Palm Beach County, helpless, helpless, helpless."

"Yes. Make me helpless, Aubrey."

~

The Anti-Chrysler made love to his Christ at the foot of Johnny the real Yuma that day and felt some life go out of him exactly where he wanted it to go.

Over the Atlantic, Marla looked down from the 747 and saw her life going toward Europe, exactly where she wanted it to go.

In the county jail, the big Junior Nelson looked at the drain in his cell floor and saw his life going where he did not want it to go.

~

A good wave feels like the top of a playground slide when you're eight. Your name is Sling Shot. You're a man-child divine balanced on a glass wand, no hands, no need. You're Chuck in the Bell X-1. You got methane playing cards in your spokes, zinging through the park on strange, jet-powered thrust coming from either the god of salt water or the fermenting bean crank you ate earlier shooting out of the crack of your ass. As a kid, Aubrey liked to think it came out of his ass, because he sided up to the idea that eating the right stuff would make you the right stuff so you could beat the other beach bum on a wave to the drop. Then he would slip away in the shudder that comes from all that and doesn't cost a doo-lang dime.

Triple Suiter loved the surfing life. He would run from Aubrey's armpit, up the stairs, through the deltoid, to a mole on the shoulder and unlatch the mole hatch, stick his head out, and scream "Ahoo! Ahoo!" until the great schizo Tater popped out of the wave's backside to do it again.

It was four in the afternoon when Aubrey met Chrome to surf. An hour after taking wave after wave, Chrome, Aubrey, and the armpit angel sat worn out on the beach.

"So, you going to tell me more about that cut-lip lady and your life, or you think I'm too nosy, don't you know?" Chrome asked.

Aubrey looked at the ocean. "I think she's a person impounded by what it says on her T-shirt: *Tell the Truth and Run*."

"Umm, after only six months?"

"Yeah, that's what I see when I throw the bones. But when she tells me the truth, she never runs."

"What's Trip think by now?"

"He's a sponsor."

"You're not so skinned you told her about that puck that moves around on your air table upstairs, have you?"

"God, no, but someday."

"Tell me more about her."

"Grew up in Miami. Was married to a cop who got into crazy dope dealing. Had one girl hit by a car and die when she was ten. Then the marriage broke up. She worked for the *Miami Herald* for a stretch. Soon we get together, all of us, and do something public or private."

~

Christaine had typed all morning, but was cleaned out for now. It was the middle of March, when the cicadas make that narcotic drone in the pines. She moved to the porch to relax and didn't notice the six-foot rattler switch backing across the lawn toward the bird feeder. Two squirrels were sifting through what the blue jays had kicked off earlier onto the grass underneath. The big snake changed directions, tongue flitting like a pervert's into a small palmetto patch ten feet from the feeder. Aubrey was off at her father's being flogged by the vicissitudes of dressage and loving every lick.

"Time to slump," she said and slid down in a lounge chair to close her eyes. The cicadas' power-line hum reminded her of dark days in Miami. Soon a slipper came to her in a dream.

"Screw the Buddhist and screw those cicadas. You kill one and there are two more right behind it, like your bad memories," the slipper said. "You can't really meditate when you've been raised in the West. Who *wouldn't* want to do that swami disappearing act in a third-world country with nothing to eat and no cigarettes?"

The slipper had come in the form of Flannery O'Connor. Then the dream turned malicious. She saw the bloodied face of Marlaine, her little girl named after her sister, mauled in the street by a driver with a cerebral blowhole, and raced to Jackson Memorial. Memorial. What a horrible handle for a hospital with horrible memories.

She'd run to critical care to stab the driver with her hatpin, but was clotheslined by an orderly at the door as she screamed at the driver's dead body, her daughter's crushed chest down the hall waiting for the morgue to show up and start a drain. The heart monitor's flat noise sounded like those locust things, those clockwork orange bugs she heard in the trees today that spit black rain on her every March.

"But you got to kick that black stuff, Christaine, that kind of puking back peel, by counting to a useless ten or pricking yourself with your hatpin for distraction. Where's the pin now, in your belt? Your hair?" the slipper said. "Distraction! That's the way to do it in the West, instead of meditating when the rationalizations don't work and you're too proud to drink and drug. You could use repression; it's an art, you know. But like art, you can't teach it."

Loud squeals by the palmettos snapped her half awake. The diamond-backed snake called Jake by the crackers had worked his plan.

Jake waited for the staggering squirrel to keel over from his poison before unhinging his lower jaw. And then the reviling process of an impossible-looking swallow by another master slimerater had begun. Christaine didn't move her eyes to anything but that. Jake had struck the squirrel in the open so everyone could see what he and Aubrey were famous for: slimming an out-of-hand object to get it down their circus throats.

The birds and the cicadas fell silent. Even the breeze shut off, and Christaine saw the car in Miami devouring her little girl like the snake, her legs kicking as the last of them disappeared through the chrome grill into the engine's teeth. She jumped out of the lounge chair and ran into the house crying. That night, she told Aubrey about the snake.

The morning after the snake, Aubrey went to ride again with Asante and then met Chrome at the beach after the high school let out.

"Hey, my old man called last night and said they had a small earthquake where he lives in New England," Chrome said.

"No shit. I didn't think they had those there."

"Yeah, he said, 'Your mother thought she was having a climax, but I told her, Mavis, are you crazy? That was a goddamn earthquake.'

Man, I hate it when your folks talk about sex."

When Aubrey got home, he found Christaine screaming on the back porch. The snake had returned and had another squirrel.

"Jesus, what's the matter? What are you looking at?"

She pointed at the coil by the pine tree. "Kill it, Aubrey."

"What...what's he got?"

"A child. Kill him!"

"Well, it's too late now, isn't it?"

But she didn't look at him, her face like rage and stranger.

"Are you all right? Why won't you look at me?"

"Kill that thing, Aubrey! Kill it! Kill it, I said!"

"Okay! I'll kill it!"

He ran into the kitchen and produced a .38 from a wood-panel hideout above the counter. Out in the yard, he turned around to her.

"C'mon, honey, that's ole Jake's job, what he's doing there. There's no reason to kill him for it."

But she was so gone, so menacing, not his soul's sidecar anymore. She staggered back onto the lounge chair and froze.

"Whatever you do, don't look at that snake doing that, Aubrey," Trip said.

But Aubrey moved toward the bird feeder, the cocked gun outstretched in a disturbed grip. When the back of the pistol lined up with the front sight, the focal center of the snake's head enlarged, and so did Aubrey's throat. The horror of that gob in the snake's mouth hit his throat, *pop!*, like a cutting torch being lit. His blood pressure went to China.

Insane. Christ on the porch, the unrecognizable harridan. Trip dancing around yelling, "Look out! It's coming! It's coming!"

The gun wobbled just before Aubrey fired and missed the head by two inches. He dropped to his knees next to the rattler, then down in the grass on his stomach on his way to the Blind Spot Cathedral. The sound opened in the dark, and the count began: one Mississippi, two Mississippi, three...*kerplooee!* The Slim Hand shoved a copy of the shrieking tree rat down Aubrey's gullet. Red men hauled him to the top of his skull, where the keloid door swirled, and a display of

X-rays appeared. A limp light pulsed to a bass beat in the rhythm of his heart, and a grotesquerie of framed radiographs—squirrels stuck in the human esophagus like breech-birth babies—hung on the walls of his skull before him. The red men made him watch it, his body hanging in the gymnast cross as they turned him slow by each and every picture. On the outside, Trip chanted their sacred rhyme, and Amper Sand typed it furiously on Trip's chest, as though their lives were at stake:

WHEN YOU CAN'T SEE, TAKE A STRAIGHT SHOT

RIGHT THROUGH THE HEART OF THE BLIND SPOT

TRUE MAGAZINE KNOWS THE TRUTH

RIGHTY TIGHTY, LEFTY LOOSE.

On one S-shaped pass, the rattler's scales brushed Aubrey's forehead with the squirrel's defecating end hanging out of its bone-lipped mouth. Then the snake joined him inside his head for the awful art show. It spoke in Reve's voice with the squirrel in one side of its maw like a cartoonish cigar.

"You know better dan to keel a sacred snake, Aubree. It is a Seminole soul, like the sandhill crane. I am the reason you believe in the forms that rise from the muck in the knee-high Serengeti. The woman, your Christ, has been possessed by one, and it is not her fault telling you to kill the snake. It is the mooch-ibonereen that lives in the flame vine and colors the belly of the skink telling her. It will pass. Christaine will come back to you."

He had a cataleptic grip on the gun. Christ was up from the lounge chair, trying to pry it out of his hand to shoot the Miami car devouring her little girl. In the struggle, a wild round hit the sliding glass door on the porch then ricocheted through the house and into Johnny Yuma's neck. The exploding hollow point blew such a hole out on the other side of the mannequin, Yuma's head landed by his feet.

"Kill it, Aubrey!" Christaine screamed again.

Aubrey started to come to and checked his throat to see if the squirrel was gone.

"Aubrey!" she screamed. "Aubrey! What's wrong with you? What's wrong with you?" She was on her knees, holding his head and acting as if she, too, had just returned home and found all of this.

Jake made his way back to the woods with the lump in his body. Aubrey lay there, staring up. He wasn't going to answer her.

~

That same afternoon, The Junior leaned against the wall of his jail cell, blue and beleaguered. He tried to remember stories from the *True* magazines he'd read as a boy describing the ways outlaws died or committed suicide when they were surrounded or incarcerated like him.

The cowboy culture had a long, oral tradition of last stands and taking one's life as the law closed in. The Junior knew the law wasn't aiming guns at him; he was only in for two weeks, and that wouldn't look good next to someone who chose self-murder because they had been sentenced to forever without parole. So he quit it—shifted into a serious drifty and watched an empty spool of bullet chambers turning on the cell wall in a narrated film piece. It told him to open the spool, insert a bullet, spin it on his thoughts, and see what happens to the trigger when the *Ouija* finger gets loose.

He saw Marla riding her grand prix horse high off the ground in flying changes every stride. Her hair shook in the suspended moments.

"Look at her, that beautiful woman. God a mighty, I'm murdered," he said in the Clorox-soaked air.

He blamed the horse for taking her away, so he spun the gun chambers in the film and aimed at the horse's head. *Click!* But the hammer landed on an empty chamber.

"I hate that damn horse. Why's this roulette let it live?" He rolled the chamber again and aimed it at his own head. It occurred to him how old he was, and she was where he couldn't surround her with his bad-boy reputation.

"Bang," he said, and the blast blew out half his brains. "I hate it, goddamnit. I hate it."

That night in his sleep, a woman came to him and held his head on her lap. She had held him before—in a jungle camp years ago when he was tied flat to a platform by his captors. After two days, a man walked into camp and shot those who held him captive. The man was South Vietnamese. The woman who held his head while he slept was a slipper.

The next morning, light flooded his jail cell. He walked over to the stainless-steel mirror above the sink and began to hear the fear, the Florida kid fear: cicadas—what Christaine could hear like a thousand dripping night faucets, the terrible tinnitus—that malarial sound that never leaves a child, even if they move away, yet no one notices it when they are happy and sane.

The Junior turned from the mirror and mumbled, "I was once, but I ain't now"—the genuine redneck inverse of *cogito, ergo sum*.

He thought about the people he knew he killed—and must have killed—in Vietnam and felt bad.

A head song came. It was Neil Young, the bleater, singing about the old man looking at his life and needing someone to love him. The Junior knew he was the old man in that song now, not the young man singing it to the old man anymore. Worse, he was a broke old man in jail, staring into a suicide-proof mirror with a shoddy shine job that dragged out his features—put there by the state of Florida and the lowest bidder so he couldn't cut his tax-paying wrists.

He studied his face more and got ahold of what he really looked like on the slow downside slide of forever young.

Chapter 10

ARRANGEMENTS WITH THE SELF

Johnny Yuma was headless. He leaned against his hitching post holding a Ball jar Aubrey had attached to his mannequin hand years ago. Inside the jar was a picture of Johnny, head still on, holding the jar with the picture inside of him holding the jar, until the picture got smaller and smaller and reached the HTML&# 8734 computer code for infinity or some other quantum doo lang those mind jocks give a supernumerary idea that jacked its box and calculated Johnny so small, he floated around with quavering quarks and hypothetical particles with the spin of 1/2 and the baryon number 1/3 named in Joyce's *Finnegan's Wake*, read variously as E-quark croak and G-quark curd— or some other top-shelf mick slang for rubbish and tripe.

Would Johnny keep on going and disappear if he got that small? Or maybe he would just get smaller than any of us can understand and stop somewhere like heaven, and that's what would happen to us, too, when we die. Just get very small. In heaven. That's not so hard to live with instead of disappearing. And Aubrey made double sure again the picture in the jar was not headless.

When he wanted to know what happened to Christaine in the backyard, she said, "My daughter..." and started to cry. She straightened herself out and asked, "What became of your parents, Aubrey?"

"My father was killed in an accident when I was nineteen. My mother died of Lou Gehrig's disease not that long ago. I felt terrible about it. Helpless, helpless, helpless. They were such good people."

She reached for his hand and knelt down beside him while the mud and memories rose around them.

"I'll never leave you in this room alone with this, or anywhere else ever, Christaine, you hear me?"

~

Aubrey left the house early for the Catheter Café the morning The Junior was to get out of jail. The spiders in the knee-high Serengeti had set traps all night for the flying insects scientists say will be the next families to control business in New York and New Jersey after humans are gone.

He watched and waited for the sun, took a pull on the toadstone bone when the light came in streaks, and flew his steam-punked truck straight up, just missing the pine tops while he looked down on his sacred Florida savanna.

At the café, he slid into a booth with a clean table.

"How you today, Aubrey?" Janet said between the chewing gum business.

"I'm good, Janet, hope you are."

"I'll get your coffee."

He looked on the tabletop for patterns and faces in the Formica's imitation marble that might resemble some artster or Catholic crap. Trip slid out on the forearm to watch.

"Did I see you moving your lips just now, Aubrey Shallcross?" Janet set down his cup.

"No, ma'am, and speaking of that, how's your husband Charlie doing with that secret friend thing he and I talked about one time?"

"He ain't got a secret friend. You don't have one, do you, Aubrey?"

He looked at her for a second.

"I knew it, Aubrey Shallcross."

"I bet you have a secret friend, too, Janet. The same one I have." He pointed up.

"Oh, well, if you mean our lord, Jesus Christ, then that don't count. It's not like that little boy in the Jack Nicholson movie where he's crazy as a wing nut."

"*The Shining*?"

"Yeah."

"Well, that's what we're trying to find out again—if there's one of those in Charlie's floor plan."

"Oh, good! Okay." She giggled. "I'll get him in here again, and we'll see if he's been seeing someone else on the side." She disappeared to the kitchen.

Trip slid out on the bicep to put his nose in it.

"I wasn't tatering just now, Trip. She thinks her old man's got a slipper, that's all. Funny. She thinks her old man's nuts while she talks to Jesus. But, of course, that's okay with these straight people, and us slipper folk, we're wing nuts. "

"I can't believe how you like to mess with people's heads, Aubrey, just to empower yourself because you're bored. Not that I'm unhappy your sense of humor is back through all these crashes—squirrels in your chest, blowing off Johnny Yuma's head. You should work more on your problems, not someone else's. Charlie's okay. I'll bet he's not even Catholic."

"Catholic?"

"That's right, Aubrey. I'm not your secret friend; I'm your guardian angel, dipshit."

~

The Junior walked out of detention with his lats spread. He didn't want anyone to think he was shaken by such an easy stretch. What he was shaken by was the ghostly gun film he saw on the jail cell wall and his face in that suspect mirror. What came to him in there was the rotten Christmas of midlife, the misery of Marla's absence, and a copy of him in andropause squatting on the cell toilet losing seven percent of muscle mass a decade and the same percentage of hair. He might try to do something about it. It was his turn to save the tiger.

Aubrey wanted to celebrate The Junior's release, so the next night, Christaine cooked a Cuban classic, picadillo, one of The Junior's favorites: rice covered with spiced ground meat, onions, pine nuts, water chestnuts, and hot habanera peppers backed by plenty of cold Dos Equis for the heat. Aubrey cut down a cabbage palm to make a chilled salad from its heart and further cool the effects of the flammable entrée. After dinner, they talked outside into the mosquito-free end of March over bowls of mango sorbet.

"So, Aubrey, ole friend, why don't you come out to the Zarnitz ranch this week and help me and the boys move the cattle to the pens for the old man? We're weaning and shipping next Thursday. Might give you that feeling when we was young, dumb, and full of come again. Oh, shit, sorry, Christ, I didn't mean to say that."

"That's okay, Junior. I'll take these plates in, and you and Aubrey stay here and talk."

"I'd love to," Aubrey answered him.

"All right, then. Hey, Christ, wait a minute. I gotta go anyway." The Junior stood. "I'm looking forward to sleeping in my own rack tonight. Thanks again for making me that picadillo, lady. Aubrey, I'll see you Wednesday evenin. Be there 'bout seven, and we'll hit the Johnny Jumper for catfish. Night, y'all."

They finished the dishes and went upstairs. Aubrey lay in the arms of his blood-borne lover, Christaine Veronica Sadacca. Enfolded in her shape, he took her warmth and watched a view of the owl's sky.

"Goodbye, March, and good riddance," she murmured in that low mezzo sotto he loved.

"I know, baby. It was a hard one, and you blew through it like a strong Gypsy woman."

"Aubrey," she whispered, then smiled the provocateur and propped up on an elbow to put her back to the outside night. He pushed up on his own arm stand and leaned in to slowly hunt her lips in the semidarkness. He rimmed them twice with damp, soft trails and pulled away so she could hunt his. He slipped his hand behind her neck to steady it and rimmed her again, then entered her mouth for a two-breath lock before pulling back for another tease.

"Where did you learn to kiss like that?"

"From a lipstick lesbian when I was eighteen."

"No, really?"

"It's true, but she doesn't kiss like you do, Gypsy woman. You the only girl I ever met who could out-kiss the lesbian."

"Uh-huh, what else did she teach you?"

"She loved only ladies, wanted to save her sisters from lousy male lovers by teaching the kiss."

"You are my heart, Aubrey," she whispered under his nose.

"You're mine, too, *mein liebchen*."

"What?"

"It's German, I'm Dietrich."

"Oh, yeah, a lipstick lesbian."

She slipped her T-shirt over her head.

They rimmed and rimmed and rimmed, everywhere and everything. The chuck-will's-widow in the pine outside stopped calling and watched them like a human until they eventually lay still. Then the plain brown bird that lives for the night flew down the shell-rock road to the main street of Florida they call U.S. 1.

~

That main street rarely broke into an open stretch anymore. If it did, you got maybe three miles at the most down the coast, then more urban sprawl, followed by urban Miami, where someone else who lived for the night sat in his car. The wind blew the coconut trees under the streetlights in Bayfront Park. It was eleven p.m. Carlos watched groups of women promenade by, still feeling the music from a concert at the auditorium and wondered which ones were in season. Watched them like that bird watched Aubrey and Christaine, but without innocence. Then he filled his nose and drove down to Coconut Grove to count his money on U.S. 1.

Chapter 11

The Cattle, The Dog, and The Junior

Aubrey drove out to old man Zarnitz's ranch, the Z Bar Up, and met The Junior on Wednesday evening, as planned. Christaine went to stay with Solana and Asante, much to their delight.

After Aubrey settled his gear, the two men parted the swinging bar doors at the Johnny Jumper Inn. The Junior told him over dinner about the catfight with Sugarcane and Marla on the dance floor months ago. They had a good laugh because everyone knew Sugarcane; Aubrey ran with her for a short time after his divorce. The Junior said Marla didn't want her parents to find out, so she swore him to secrecy at the time.

"So you think you still know how to ride a cow horse after hanging out with Asante on them German dumb bloods?"

"Oh, hell, yeah, and don't be giving me any shit about dressage in front of those guys tomorrow."

"Sure, as long as you don't show up in the tight pants." He swallowed a hush puppy without chewing.

The alarms sounded at four a.m. on the big spread. Everyone dragged over, still asleep, to the main house for breakfast. Aubrey watched the ranch's cook dole out red-eye gravy the old-fashioned way: liquid ham fat from the pan, a rufous liquid spoon-pressed into each serving of grits to resemble the red eye's iris, then a pinch of used coffee grounds in the middle for the pupil. The albescent circle of grits on the outside of the gravy creation made a perfectly flecked white eyeball that looked bloodshot when the thin red juice seeped out in walking lines toward the plate. Aubrey had grown up on the parochial concoction and was doing to his spoon what he did to Christaine's lips at night.

The old man got to his feet at the end of the table and asked for silence. Caspar Zarnitz's ranch was twenty thousand acres, not uncommon in south-central Florida, a part of the state that supported cattle herds on hundreds of square miles of improved and unimproved pasture. The calves were weaned each spring at an average weight of three to four hundred pounds then shipped to feed lots in the Midwest to be fattened before they followed a Judas goat down the orthodox path of sacrifice and slaughter.

"First thing I'd like to do is thank everyone for showing up on time for breakfast," the old boss said. There was some scattered titter. "And I wanna thank Aubrey Shallcross for coming out and giving us a hand for free." The titter got louder. "But then he oughta, considering all the goddamn trucks I've bought from him over the years.

"Okay, boys…same old rules. Nobody gets too wild out there and runs the weight off my calves going to market. I want the highest wean weights I can get. Weight is money. At the same time, I don't want anything to get left behind in the cypress heads or sloughs, 'cause that's money, too, so if they get up in those cabbage domes, you send the dogs in and get 'em out. Don't try to be a hero and cripple one of my good horses in the bogs." He stopped and sipped his coffee.

"Also watch out for particular ones that'll come after you, that number thirty-nine brindle cow and the banana-horned bull we call Chaucer. The supply truck with Marty will be there at the cow pens with everything you need. And finally, you know Junior is the boss out there, and I ain't gonna tell you to mind what he says because he'll take care of that if need be. Okay, eat up and saddle up, 'cause Demitrio done got up before you did and fed up your horses."

Eight mounted men, all seasoned cow hunters except for two excited high school boys from the neighbors, streamed through the gate at first light. They followed a dirt road aimed at a long windbreak of Australian pines across a prairie of perennial pangola grass. The men could judge the distance because the faraway trees looked blue instead of green, and that meant one thing to a local: It was at least three to four miles away. The pinewood's unimproved area of grazing started beyond those trees—the same wild topography De Soto and Ponce de León marched through looking for the fountain to keep Queen Isabella forever young. The Indians swore with straight faces that it shot up out of the ground like spermatozoa. The cattle were in the wild part of the ranch that had been controlled-burned a couple of months before, and it made the new grass grow like something on fatback and iron pills.

The riders eased their horses into a slow endurance trot. Three dogs, formulations of pit bull, hound, Rhodesian ridgeback, Catahoula leopard dog, and any other interloper that had gotten to a bitch, followed behind. Okeechobee curs, they called them, like some redneck breed of their own the American Kennel Club didn't know about. They knew their jobs and were fearless and obedient, or they'd get the worm medicine kicked out of them. Tough love in cow country for everything. Even kids.

The crew reached the tree stand in an hour and came upon the first cattle, which took off like deer and disappeared into the scrub. The Junior told everyone to stop and watch that the dogs didn't chase as they rode another half-mile around the cows out of sight and came in on their flank so they could turn the herd down a woven-wire fence line while the riders spread out behind.

They'd push them north another mile to the pens. It took genuine cow sense to work this feral stock—to gather, control, and cajole them to a destination, especially in palmetto country, where they can snooker you like snipe.

In a half-mile, five cows with calves and the bull called Chaucer got through the young neighbor boys and took off across a marsh into a cypress head, the higher ground stand of trees and foliage God put in the middle of a wetland like a power plant—what the white man calls an ecosystem and what the Indians call a church. One of the boys, a sixteen-year-old, tried to follow, but his horse sank down to his belly in the bog twenty feet into the saw grass.

"Goddammit, Danny, you stupid kid, now look where you at!" The Junior screamed. "I swear to God, I've told the old man not to make me babysit you girls on these drives."

The kid stood there, hanging his head beside the stuck horse.

"Well, all right, don't just freeze up like a no-count, son. You know what to do, now get to doin it!"

The boy started digging out the horse's front feet to turn him toward the entry point. Hopefully, the animal wouldn't panic and wreck his stifles.

"Okay!" The Junior yelled. "Send them dogs in and get them cattle outta that head. C.W., you tie your horse to that tree and jump in there with your school buddy and help him get his horse off this bog."

Trip looked out the deltoid mole hole Aubrey cleared by rolling up his T-shirt sleeve so Trip had a view. There was nothing to see when the dogs went in at first, only the sound of wheezing, blowing, and clicking teeth. The surrounding wetland exploded from the invasive commotion. Snipes, rails, marsh rats, wood ducks, and killdeer ran from the ruckus behind the low fronds. Then the first cow emerged through the trees with bleeding ears, the calf behind her untouched. The second and third cows and calves showed, followed by the rest, but no bull.

The first cow trudged her way up the edge with her calf onto dry land. Two men roped her and pulled her in a slow lope to the rest of the bunch so she couldn't run the opposite way. The other cows followed the caught cow and calf, compelled by the herding instinct.

"C'mon, dogs, catch him, boys. Catch that Chaucer bull now, bring 'em, bring 'em to me, ooh-aye-ee, oh-ooh-aye-ee, oh! Catch 'em, catch 'em, Maxey, boyeh. C'mon on, dog!" The Junior hollered at the hammock, where it sounded like hyenas in scrum. Finally, the bull had enough, and here he came.

The two-thousand pound Brahma slogged across the slough slow, bogging down like the horse, but his male power managed to pull and blow against the belly-deep sump, even with the torturing dogs. He was plenty mad when he made the bank, and so was the dog called Maxey beside him. Maxey locked onto the monster's nose, and the bull tried to shake him off while he ran then tried to flip Maxey up over him. That didn't work, so he lowered his head, pushed the dog into his front legs, and fell on him. When the bull got up and headed for the herd, the dog didn't. The Junior and Aubrey rode up to Maxey, and Aubrey got off his horse.

"I don't know, but he's not movin."

"Shit, is he dead?"

"No, he's breathin."

"Leave him there. He either gets up, or he don't. We gotta keep going, and somebody can come back later to see if he's done or just stunned."

"Your drive, boss."

The backs of cattle were pushed together like a hair-covered logjam, the cowboys spaced correctly behind them. Foot stomps and low bovine singing drowned out the meadowlarks, redwing blackbirds, and bobwhite calls they had heard on the ride out that morning as the herd funneled down the tapered trap lane to the pens.

Aubrey looked at The Junior and nodded. This was heaven and had been since they were kids raising hell in triplicate.

"Hey, The Junior."

"What's that, college boyeh?"

"You remember, you and me like those two high-schools digging that horse out back there. I said to you once, 'Don't ever let me grow up to be anything but a cowboy.' You remember that? And remember how we used to run to the magazine store to buy the *Western Horseman* from that guy Sonny who worked there? Sonny would visit my mother when she was dying. Whatever happened to him?"

"Moved out on the South Fork somewhere. Lived like a hermit, I heard. You woulda been a cowboy if you weren't goin flat out with that binness shit of yours and those other personalities you was runnin."

"I love the smell of cow shit in the morning. Who said that?"

"Duvall, only he said napalm, Aubrey."

"How do you know, The Junior? I was with you when you walked out of that movie."

"Yep, it was right after that line, remember? No Nam crap now, Aubrey, I wanna enjoy myself out here."

"Yeah, I was just...shit...you're my oldest and best friend."

The Junior threw him a kiss, and Aubrey smiled as he spaced himself out behind the herd again.

The cattle were in the pens by noon. Two steel squeeze chutes were positioned strategically for branding, castrating, dehorning, and other husbandry.

Later that day, they separated the calves to be shipped the next morning. It was Danny's job to run the calves down a narrow lane that filled with manure as the day wore on.

"I hate this cow shit!" he grumbled to an older man sitting on the fence.

"Aw, son, after you been doing this as long as I have, you get to where you can spread that stuff on your bread."

Some bull calves the ranch was keeping for meat were run through the squeeze chute and castrated by a man with his pocketknife and antiseptic. He called the two high-schoolers over and told them they had to join the cowboy club, or they would never be real cowboys or work on this ranch again. He castrated the next calf and held up the grape-sized bloody nuts, then swallowed them to show what he meant. The men sitting on the fence were loving it.

The next calf was for Danny. He closed his eyes, and the oysters were dropped one at a time into his mouth. He got them down right away, much to his delight, probably hoping he'd redeemed himself for bogging down his horse. The other boy gagged and gagged—kept spitting them back into his hand until he made it on the third try, blood on his lips, then disappeared behind one of the stock trucks to hurl.

The cattle settled for the night. Marty the cook grabbed the vet box with his suturing, Xylocaine, and antibiotics and went to work on a horse that had been horned superficially at the tip of its butt. Danny stood beside him and tried to avoid the onerous Junior.

The sun sank to the palmetto tops, slow as an orange jawbreaker in thick glycerin, while the men tied out the horses for the night.

Marty and Danny served a supper of chicken and black-eyed peas with biscuits. Marty fried extra dough in a pan and threw it to the whining mutts to keep them from begging off the men, saying, "Hush, puppy," to make the men laugh. Then the men wanted hush puppies, too. Everyone ate two plates and talked through stories and the news until ten while they leaned back on their bedrolls, smoked, and drank a shot or two of whiskey someone passed around. All were thankful it was April, the dry season, so mosquitoes wouldn't keep them awake.

The Junior threw his saddle over his shoulder and started for the horses.

"Hey, where you goin?" Aubrey asked with the moon coming, big as a plywood stage prop over the theater of the pangola prairie.

"Aw, hell, I gotta find out what happened to that scrappy dog."

"Me, too. I'm goin with you."

A fog rose from the floor of the woods, and the night-feeding killdeer flew up from their approach and scolded the two riders for the interruption as they backtracked to the cypress head where the bull had fallen on the dog.

Aubrey thought he saw movement in the trees, some clootie maybe, or the evil-storied moochibonereen Reve had said was there. It still gave him juvenile chills when he saw a ground fog because of her, but it was more amusing than scary now, and he tried to conjure every old feeling he could on this drive to revisit his boyhood. He remembered Freud said, "What you are and where you are from one to twelve years old, you are the rest of your life." He believed it, and it brought back a pleasant, interweaving fugue of boyhood memory that he thought he might have lost. He guessed he never would forget these smells and sounds, even if he moved up to that moon over his head. He rolled up the sleeve on his left arm again for Trip and told him to look out for skunk apes and giant skinks in the woods. Trip got right into it and overacted his part as he scanned the palmettos.

The Junior finally spoke. "Hey, Aubrey. How come you roll your T-shirt sleeve over that shoulder? And how come only the left one? That some kinda half-ass James Dean look?"

"Don't know. Don't even remember when it started. Must be a nervous thing like Punky used to do with paper clips, remember? He'd bend them into triangle shapes and leave 'em around everywhere."

"Yeah, I remember that. You'd know where he'd been 'cause you'd find a trail of those things."

The sun on the other side of the Earth bounced its own triangulated trail off the moon and down to them as they talked about their dead friend. Dead friends always leave trails—easier to see it when the moon is up.

Maxey's whimpers led them to him in a clump of tall burn grass on his stomach, his hind legs splayed behind him. The catch dog had crawled at least thirty yards from where the bull had crushed him.

"Hey, Maxey boy, how you doing out here all by yourself? You been waitin for me to come and get you, haven't you?" The Junior said like a child as he dismounted and bent over the dog.

Aubrey tied up the horses before they knelt silent in a diagnostic state.

"He's a good un, this boy. He's born on the ranch. His daddy was from the Maxey Ranch, so we named him that. What's wrong with you, Maxey boy, huh? What got you pinned down? Don't you want to get up and get another piece of that bull, you tough little bugger?"

The dog perked his ears at The Junior, clawed at the dirt, and pulled himself a few inches with his front legs.

"You know, he's not moving those hind legs," Aubrey said.

"I know, and he ain't wagging his tail, either."

The Junior pushed his pocketknife gently into Maxey's hind end and feet. No reaction. They tried to lift him onto a saddle to take him back to camp for Marty, but he screamed in such agony they lowered him back down.

So there they were—two grown men and a broken dog with broken brown eyes exchanging the same trampled looks over a sorry plight served up on another crossroads job. Neither one of them wanted to speak the inevitable, but it was The Junior's show and the ranch's dog, so he committed.

"Much as I hate to say it, I guess we better do what we's taught to do growing up when a creature is sufferin, 'cause lookin at that crook in his back and him not havin feeling in them legs tells me his back's broke. He wouldn't have no kind of life."

Aubrey could see the dog was watching The Junior's face, trying to pick up on his tone.

The Junior walked over to his horse and pulled a .38 out of the saddlebag with a piece of jerky in a wrapper. He stood with his head buried into the horse's flank, as if he didn't want to turn around. Aubrey saw a jaw clench ripple his face before he backed away and turned. He had the out-of-context look, a contra expression, a smile in these circumstances. He bent down to give Maxey the jerky. The dog just sniffed it and licked it once.

"Yeah," he said with that wrong smile. "I don't feel the way I used to about making decisions, so I'm gonna let ole God do it for me tonight."

He unloaded the gun, inserted a bullet back into the chamber, and spun it.

"Oh, come on, man. What's that all about?" Aubrey said in disbelief.

"Don't give me that man shit, Aubrey. That Sixties man shit." His face changed to mean. "I'm not gonna make these decisions anymore, Mr. Head Wound, Mr. Ambrose fuckin Bierce, Aubrey. You always wanna talk about Nam stuff. Everyone I know like you who wasn't there wants to talk to me about that mess. Well, maybe you'll get off on this, rich boy. You liked *The Deer Hunter*, didn't you? I 'member you tellin everyone how cool you thought it was. I know the story listening to you and your friends talk about it, because I wasn't about to sit through that crap. I walked down a few of those back alleys over there in the capital myself. I saw that Christopher Walken-Russian-roulette shit goin on like your air-conditioned movie experience…like you was watchin *Gunsmoke* when we was kids. But it ain't the same. It ain't *Gunsmoke*, Aubrey. Wanna see *The Deer Hunter* again?"

He put the gun to his temple and pulled the trigger. *Click!* Aubrey couldn't speak. The Junior spun it again and pressed it against his head, paused, then pointed it at the dog's head and let the hammer go. Maxey's body lurched forward.

The Junior fell to his knees. "Oh, no, wrong one again."

He started to sob so seriously the woods fell quiet. Aubrey rested his hand on his friend's shaking shoulder. The Junior was broken, and Aubrey didn't know how to fix him or even how to get him to stand again.

After some silence mixed with crying, the Junior stood on his own, but he wouldn't look at Aubrey. He walked a few off strides to his horse and pushed the pistol back into his saddlebag, stepped up, and rode over.

"Would you lift him so I can take him with us?" he asked Aubrey. They balanced the dead dog across the saddle and headed back to the cow camp.

Aubrey spoke first. "Listen, there's something I always wanted to tell you but was afraid to. I ain't as together as you think I am. I mean, I have personal problems I've never told you about."

"You saying this to be clever so I won't think I'm so weird, 'cause if you are, I ain't gonna bite."

"No, really. I feel guilty I'm talking about me instead of asking you what's wrong."

"What's wrong? The heart don't work 'cause a vandal took the handle."

"You mean, well, I don't know what you mean. I mean, I know the other version of the line, but—"

"Since she took the handle, Marla, I mean, what's pumping for me besides fuckin liver bile?"

The Junior pulled to a stop, the draped dog in front of him dripping blood from his head down the horse.

Trip jumped on the quiet spot with the inner voice. "What the hell are you doing, Shallcross? Trying to get him to listen to some problem of yours you think might be smaller than his so you can feel better and take over the night? Look at him! He's in pieces. What are you going to say your problem is anyway, asshole? Schizophrenia?"

"I don't want you to be alone in this," Aubrey said to The Junior.

"But I am. You ain't in it, Aubrey."

"Well, maybe I'm...there's this thing that happens to me like what happened to you back there. I mean, where you feel captured by something, and you can't make the decision or stop it. Am I making sense?"

"Maybe, I don't know. Nothin does lately."

"You see, I have these blackouts. I can't stop it, kind of like a seizure. Some other part of me makes that decision, and it just happens."

"No shit?"

"No shit, The Junior, swear on my mother's you know. It's something I've had since I was young, I want you to know this. Maybe we can pull one another outta this trouble to the fence, me and you, like the old days. Are you sure your vandal is Marla?"

"Maybe I'm my own vandal."

"Me, too. You know, I felt that way when Leda left me, and even worse when she and Arquette seemed to leave town at the same time. Why torture yourself? Then you *are* your own vandal. They say the best revenge is to let the other man have her."

"Now you got it, Tater man," Trip said inside Aubrey's head. A cloud crossed the moon in a clearing and dimmed the night to the twenty-watt look. A bull from an adjoining ranch a half mile away brayed his tuba along a fence line, the boundary that kept him prisoner only the man who built the fence understood. Aubrey could see The Junior's tanned face straining to talk; he knew how hard it must be for a man like him to speak naked, nudged by the push rods of male misery—the ones that let a Joe show another Joe, dosed in toughness and self-defense like him, that he has a certain amount of sensitivity, humility, and weakness, next to the load of weaponry on the backside of his sternum in case some Jack pops his box and tries to gang-rape his head or loved ones. That's when he'd want the other Joe to know he'd cut out Jack's heart for righteousness's sake.

He thought The Junior might be ready to show this other side to him but would want to step over a few things, and he couldn't blame him. Even though they were best friends, they knew they were very different, and Aubrey's upstairs rooms were something The Junior had never seen—rooms that could be full of black-hearted Jacks as far as The Junior knew.

"I think I may be done here," The Junior said.

"You mean—?"

"Yeah, I mean done here, carburet it. Finished."

"You mean the other finished?"

For the last half mile, the big man spoke of a dogging sadness after Marla left and his roulette apparition on the jailhouse wall that played out, then played out for real tonight with the dog. He talked about the metal mirror in his cell polished all wrong…or maybe polished all right. He said he never thought he would feel like this about getting old, and Marla being so much younger than him probably had plenty to do with it.

"I shoulda listened to you at the Goose that first night, Aubrey, and not got bogged down in her like that kid's horse back there. Course, it's not her fault; she'd kill for me, I know that."

The campfire and the cow pens came into view.

"This is something we're going to have to take time to talk about," Aubrey said. "I didn't want you going to sleep tonight thinking you're all alone in some fucked-up struggle."

The Junior nodded.

"Hey, just remember Punky's bumper sticker," Aubrey said.

"What about it?"

"You and I are not going to let C. Jay die for nothing, and we're gonna stick around and get our money's worth. And have you ever heard this one? 'Everything you always wanted, you probably already have.'"

The Junior pulled up his horse and looked at Aubrey. "No, I never heard it, but I like it."

They rode the last fifty yards into camp and settled in for the night. Aubrey lay on his bedroll, and Trip slid out on the forearm. The hallucination had a smile on his face, and Aubrey did, too, because he knew he'd sacrificed something, and so had Suiter. It was a non-Tater move to offer his hidden weakness up to his friend in such misery, especially when it meant so much to keep it in the wings for the strong image he wanted to present to everyone. The Junior then would become someone who knew about this part of him, like John Chrome. That bothered him, because he hadn't even told Christaine, even though he was sure she could field the model, but he didn't have the nerve right now. On the other hand, The Junior was the antithesis of Chrome, and Aubrey never thought he'd see the day he would show him a piece of his air puck or the cracks his toothbrush ran over at night—the ones that tore down the runway of his hometown heart. But now he had. Had to.

The penned cattle were loud and unhappy. He checked for thunderheads over the pangola prairie, but a high-pressure cell was on top of the state, so he closed his eyes.

"Aubrey, don't forget to pick a film tonight," Trip said. "And don't forget a trazodone so you can sleep."

"Should be a western around all this."

"Which western?"

"*Lonely Are the Brave*, with Kirk Douglas."

"Is that a real western?"

"You bet your small ass, and it's the most red and swollen movie old Spartacus ever made."

In a half hour, the pill took him down to the Trazadone Lounge, where he fell off into the Organ Mountains east of Las Cruces, and here came Kirk on that dark bay mare named Whiskey inside the high tree line, trying to beat the sheriff to El Paso and cross the border near Juarez into Mexico.

Chapter 12

THE MOUTH IN HAND, THE MISE AU MAIN

He tried to hook up with The Junior the next two days for their promised talk, but couldn't find him. He called the Zarnitz ranch and spoke to Demitrio in the barn. Demitrio said Señor Junior hadn't been around and had been going to the Johnny Jumper Inn with the guy who fixed up those dead animal heads for people. Aubrey knew who he meant: the Tax Man.

Come Friday, he told Christaine he was worried enough to go look for him.

It was a typical weekend night at the Johnny Jumper, thick—everyone breathing in and out at the same time, talking, dancing, drinking. Aubrey made his way to the back and politely nodded to people until he found the man he wanted: Cabbage Pinley.

"Mr. Shallcross, what brings you to west county?"

"I'm looking for Junior."

"Oh, well, I wish Junior'd start lookin for Junior." Cabbage leaned closer. "He's on some kinda tear, man, but I couldn't tell you why. He's been comin in here with Henry, you know, the taxidermy guy, and he's drunk every night. Henry said he's lookin out for him at his place till this passes."

"Thanks, I'm gonna go find him."

Aubrey walked out a side door across the wooden porch and saw *Chicken-Necker Hook* scrawled in Magic Marker above a three-inch brass peg—the very one The Junior hung Marla's grab-ass interloper on, he guessed. He smiled, shook his head, and headed for Henry's.

The house was a hundred yards from a locked gate, and a button on the gatepost rang a doorbell inside like some big-deal security thing.

"Who's that?"

"It's me, Aubrey." He could hear the crowd and the hoodang music in the background.

"Who?"

"Shallcross."

"Hey, thank God. I'll hit the gate."

Pickups covered the yard—Tax Man hangouts marveling at the still life. The resurrectionist himself was standing next to Aubrey's truck before he could kill the engine.

"Hi, Henry, how you been?"

"Exhausted, totally fucking exhausted, man. It's Junior, man. He's trying to disassemble himself or something, and it's all over that young girl, that horse lady who took off to China or somewhere. And then he's talking about getting old and being good for nothing, and after that, he'll start talking about Nam, which ain't like him. And then the stupid motherfucker, you know what he asks me? If I will tax up his body after he dies and keep it out here standing in my living room 'stead of the cemetery."

"He said that?"

"Hogs screwin in the ditches! And it was in the morning, sober over coffee, so you're here to either relieve me or come up with a fix that gets him straight." Henry stopped just before they went in. "My dad used to say something somebody said, 'We seen the light at end of the tunnel and it was turned off.' That's our boy, all right."

Henry's place was built out of concrete block, a twenty-foot crowned ceiling in the living room. A long, institutional hallway was off the kitchen. Each room down the hallway was dedicated to certain creature mounts: the coon, the armadillo, the bobcat, the bird, and the reptile. No mounted fish, though; Henry had vowed never to do another stinky fish for a chicken-necker now that he had money.

Couches circled a wagon-wheel table with a glass-top lazy Susan. The boys spun lines of coke to the next man back in the low-eighties on that table, and one time, someone smacked down a sticky ball of smoldering opium the size of a kumquat. But Henry had outlawed hard dope since then, and everyone was back to the alcohol and weed their daddies raised them on to make gimcrack resolutions and blab blind Tater stories about hunting, monster trucks, and "Git 'er done."

A few rebel yells went up when Aubrey entered, especially from the guys who drove Dodge trucks. He dropped on a couch with the off-duty hunting party and saw The Junior drizzling his throat by the refrigerator. The Junior turned and shook his head at him.

"Hey, boyeh. Henry's got a little cheap gin, but he ain't got that orange licker you like, that cointro. There's some fresh squeeze, though. You want me to make one?"

"Yes, I would, please and thank you."

He handed Aubrey the drink and turned a chair around with his elbows over the backrest. "So...*que passa*, A.C.?"

"Well, I been looking for you. I thought we were going to get together this week, like we said, and—"

"Yeah, here I am, yep, holed up with ole Henry and his stuffed buddies, so I got plenty of animals to talk to, includin the human ones 'round this table—goddamn bunch of shit-kickin whiteys, ain't they? Old man Zarnitz breeds better stock."

Aubrey tossed his drink and eyed him. "You feel better about the things we talked about in the woods?"

"What things? Oh, that? Yeah, I do, Aubrey. In fact, tonight I feel better 'n I've felt in a long time. It just come over me yesterday, and I got this stuff figured out. Finished."

Aubrey thought he looked wrong; his features seemed to cant the way they did the other night walking back from his horse to shoot Maxey.

Henry came in from the hallway after one of his storied tours holding a live version of the deadliest thing in North America: the coral snake, named for its bright orange, black, and red colors, resembling the ornate fish on the coral reefs off High Beach. He knew how to handle the creature, which is not that aggressive unless provoked and can only bite where the skin is as thin as the webbing between fingers. Every man there wearing at least one piece of camouflage knew exactly what Henry was holding.

"Now a guy brought me this unusually long coral a few days ago," Henry said, like a park ranger. "I guess, oh, he's about thirty-four inches long, and the dude wants me to chloroform and raise him up in a terrarium scene for his house. They won't hurt you if you handle 'em gently, but I think I'll keep ahold a him behind the head, all the same." The boys laughed. "I also turned up his cage light to make him sluggish for added insurance."

Everyone was listening, except The Junior, who'd gone back to the kitchen for another drink.

"I remember my old man told me the way you know this poison one from the king coral is you look at the colors on the head," one of the men said. "You start with the nose and say, 'Black touches yeller, kills a feller. Red touches black, okay for Jack,' and this un here sure ain't the fake one."

Henry nodded and showed the snake around the room once more before returning it to its cage as the stars above his house moved righty-tighty over the dais of Earth's drier parts and lower oceans, waiting for something to happen.

The subject of a new freeze-drying taxidermy technique came up when Henry returned to the living room. He told Aubrey he was hard-core; he wouldn't change the traditional ways of the old taxidermy masters. He liked gutting, skinning, working bone armatures, cotton, sutures, blood, all that gory stuff, and wasn't about to turn out a piece by flash-freezing it in the new machines.

The Junior interrupted when he marched to the living room from the long hall wearing a bed sheet like a toga over his clothes and carrying a cigar box. The group started laughing and slapping their knees as the big backwoods Roman danced to the party's electric country music and waved the mysterious box in front of him like it contained a treasure—Thumbelina in a thong, maybe—for the redneck boys tonight.

"So what the hell does this mean?" Henry asked.

"I don't know, but he told me he was feeling better, so I guess he feels like prissin around," Aubrey said.

"Last night, Shallcross, he crawled across my yard with a stinkin gator hide on his back, feeling better, too, after drinkin 'bout a quart a that Russian kickapoo juice."

Then *kerplooee!* The Junior pulled the coral snake out of the cigar box. The room didn't know whether to clap or freeze. Henry jumped up and demanded the snake, but The Junior fucked him off with a look that told him to sit down. He shot Aubrey a *watch this* look and continued to dance with the snake.

He two-stepped across the floor and shoved the snake's head in each of the men's faces to make them flinch, but not Henry's or Aubrey's. He looked whacked in this solo performance for his white rat pack. He spun and pushed the snake head at his own back and forth again and again, teasing the poor creature, who only read for villain parts, while it cringed and flicked its tongue, and The Junior flicked his back at the snake.

"Henry," Aubrey said.

"What?"

"That thing's not going to bite him, is it?"

"I hope not. Damn thing might try. Its fangs are far back, so this particular kind has to gnaw or find some thin flesh; it likes the webbing between the fingers, kinda like that sick fuck Tin Snip, who killed those women. Remember? That murdering son of a bitch would snip a woman's thin parts wherever he could when he'd kill 'em? Then stuff their bodies in those old refrigerators that had been dumped in the woods. But goddammit, see now, Christ-a-mighty, this is the kind of shit he's been doin all week, and I've had enough. He better not damage that thing so I have to patch it up."

Henry was about to come off the couch again when The Junior wheeled around and slipped his hand back six inches from the coral's head to show his nerve. The snake and the snake man circled the room, feinting moves at each other's faces like boxers, closer and closer, until it was tongue flick to tongue flick.

And as it is said so many times, when the timing is perfect or lousy, The Junior came in for the last time with his moist membranous part glistening like a reptilian rival, and the snake got it right. He released the short coil in his neck and nailed The Junior's tongue like an earthworm. The curved-back fangs did not have to gnaw on that lean carpaccio; they injected their venom into the rich blood area, and the hollow needles seated in the flesh of the glossal organ until the coral was stuck.

The Junior's eyes grew wider than the war he had fought in. He tried to pull the snake back and pry the jaws, but no good. He froze. His lips seemed to form a coming kiss that encircled the snake's neck like a sex act. Then he bit the head off inside his mouth and dropped the writhing body to the floor.

Stunned, he staggered around with his tongue out. Everyone could see the bright-colored stump and its last blood running down The Junior's chin. He turned to a mirror on the wall...wobbled, fainted.

Aubrey got to him first, The Junior's head back, his mouth open, the decollated animal part clamped on like a decorative tongue stud, and he thought he might fold into his own oral predicament. He flashed back to the rattlesnake with the squirrel in his backyard, but Trip was right there with their rhyme to stem the gag.

"What are we gonna do?" Henry asked, his face all torqued. "Call 911?"

"Hell, no. We're gonna get him in the bed of your truck and drive to the hospital, or it'll be too late," Aubrey said.

The Junior was coming around dull as the venom spread through his body. He tried to talk, but the head distorted the words. Aubrey leaned over the languet part lolling in and out of his bleeding mouth, and it started to make him sick.

"Ge da ucking ead ah ma ongue," The Junior said.

Henry already had flown to the back room to retrieve needle nose pliers and a mini-screwdriver. He wedged the screwdriver between the deadlocked jaws to pry them, but no go.

"Aubrey, I know it sounds gruesome, but let's leave the head there, because any pressure on them fangs will release more poison. We get him to the hospital. Time's everything, and it's twenty fuckin miles."

They turned onto the state road, throwing gravel thirty feet in the air. Aubrey hovered over The Junior in the truck bed, nervously telling him he would be okay and to try to slow his heartbeat. The Junior nodded to him with his twenty-watt eyes and let them wander across the night sky, as if thinking what humans think in crisis when they look up: *God.* Anybody's God.

Trip thought he saw something—a green glow from one of The Junior's nostrils. Maybe it was the mixed colors from the truck's running lights, but it looked like a slipper's light trying to leave The Junior's body.

Aubrey's mind was flying, carbureting kinds of triages in his jar. He thought about Coker and Reve, and the can of alum that had saved Reve's father from the snakebite, and stupidly reached inside his pockets.

He felt The Junior's hand squeeze his arm and bent closer. Broken blood vessels around his friend's lips and proximate skin looked like a croton leaf. The Junior's words sounded like pig Latin.

"I tow ya ah ad ii aw wauked ow."

"Just nod if I understood you!" Aubrey yelled over the road noise. "You said, 'I told you I had it all worked out,' right?"

The Junior nodded.

"You're not telling me you did that on purpose, are you?"

The Junior looked at his Anti-Chrysler like the "Rocket Man" must have looked at his wife for the last time, knowing he was never coming back. He opened his mouth the way a child shows you their chewed food and smiled.

His eyes moved past Aubrey's head to the night sky again and closed. He nodded his head twice, as if answering yes to Aubrey's question, then rolled his head side to side, no.

"The Junior! You listen to me!" Aubrey yelled above the wind noise. "That hospital is getting closer. You can't die on me. Remember Punky's bumper sticker? 'Jesus paid for our sins, so we get to get our money's worth.' You gotta stay here with me and do that, Biggie. Stay with me, goddamnit! I'm a certified saver, do you hear me? Certified. I'm saving you tonight, by God." Tears ran down his face. "You and me, Biggie!" he screamed in the wind. "There's money in my bank. This is why Jesus paid, for you and me and the money, boyeh. We made promises when we were kids, remember? We promised we'd go through life wide open, even if we didn't get the money. But I got it, didn't I? You hear me? For us! You're my brother, my brother!" he yelled out at the night. "Don't you disappoint your Jesus and leave me with that goddamn money, don't you do it!"

The Junior opened his eyes one more time, nodded his head, gripped Aubrey's arm tighter, and lapsed into his sacred coma— the one that doesn't cost a goddamn dime.

Aubrey stared at him in the dim of the truck bed, the snakehead protruding like some lost tribe jewelry. He thought he saw a flame vine stretch across The Junior's neck as the wind streamed ninety miles an hour from hot tires racing the Dodge and its bright lamps on a highway seen above by rising souls and one giant Blue Heroness on her way to a silver-topped pond in heaven, with The Junior riding on her back. Aubrey's eyes watered and burned. He looked through the truck's windshield at the head-lighted road and saw hundreds of hallucinated road kill crosses lining both sides the last mile to the hospital. A homophonic song played an assassination rag that he and John Chrome listened to in the seventies, their bloodstreams flush with the drug MDA, so they could slip away.

I SAW MCKINLEY ON THE TRAIN
HE RODE TO BUFFALO.
I SAW OLE LEON WITH THE GUN
AND AIN'T NOBODY KNOW.
TWO BULLETS HIT THE PRESIDENT
HE KNELT DOWN ON THE GROUND.
SOMEBODY GRABBED THE ANARCHIST
AND TOOK OLE LEON DOWN.
HE'S GONE, HE'S GONE, HE'S GONE,
ROOSEVELT GOT THE WHITE HOUSE
MCKINLEY GOT THE GRAVE
ROOSEVELT SLEEPS ON SATIN SHEETS
MCKINLEY ROTS AWAY.
HE'S GONE, HE'S GONE, HE'S GONE.

The Junior's body arrived under the hospital's portico suffocated by a nerve toxin even his Vulcan rib cage couldn't beat. The doctor said if he had made it to the hospital alive, the antivenom from the Miami Serpentarium rarely worked on a bite in such a vascular spot, anyway, especially from a coral snake.

"What about alum?" Aubrey asked.

No one knew what he meant. He broke down in tears, and Henry and Trip tried clumsy man stuff to ease the pain for their friend, the schizo car dealer from Jensen Beach who believed he'd failed as a certified saver and a catcher in the rye tonight.

~

They buried Junior in a coffin made out of tongue-and-groove yellow pine and tidewater cypress, so he'd have the backwoods smells with him until the second coming, whoever showed up, C. Jay, or the Martians. Aubrey tried to sit by the grave at night, but Trip said he had to let him go.

Marla had rushed back from Europe the next day before the burial. She asked Aubrey and Christaine to take her to the morgue to see The Junior's refrigerated body. When she leaned over to kiss his cold face, Trip saw the faint light from The Junior's nose he saw in the truck bed when the man was dying. Trip knew who and what it was: an old friend, Lucinda, a 300-year-old slipper, shivering and barely alive, left The Junior and entered Marla's nose to soak up her warmth and life.

Marla was out of it the next week, hysterical at times, running through the bruising darkness with her eyes closed and bashing into trees like her sister after she kissed the Burdines Jesus.

Aubrey knew. He had sought the same distraction of psych-asthenia through cuts and contusions after his father's death, wanting to take the deathblow himself through the soughing and wails that came up from his cecum—a spasm that never vomits, but dry heaves for days.

He told Marla that kind of stuff never gets off your plate, that you learn to eat around those dirt spots, and everything you were taught about a clean plate, clean heart, and clean thoughts takes on a different look with that spot weld of lunchroom crud stuck to your madness and history.

He and Christaine kept her at their place most of the time. When Marla suggested The Junior's death might be her fault, Christaine spoke to her in Romani and raised her hand, but didn't slap her. Marla didn't mention it again, but drove to Fort Pierce the next day to have a coral snake's head—black touching yellow, that kills a fellow—tattooed into the oval frame at the base of her spine. She was sure it was she who had bitten The Junior...the *chica loca*.

~

Aubrey, tired and alone, lay down on O'gram's bed days after the funeral and tried to conjure something acceptable in the jar about all this.

Tied to his RKO, he pressed on a gear of soothing shapes and pulled on the toadstone rock until the wrong whittle monster got loose.

A foreign squeeze formed another figure of high resolution in his jar. He hoped it would be The Junior, so he could talk to his spirit, but it was a copy of himself tied to the tower, holding his jar with a picture of himself inside the jar, holding the jar tied to the tower, racing toward the infinity of HTML: & # 8734, getting smaller and smaller like Johnny Yuma's picture downstairs.

Now he was forced to watch the animate equivalent of himself as an intruder with its own frog-bone fuel stone to fuck with.

The intruder showed him the Tax Man mounting The Junior's gutted body: pulling out his eyes, dropping them in the trash, and installing glass ones from the mall. The Tax Man worked cotton into the cavities and wet spaces while dripping sweat and The Junior's blood, as Aubrey dog-kicked under his FLORIST sign, his eyes forced open, like little Alex's in *Clockwork*. The McKinley assassination rag played over counterpoint screams in the background: "He's gone, he's gone, he's gone."

142

The Junior's spirit appeared as a speck at the far end of the Tax Man's hallway. He started coming, getting larger, closing the distance. He took four steps forward, then one step back, like a sidewalk jive walk man, until he was skin-pore close to Aubrey's face.

He smiled a grille of chrome-street dentition and parted his silver teeth. The snake stuck his head out of The Junior's mouth and smiled, too, as if he had found his dream house in The Junior's transcendent corpse.

"Black touches yellow, kills a fell—" the snake's voice stopped in the middle of a word. Then it spoke in Reve's Québécoise voice. "Luk at me, Aubree...I am in the other realm, which of course is the same realm you are in, so nothing really changes, does it? A predator is in your life, but that was not him in this snake and in your jar; that was the Slim Hand. He ran when he saw me. Watch for the sand skink a comin, something's going on with dat lizard."

Aubrey woke like a blowhole. When he went downstairs, Christaine could see it on his face and closed her arms around him. "You know I love you, Aubrey?"

"Yes, I do." He made the sign of the cross. "You are my Christ now, my soul-eyed *belle tournure*. I drown in you."

They climbed the stairs to the top of O'gram and lay in bed with the lights out. A soft rain started falling on the tin roof and Aubrey breathed better; no white noise machine in the world could stack up to that sound of real rain.

Chapter 13

FEAR IRRATIONAL AND SALVATION EQUITATION

Marla flew back to Germany to continue her riding. When she kissed Christaine goodbye on the lips with tears in her eyes, the slipper, Lucinda, who had come to her from The Junior's body, traveled from Marla's nose into Christaine's.

~

One night, Aubrey was stretched out on the sofa looking for shapes in the wood ceiling when Christaine walked into the room.

"How are you doing with the riding?" she asked him.

"I think I've had one of those eeeephifanees. How are you doing with the writing?"

"Personally, good. Financially, good thing I've got you to take care of me."

"Come here," and she sat beside him. "It's a good thing I've got you to take care of me financially."

"What's that mean? You'd be blowing money on stray shank if I wasn't here to get you home every night?"

"Yep, how'd you know?"

"Gypsy stuff." She shrugged, bit his hand, and pricked her own with her hatpin, then pressed their wounds together and spread out on top of him.

~

Asante handed Aubrey a scarf to use as a blindfold and led the horse to the rail.

"You ride a little backwards in your head, my friend. You are trying to make him round from front to back with too much rein instead of back to front by riding forward into the bit and a receiving hand. I will try to give you a taste for that feeling of a pure collection from a horse with the forward feel, but he will be on the spot, and you have to let him step into it while he is there. You have a horse here that can do it, my friend, so you say a *Deo gratias* for that."

Asante raised his whip. The horse began to trot in place. This was Aubrey's first time on a classical movement the cognoscente call "the piaffe."

"I feel it!" he said, excited. Asante stopped the horse.

"That's good you feel it, because I cannot make this guy do it all day. Good thing he's a Lusitano and was born to do it. And take off that blindfold for a minute."

"This blind stuff really works, Asante."

"What do you expect, that I am bad teacher? Of course, it works, but not on everyone. *Ho porra*, you don't think every blind man can play music? I tell you it works because it is you who took the eyes out of your head and put them in your seat bones. It is also the eyes in your mind that count for this, Aubrey, like Mr. Ray Charles."

~

"What subjects are you writing about lately?" Aubrey asked Christaine that evening in the living room. They usually didn't discuss her work or his riding—a rule they had about familiarity's contempt, but hard to stick to.

"Short stories."

"What subjects?"

"Many."

"Oh, just toss me one. Come on."

"Okay. The reporter asked the Hungarian farmer why he hates the Gypsies."

"Why does he?"

"Because the farmer says everyone knows the Gypsies train foxes to steal chickens for them."

"Good one. Tell me another."

"Um… There's an armadillo called Strike, because he can snap his toenails together and make a spark to start a forest fire whenever he wants."

"What for?"

"The worms and grubs come to the top to breathe after the vegetation burns off, and the armadillos get to eat until they bust. So Strike is the new king of the Dillo people, and he's good at checking which way da wind blow." She winked.

"*True* M?"

"Yep, *True* magazine, and what about you and your schoolmaster horse, Rigoletto?" Those coffee-pond child eyes of hers widened.

"Your father asked me to look into Rigoletto's eye a couple of days ago and tell him what I saw."

"And?"

"Well, it just hit me I missed something."

"Yeah?" She nodded him on.

"A horse's eye is more appealing if very little white shows in the whole ensemble, but it's the opposite with a person, especially when it's a man like me looking at a woman like you, and by Yahweh, you should see your eyes right now."

"What? What about them?" She started to read him.

"They are so…big, big, beautiful lights, and they lob that light at me. I can see the moisture they're bathed in and that wet, and well, I know it's yours, your body's and—"

"Come here, horse man."

She sexed her eyes, and he moved in without touching her, at first. An insuperable traction came from the way he held his hand an inch off her place. It felt dangerous, compulsive, and he had an urge to wolf it—be sensually slaughtered by the endings lovers consider: dying with one another or by the other's hand, should they dance the little death too near the larger one, their hand on a throat.

They stood together and stripped. Christaine slipped under him in her luscious sprawl. He teased it until she pulled him in. When he reached the center, he wore what he craved on her mons until everything inside of them shattered and he lurched forward in a sweet strain. "Christaine, slip away," he whispered.

His mind put him in the cane field. It was as if it had just rained. A huge mockingbird egg was where the tower should be. Was it his room or her womb? Tailed blood types snaked through the cane toward the bird egg. He thought he saw one bore through to start a life of original sin—that crack his grandmother said God put in everything. It took only one schizo-seminal hero to do that that night from an Adam bomber like Aubrey Shallcross.

He twitched again. She picked up his post-lovemaking face with both hands and asked with a smile, "Did you tear any muscles?"

He said she may have to tape his groin later.

She wriggled out from under him and walked to the kitchen. Her temperature had been running ninety-nine or higher all day. Soon, the bird egg would churn like corn mash, working inside her until it cooked off a crossbred wonder of them. Another unknown soldier with an unknown soldier in its shoulder, in its shoulder, out past the infinity of #8734 and Keir Dullea, in the space womb at the end of *Two Thousand and None*.

She walked back to where they went down on the floor. He was sitting on the rami of his seat bones, legs pulled up to his chin. She bent over with her clothes in her hands and kissed him on top of the head.

"I'm tired and all woman now, *gadjo* man. I'm going up to the neon headboard and knit the penless story. You coming?"

"No, sweetie. I think I might go out to the music room and tinker."

"All right. When you slip into bed, be sure you don't touch that spot on my back between L5 and S1, or I'll put you back to work."

"It would be like shooting up again, you drop-dead, chicken-stealin Gypsy woman."

"I can sleep on that, Johnny Yuma. Don't stay up too late. Night," she said, as she climbed the stairs.

Aubrey got dressed and started thinking about the broken-back cow dog, Maxey, in the woods for some reason. He flashed on Maxey lurching forward from the bullet when The Junior shot him, as he did a moment ago when he came with her. And what would he do the rest of his life if he was paralyzed from the waist down like Maxey? Was it the swollen sex he'd just had that made him think that? But maybe it would be all right if he was. He wouldn't need to have sex again after such a beautiful meld with his lover, would he? He could just live the cerebral life, right? She wouldn't leave him. The stun shot up his back, and the subjective cookie he always dipped into the milk of possibility and prolapse exploded. There would be no more riding horses, and The Junior wouldn't be there to put him down like Maxey. He saw President Roosevelt coming at him with a big smile, smoking the famous cigarette in its holder. Only a pair of slim hands pushed the president's wheelchair.

Out of the house and down the path he walked, weak, and sat on the old pine stump. Ready as ever, Johnny Angel slid out onto the bicep to talk with his man, who had just slipped on the backside of free will into a look at self-destruction.

"Sweet mother Mary of Swirl, what was that?" Trip spit over the side of Aubrey's arm.

"Oh, well, that was…that was a bushwhack whack."

"Right, but that's not the answer. What was that really? I mean objective world really? I mean base of your tower righty-tighty really? It was an irrational fear, Einstein! You shove yourself back to clockwise right now and scratch a zero here in the dirt for the odds you're going to be paralyzed. You're doing 'it is what it isn't' again because you do that black fetter now and then to see if you can handle it. You know what I mean, Aubrey: Monkey see, monkey don't do that shit, carburet it?"

"I can't scratch that out in the dark here, fucker."

"Then do it in your head, goddammit. Dramatist!"

"That's the Lord's name in vain on you, you semi-pious little prick."

"Even God says goddammit when he's fed up, Aubrey. Now get off this pine stump and go to the sound barn and write one before you get as stuck in that fatuous shit as this amputated tree in the ground."

He sat in a chair with the lights low. Christaine was medicine, he knew it. She was extreme unction. He'd be the walking dead without her, or God help him, paralyzed like the cow dog.

The first line of lyrics drifted into his jar, and he flew the words around the tower in the pure lefty of his creative loose.

My heart's like a rainbow my mother designed.

Me , I'm a madman with a romantic mind.

My love is just like me, she got X-ray eyes.

When she looks at the ocean, she can see the far side.

So I'm asking you simple, Whacked-out existentials

Trapped in the no-fly zone—

Are you having a good time?

Or is your life a dull crime?

Tell me the truth, balls to bones.

Tell me the truth, balls to bones.

You get what I got

You'll fly through that blind spot

I'm talkin the truth, balls to bones.

"Good," Trip said, when Aubrey came out of the big room. "Big Indian! Juicy Fruit, et al. Finished"

"What? Too cheesy? Too maudlin? What?"

"No, I really liked it, especially that blind-spot line in the last verse. Your movie, son, your air puck, Head Wound. Love works, Aubrey."

"Maybe."

"Maybe? Why don't you admit it? It's fear again, isn't it? You're afraid of that cripple thing and your dependence on her. You old single guys get like this. Can't take the pressure of a real-deal relationship. That's so stupid. Don't you know what life is all about? Loving, dying, hurting, fishing, dreaming, laughter, tears, and laughter. Wait, was that a book?"

"It was a big line in Gibran's book, and maybe some movie. I can't remember," Aubrey said.

"Who cares, schizo? You and I go around all day doing lines from the movies because you said in college you were sick of the Greek those prigs used. I'm trying to make a point here, and I'm not going to mention Prometheus."

Aubrey nodded.

"Where do you get this fear crap, Ambrose? It's from smoking that toad part all day."

"Maybe, Trip, but I'm not giving that up, no way."

"Well, then, smoke more rational things. I did like the song, especially that part about 'whacked-out existentials.' That's you, boy."

"I'm tired. I'm goin to sleep, Trip."

"Oh! Well, be sure not to touch her between L5 and S1 when you slide into bed if you're that tired. Be very quiet and pick a film, Aubrey, any film…except one about Franklin Delano Roosevelt. Not that one tonight, whittle monster."

Chapter 14

FRIDAY NIGHT AT THE GOOSE

The night before John Chrome was going to meet Christaine Sadacca, he had a dream about the actress Katherine Ross. That hometown stunner who took him over at the age of twenty-four in 1969. The astonishing American girl whose high school facial cast ended up doing Butch and Sundance naked at a place called Hole in the Wall out west after dark. The girl in the dream was a slipper.

Chrome climbed in his car the next evening and headed for Aubrey's, still thinking about the dream. He was going to meet Christaine Sadacca tonight, and from what he had heard about her face, it might be the same shot to the stomach the Ross girl gave him.

The plan was they go to the Blue Goose, the palmetto pantheon of young Turks and old galoots with no-lace sneakers titrated on rum and rope.

Chrome stopped at the head of the driveway to take in Aubrey's house lit against the night sky. The big thing hung in the poles like a billboard dog. It seemed to recognize his Ford wagon, the car with three hundred thousand miles he'd owned since Harry Nilsson left his bank job and Duane Allman kissed a truckload of peaches in Macon, then went upstairs to sit with Frankie Lymon.

At this house, a surfer girl they called Outrageous stunned him when she asked to massage his prostate before they made love on the high platform under the stained glass eye in the big silo. He let her because that was the deal to do it with her normal next, her knees in the air on the pine rail hollering, "Oh, oh, oh…get it, Chromie! Get it, Chromie, Chromie, Chromie!"

Looking at this house made him feel embarrassed sometimes, yet gave him a peace that passeth all understanding. Splendid, stoned, self-exalt Tater moments happened here when the acid took him into the back peel and let him hand steel balls to hallucinated cripples so they could walk again.

He'd said good things and stupid things in this house—crap cliché advice he gave out drunk: "The sun'll come out tomorrow," or worse. Revelations from psychotropia Peter Fonda promised happened in this house, and revelations Peter promised that never happened.

Once, he and the love of his life, Rose Mothershed, bought ten pills of first-class MDA from Arquette Orlander here for wondrous ascensions. Chrome told her the pills were the steel balls he had handed the crippled people—the same ones Jeff Bridges had in the *Starman* movie when he crashed into the lake and then drove to Arizona with the young widow.

Rose rented the *Starman* movie a week later, and she, too, drove to Arizona, to find Jeff. Rose was never seen again. Losing Rose broke Chrome's heart. Thank Yahweh she didn't want to massage his prostate, because he was beginning to wonder after that beach bunny if it was how wiser women gauged the potential size of a man's orgasm—some girls' bathroom throbbing rumor that the bigger the gland, the bigger the blast of seminal kerplooee, making it all the more appealing.

Oh, man, too weird. He smiled and shook his head. *How have I been able to live this long this stupid?*

The stained glass eye in the silo winked when he looked, as if remembering that night on the top deck with the beach bunny, then the whole riotous residence began to shake like aspic. "Everything moves all the time anyway, sure it does. Everything's aspic," he said to his rearview mirror. He'd confirmed that years ago as a stentor protozoan, blowing his horn in the hammer lane at slower-moving rhizopods in the red mangroves of the Indian River after swallowing two pills of LSD windowpane on an empty stomach.

He shifted his beach-sand Ford into gear and pulled into the front yard.

"Christaine, Mr. Chrome is here!" he heard Aubrey yell.

"Why do you call him Mister?" she yelled back.

"Because he's a schoolteacher!"

Chrome stepped up on the front porch as Christaine dropped one leg at a time down the stairs in tight jeans and a high thread-count

T-shirt with a human hand painted on the front. Chrome watched at the open door as Aubrey put his own hand on her chest after the last step. Chrome remembered Aubrey had told him women feel better through that kind of thread count than they do naked.

"Well, I look okay?"

"Jesus, Christaine, if I was born with that corpus of yours… Hey, John! This is Christaine. John and I have known each other since the Romans."

"Good to finally meet you, John, and I think you ought to admonish this man for not having you out sooner."

Chrome bowed.

"I'm going to get a step ahead of the bar bill tonight and have a drink," Christaine said. "Would you like something, John?"

"Yes, uh, I'll have, uh, a sidecar." He winked at Aubrey. "No, just kidding, a beer is fine."

"How about you, Chrysler?"

"I'll hold off. Singin with the one and only Frank Clark tonight, if they'll sit through it."

"You're singing? What song?" Chrome asked.

"'Seven-Eleven Outlaw.'"

Christaine made sidecars anyway, the drink that made metaphor history in the psycho-*doppelgänger* world of Aubrey and Trip.

1-1/2 OUNCE BRANDY
1/2 OUNCE COINTREAU
1/2 OUNCE BENEDICTINE
1/2 OUNCE FRESH LEMON JUICE
SHAKE WITH ICE

"Ooh, look at this," Chrome said, when she came back with them. "Real sidecars." He bowed like Japan again. "I'd love to walk the windows. Any new? I see these in my dreams, and I'm hurrying a little to get around the corner to Yuma."

"Oh, him. Well, don't be shocked, John. Aubrey blew off his head," Christaine laughed.

"Who blew his head off?" Aubrey said. "You did, Liberty Valance."

"God in cowboy heaven, and there he is, decollated, for sure." Chrome slacked his face. "I suppose there's a story with this, but I won't ask." He stared at what Johnny held in his hand and murmured, "The jar," then returned to the living room to drain his drink. "What'd ya think? Drive into Jensen Beach?"

Chrome and Aubrey skipped checking out Punky's barstool when they passed through the doors of the Blue Goose; Christaine headed for the ladies' room.

"Do you feel down about The Junior when you walk in here?" Chrome asked.

"A lot of things land on me in here. I mean, I can see my parents stretching their arms toward me on the dance floor. They used to bring me when I was a kid, and I always see a trace of Leda in one corner and Arquette in the other. 'Course, he never was very far from Leda, now, was he?"

When Christaine came back, they sat at a table for four. Frank Clark looked up from the stage and nodded. Chrome heard Aubrey tell Christaine he would sit anywhere except near the jukebox. Too much of The Junior there.

"Now I'll have a drink." Aubrey set his guitar case down next to the chair and ordered conch fritters for the three of them and a Bombay Sapphire for himself.

After the band broke, Frank Clark walked over and patted Chrome on the back. They introduced him to Christaine.

"Aubrey, you wanna step out through the kitchen with me while the band smokes one? And bring your axe so I can hear those chords to 'Seven-Eleven' again."

Now Chrome was alone with her, squinting from his second sidecar, but wanting to stay half-sober for this rare moment.

"Aubrey told me you used to write for the *Miami Herald* and you still write every day," he said.

"I do show up to do it…"

"I know what you mean."

"Oh, you write?"

"When it comes."

"What's it like teaching teenagers?" she asked him.

"Good. I like their head at that age. Oh, that came out funny."

"No, I didn't even get it. So what are they like?" Christ asked.

"I'll probably sound old, but I see a lack of intimacy among the sweethearts. They don't hold hands anymore. I saw a boy with a T-shirt the other day that said, 'Define Girlfriend,' you know, that kind of wiseacre stuff. And I think it all started in Detroit with the advent of the center console. No more bench seat, like when I was a kid. Now they just reach across that cup holder and tap on a shoulder or something."

"I hope you write that kinda stuff. I think you're a romantic, John Chrome. Me, too, I'm a romantic."

Don't stare at her eyes too long, John. "I like that. I mean, uh, that you are a romantic," Chrome said.

"When I write, John, some days are chains of melody, some days just chain link. You agree?"

He nodded.

"You know?" Chrome said. "I've put my thesaurus away." He swallowed a fritter almost whole. "Lately, I take my adjectives and nouns from the *Fix It Yourself Manual*—like, 'He snapped like a throw bolt.' Or, 'She was a powerful helix in the solenoid of his soul.' I've started going to hardware stores and using their product names to describe a *glazier*-point personality, a *slot-head* attitude, *square-head* taste. I'm giving up my nineteenth-century background in lit. I don't think about writing to get read or make money, any more than I think about eating these fritters to jet them in the morning, 'cause that's what they make me do, but I...I am doing it. I, eating the fritters and still writing, I mean, to just enjoy and then jet it—the writing, I mean. Not about recognition."

You just said fritters make me shit to Katharine Ross here, John.

"Hey, John, has Aubrey always talked to himself?"

"Like what?"

"Like what? That's what I hear him yell out of the blue when he thinks he's alone. And then I hear, 'Trip' or 'Tripper,' like falling down or drug tripper, and of course, he says, 'Finished'!"

They laughed.

You better play dumb, John. A woman like this could get you to tell her anything.

The band returned for another set. Frank Clark walked around the stage fingering the Les Paul he played for most of his life. Chrome had heard it was the instrument Frank honed as an asthmatic teenager stuck in his room.

"I got lots of good friends in the room tonight," Frank said from the stage. "So I'm gonna sing an old Tom Rapp song from Pearls before Swine called 'Another Time,' and it comes from another time… when things moved around out there in the colored air and wouldn't stop, would they? And after that wore off, they never stopped again, did they? You remember that, don't you, people? Another time." The townies applauded and whistled.

"Oh, and yeah, most o' y'all know Aubrey Shallcross up here with me. He's gonna sit in, like when we were in his old band, Sock Puppet…another time."

It was a five-member group: Aubrey on rhythm guitar, a girl singing harmony, the bass player, the drummer, and Frank's lead. The intro lasted a full minute and became dreamier, then tangerine dreamier. A spell rose among the middle-aged in the room. Frank licked his lips, and one of his numinous fingers licked the guitar neck with his slide as he began.

The end of each verse asked the crowd, "If they came by again to die again," then told them they'd have to try again another time.

Now the place was quiet, even the bartenders. All eyes had crystallized during the instrumental bridge in the windowpane tones of the times until the last line in the song asked the room, "Ever think the world outside might be just inside your mind?"

Applause thundered, and people stomped their feet. Christaine leaned over to speak to Chrome, and he froze when her famous lips brushed his ear runnels.

"Look at Aubrey up there. He loves this music. Is that the trippy stuff he cants about around the farm when he thinks he's alone?"

Chrome couldn't help it. He had to, even though he'd been sworn to secrecy. He made the face—the superior, enigmatic, *I-know-a-*

secret one. The one a man makes for a woman so she'll think he's as cool as Johnny Yuma. And she saw it.

"Now we gonna change it up some," Frank Clark announced. "Aubrey's gonna do the 'Seven-Eleven Outlaw' song we used to do with Sock Puppet for old-time's sake."

The crowd went through the noise again. Aubrey took a breath at the mic. "A-one, two; a-one, two, three, four." The rock came, cooking the place in it. When the Tater King caught the end of a four-count, he came down on the first line:

Do you remember me back in 1980,

Livin in Georgia with a southern lady's brain?

I stole everything.

I rode a Ford with a macho mannequin,

We looked married, and we rode 'round for fun,

Then I'd pull my gun.

Say, 'Get your hands up, son!'

I robbed 7-Eleven food stores

And then I'd run.

I remember when I was Marlon Brando,

I never talked, but I used to mumble songs about boys gone wrong.

I got in fights over lots of outlaws,

Pretty Boy Floyd, he was my hero, too.

He was an artist true.

They said I was too, oo, oo, oo.

The people say, 7-Eleven outlaw, we love you.

I had to rob to be freeee,

I had to rob to be meeee,

And I robbed for everybody's outlaw fantasy ee ee ee.

And so the old Blue Goose began to shake like Chrome's flashback aspic, the drinkers singing with each chorus, especially when Aubrey quivered his voice like Gene Pitney, his eyes shut, and headed for the Orbinson high note that shook the fronds on the big rum shrine. He reached the last part after two more verses:

> *And life is yours and all your daydreams of being an outlaw and living your fast scenes where? Where you're never scared...in your TV chair.*
> *So here's to all you 7-Eleven outlaws out there.*

To the final thump! He bowed during the applause and walked back to his seat, slapping hands with the crowd.

"Master blaster," Chrome said to him.

"It was wonderful, Aubrey." Christaine beamed and kissed his cheek as a young man cleared his throat by the table.

"Uh, Mr. Shallcross? My name is Jimmy Ordway, and I just wanted to say I loved that song, and uh, I got the message."

"Well, thank you, Jimmy."

The man nodded and was gone.

"You see, honey? He got the message."

Aubrey leaned back and watched his little river town's dance floor. Chrome heard him say to Christaine, "I see my parents dancing in each other's arms in this room, smiling at me as if romance is the only religion...and because of you, heart, it's my religion."

Aubrey put his hand under the table on the holy shank of the woman he loved, Christaine Veronica Sadacca.

~

In Miami that night, he, too, was on the shank of a woman and that other shank, the two-faced blowgun nose relief the cocaine cowboy rides. Carlos O'Meara, nicknamed the Mick Spic by the Anglo law, had some good times until the rat-dance boss ratted him out and shortened that ride. The city of Miami sent him to prison for three years with no parole.

Two women aborted his children because they hated him that much. Others had lied to him about their cycles. In prison, he thought only of her, his obsession, his last shot at life and his dead daughter's return—the woman who lived in Jensen Beach called Christ Sadacca.

Chapter 15

REDHEADED THUG

Drayton Sadacca Shallcross let out a paint-peeling scream in the backyard as a blood-hungry horsefly tried to bore through his baby-slim skin. His mother pinched it dead before it could get into any gore. Christaine and Aubrey were inebrious over the child they had named after Aubrey's father.

"It's all right, Drayton. I killed it. I killed it." She tried to rub the spot, but the two-year-old slapped her hand away as if his mother had bitten him. It was the fall of 1990, and the first break in the heat had come from a weak cold front.

She opened a gold cigarette case. Drayton's picture on his first birthday was above the magazine load of Gauloises, a white-tubed fag in the spring clip ready to go, plucked and foreplayed with her right hand. Her brain went sweet when it wobbled and blew hot. She remembered an actress who two-fingered one into her lipstick, exhaled, and picked a piece of tobacco off her tongue that flashed some pink at a man. Very sex. Less smoke around today; she missed the oral show in movies and in real life.

Aubrey had given her a silver Zippo for her birthday with Christ inlaid in gold on the cover. He liked smokers—considered them chatty and enjoyably uneasy. She was comfortable around him with it and had taken it up again after the baby was weaned.

During the final months of her pregnancy she never let him see her naked and didn't allow him near the delivery room until she was covered in bed, despite the imprecating looks from those natural nurses. Her ex-husband had been there for their daughter's birth, and Christaine was convinced the sight of all that baby blast made him lose reverence for her body, and she knew he was seeing another woman, even while she bled on the fourth floor of the hospital from the destruction of borning.

This man, this Carlos O'Meara, an ex-police detective, still called her once a year; she kind of hated him. The end came when Internal Affairs coughed him up as a dirty-money dick in the maggoty Miami side of *Scarface* wannabes, and of course, somewhere in the real satellite shot of Miami, the real *Scarface*. Carlos, the bitter cop, became the bitter thug after he was fired from his job. As much as she tried to go on with their life after his inquisition, the fallout crazed him, and he began to sit in with the same bad people who had trolled for him.

He was well trained in stealth and tracking and could find her on a phone anywhere. Christaine and Aubrey had made a deal to not talk about their past, only their future together, so they never discussed ex-spouses or lovers. One morning, Carlos called when Aubrey was riding with her father.

He was apologetic and said for the umpteenth time that he wanted her to know he always would be there if she needed him. She clinched her hand over the trashcan in her chest, where she kept things like him, old feelings, certificates of pain, and trespasses she'd dismissed with prejudice, in case a somebody claimed it never happened and she had to take it all back. She was tougher than her sister, Marla, even though Marla acted tougher.

She slightly indulged Carlos with a par question or two to be decent, because she remembered how much her daughter loved him.

"How have you been, Carlos? I talked to your mother on Christmas. I hope she is doing okay with the chemo?"

"It was ten years we had," he said, "and I'm the one who screwed it up. I still miss you. I know you're happy with that country boy, but I think about you every minute."

He told her he was just out of prison. She didn't answer him.

"I know, I know," he said and hung up.

~

"Aubrey, try it again," Asante ordered from the side of the dressage ring. "And I want you to think about this. The canter pirouette is not about turning; it is about the forward riding in the collection and the quality of the canter underneath you. You are thinking too much about the turning part. Come on! Turning must be your second thought. The horse's energy must go through his frame on every stride, active and balanced, then you bring him around in five or six jumps from a long inside leg. Now tell me how you do this, like I would tell you."

"With the turning seat, the way Steinbrecht says in his book. My inside hip pulls forward with the horse's hip, and my inside shoulder goes back to match his shoulder. It creates a torque in my body that marries his shape and allows me to turn him almost without any rein when I increase it."

"Ah, yes, *monsieur*, now I know you think about it."

"Yes, I do, my sensei."

They walked up to the house and stopped next to his truck. Asante told him he must be humble when he looks in the mirror and to thank God for sending him these beautiful animals that put the same wind in his face they put in their own. In fact, he told him to thank God for every day of his life, a life his friend, Junior, had lost. His eyes were a sorry wet, and Aubrey's, too.

"I do miss that boy, son, and..." Asante choked and looked away.

"Yes, he's gone from me...tragedy," Aubrey said.

He drove to the beach from there. The fall surf was roaring for the green-room searchers to overdo it in the bull sections—pure levitation crank for the testo-haunted hominids who could give a shit about tomorrow, flying down the water walls of the breaking left pearls.

"So...how's that nasty get of yours doing?" Chrome asked.

"Building immunities every day, puts anything in his mouth—dirt, horse shit, his shit."

"Yuck."

"Yeah, I told Christaine she better put our kid on the same schedule for worming as the horses, or he'll be a midget."

"Yuck again. Hey, I got something for your Ball jar. You wanna listen?" Chrome was lit, not his everyday poky-word drone.

Aubrey nodded.

164

"It's this guy I've known forever. He's the real-deal science guy, you know, perfectly cut canals in his brain. My brain looks like a diseased root cluster. Anyway, he's a neurosurgeon at Miami Jackson and works in research."

"This isn't gonna be a psychotropic drug study, is it, because I'm ineligible if it is."

"No, this is a device that gives you similar, though weaker, abilities of a quasi-savant."

"Like *Rain Man?*"

"Something like that. Well, not that intense. He wants me to try it, and I told him about you and the way you open containers."

"Savant qualities without leaving you a savant?"

"Yeah, they monitor your brain with this topical electrode hat. They can make the machine enhance part of your mind by slowing down the other parts of it, as autism does. It's called TMS, or *transcranial magnetic stimulation.*"

Chrome stopped talking and pointed at the water. An eight-foot shark was sliding through a wave wall lit by the low afternoon sun shining off the dune behind them.

"So one day, he asked a patient to start counting with the hat on, and the patient whizzed through square root questions. Get it? Yep, Dr. Henry Brown, you know, like the old Dr. Brown…what we called heroin back when Nixon shut the store down in Turkey and it all started coming from Mexico in a brown color. You remember, we snorted it like coke. Come on, you have to open your mind to new things again, Chrysler, even though you're a father now. Don't act like a Luddite."

~

Four days later, Carlos stood next to the pay phone in the Catheter Café.

"Carlos, are you in my town?" Christaine asked him.

Silence.

"Carlos, did you hear what I asked you?"

165

"Well, I am close by."

"What do you mean you're *close by*? I'm asking are you in Jensen Beach?"

"Yes, because I'm on the way to Jacksonville on business."

"So, where are you?"

"Why? You want to come see me?"

"No."

"I'm on the turnpike, not right in your town," he lied. "I'm getting some gas and wanted to say hello. I'm sorry I got emotional the other day." He switched the phone to his left ear when Janet put the lunch special on his table.

"You know, Carlos, it just makes this old thing linger like chronic, and that's bad for both of us."

"Maybe, but I, I am an expert at chronic. In fact, what other people call chronic is just a way of life for me."

"Carlos, I'm not going to get into a discussion about anything with you." She hung up.

"Can I get you something else?" Janet asked him.

"Just the check and local information."

"I'll get the check first. Now what is it you need to know?"

Janet turned as someone walked in for lunch. "Hi, Aubrey."

"I don't need that information anymore," Carlos said.

Aubrey drove to Asante's early Sunday morning with Christaine and their boy. They were all going to a dressage show in Wellington, just south of there. Solana was watching the gate and eager to hold the baby when they arrived, so he could giggle from his grandmamma's attention.

At the show grounds, they waited for the grand prix freestyle, the riding test performed to music much at one with the ice-skaters on television, except with a horse. The small town of Wellington in Palm Beach County was the epicenter of the sport horse world from January to April: world-class polo, grand prix jumping, grand prix dressage. All were there to light up the fans and competitors for the halcyon months of Florida's famous winter.

Aubrey raised acres of goose bumps when the freestyle started. It made him more fervent about his riding, and he was determined to reach this level one day.

Asante drove home on the turnpike with Solana next to him holding the baby. In the backseat, Aubrey's lips touched Christaine's ear. The noise from the Cummins engine kept the declarations to his heart beside him off the front seat.

The flatland streamed by like a stuck space bar. When a shell-pit lake appeared, he thought about the altar-boy story she had told him that first night in the *Tell the Truth and Run* T-shirt, and she did run— back to Miami. He thought he'd never see her again. Now, here she was next to him, with their boy in the front seat, going home.

"Christ, look, we're passing a shell pit. Ain't it swollen?" he whispered.

He saw her mannequin in its cassock and surplice again, sinking into the flooded catacombs under Miami, and felt a carnal stir in his knees. He slid an index finger over the inside of her thigh, the way a hospital practitioner does when they test for nerve damage. She flinched like a chill. He did it again.

"Hey, you, Gypsy lover," she whispered. "You gonna have to follow up on this tease you're working or die by the hand of a hysterical woman. Finished."

"I always make good on my teases. Not finished."

"What's the plan for the rest of the afternoon?"

"Let's leave Crib Death with your mother, pick him up later in the evening."

Christaine smiled the look at him.

At home, on O'gram's second floor, he laid down a piece of cardboard for her nude body at the top of the circular slide, then walked downstairs naked as she was and counted to three.

She stretched her arms out in front of her as she spun the drop through two floors and wrapped her legs around him at the bottom like pretzel syndrome. They played it out around the room, up against things, on top of things, between things, and finally down on the coffee table by the sofa until their feet stopped kicking.

"You murdered me, monster, you lady killer," she said.

"You murder me, Christ lady."

Aubrey lifted her off the coffee table and carried her outside into the swimming pool, chest deep. "Your turn to direct, girl. Want me to sink like the altar boy?"

"No, I want you to be the kingfish and keep driving that fin of yours. Crimson and clover, you know."

They rolled in the sun-cooked water like spawning fish. The blue mammalian eye painted on the bottom watched them like something from Syria, while something from Miami with the strychnine eye watched from the woods.

Chapter 16

DEVOTION

Aubrey walked the path to his music shrine after picking up Drayton at Asante and Solana's on that perfect day—his first look at a dressage show and the naked terpsichore with Christaine around the house and in the pool. He had an old habit of blowing his breath out on his forearm to spark the spore of a skin whiff, but the chlorine smell from the pool water had ruined it. He sat on the pine stump.

"Hey, Trip."

Trip sprung out of the armpit armory. "I am here. The chlorine blew it for you, huh?"

"Oh…yeah. Hey, do you think I'm doing better with how precious I make things I'm afraid I'll lose?"

"Yes, I do, Aubrey. And I think you are learning something about irrational fear, realizing you are not alone in this time of your time with these feelings. Many people deal with this."

"Aren't they something, Trip? I mean Christ and Drayton."

"I never told you, but I wrestle your same fears when it comes to both of them. I love that child, and I love that girl, and I'm so happy I kicked your ass into all this that I could kiss myself."

"What you mean kicked me into it? I did this."

"Yeah? Well, who told you take up this riding and get to know these people? And what a wonderful thing this is instead of staggering around the parking lot of the Blue Goose with a Hamilton Beach jacked out in your throat. Finished."

Aubrey rolled his neck back around his shoulders. There he was again, giant-like under the stars, thinking of the universe as the only real God and at peace with it. It made him look up at the diamond sky and say, "God!" the way people do. The way The Junior did when he was dying in the bed of the Tax Man's truck.

170

Inside the music shrine, he sat with crossed legs as his father used to. He could see his beloved old man with his pipe and tobacco pouch pressing a thumb into the bowl of leaf before lighting it up. Aubrey still had that pipe in a box somewhere and once bawled like a baby when he put it up to his nose.

A drifty walked on. He stared at the drywall in the room and imagined the hollow space behind it between the studs. Then words came in snowflake letters—white font falling against the foil of a black Gorky-treed sky and floating in the solar monstrance of his prolific carburetion jar. He rose out over the cane field in his mind, singing the love song he'd written for her two days ago:

CHRISTAINE, SHE'S AN ARTIST
FROM THE JEWELRY WORDED WORLD.
SHE MAKES FLYING LINES FROM DIAMONDS,
SELLS 'EM TO THE BOOK-HEAD GIRLS.
SHE STANDS LIKE A PRIESTESS,
A VENDOR ON THE STREET.
PEOPLE BUY HER SILVER CHAINS
JUST SO HER KID CAN EAT.
SHE PULLED MY HEART FROM MY CHEST
FROM FIFTY-FIVE FEET AWAY
AND IT NEVER CAME BACK TO STAY.

'CAUSE I BELIEVE IN THE FIRE
AND THE HEART IS THE PART THAT GETS HIGHER.
AND I BELIEVE YOU SUSTAIN
THE HEAT OF THE LOVE YOU EXCHANGE.

SO I'LL BLOW ON THE FLAME
WHILE I ROCK YOUR FRAME.
I LOVE YOU, CHRISTAINE.

Carlos leaned through the car window to thank his puzzled friend, Manny, who he'd known since childhood. It took only a minute to unload his gear.

"I'll call you when it's time to pick me up at this spot. Don't tell anyone where I am, as we discussed, Manny."

"But I do not understand. Why can't I help you with this?"

"It's my business. It's between me and her, *comprendo*? This has nothing to do with our money and product. It's personal."

"Women are more dangerous than what we do for a living, Carlos. We always have looked out for each other, man, and we made promises. I am worried."

"I'll handle it. Now go, before someone sees us on this stinking shell road. And thank you."

"Hey, amigo, look where you walk. There is snakes in these woods."

"I know, Manny. I'm one of them."

Carlos jumped the ditch and leaned over everything he'd need to live around O'gram for a week: tent, bedroll, dry food, canned food, dope, weapons, and batteries. His mission had at least three backup plans to kill that redneck or mess him up and take back his woman. Be what his suppurating brain called a "righteous quadruple motherfucker." But what was he going to do with their boy? Maybe some kind of accident, or he'd sell him in Miami.

He took three trips in to set up camp, walking with his chest out like Crazy Horse in a bulletproof ghost shirt, with the black grease smeared under his eyes for no reason.

He lay back to rest in the low-water hammock and stared into the mesh of tree branches and hanging moss. "Why do they call that Spanish moss? Oh, yeah, Ponce de León," he mumbled.

Resurrection ferns covered limbs. They appeared dead, but Carlos knew about that, too: They would sit up alive for rainstorms, and so would his Christaine for him, revivifying their love as he spread his moisture like the rain inside her to resurrect their daughter, Marlaine. That's what the ruined knuckle of his mind told him. That's how far this had come with his interest in scarlet sin and voodoo. Where was the buffer? The moral filter? The designated agency in his head, called the super ego, to protect us from a rabid tortfeasor like Carlos and ourselves loose on the world?

~

Aubrey turned into the parking lot of a beach access known as the Rocks. The Chrome Top pulled in next to him.

"Jesus, I could hear this surf when I stopped for fuel on the river side once the pump shut off," Aubrey said.

"What pump?"

"The fuel pump. It does make a *whomp whomp* sound, don't you know?"

"Smotes me. I only care about that surf pump."

After an hour in the water, they breathed from their stomachs, perfectly correct on the beach. Two minutes of silent sky went by.

"Hey, I didn't tell you, but I hooked up with my doctor friend last week, the one with that hot-wired *Rain Man* hat I told you about in Miami. We played around with it, and I became kinda Too Loose Lautrec," Chrome said.

"What happened?"

"I picked drawing to focus on because I can't draw. The thing also works as a turbo memory enhancer."

"Right, and?"

"I got pretty good by my standards. This technology is really kind of amazing. I didn't produce anything I could sell, but I did a couple of sketches miles above my usual abilities."

"First step to Savantville."

"Yeah, right, too loose. So you're next, Chrysler, man. I'd love to see what you'd take off that hat with your swollen drifties."

"Long as there's no Hunter Thompson involved."

"No, no chemistry, no winged horse."

"Reminds me, I gotta leave for my training as the world's greatest up-and-coming dressage rider."

"Oh, yeah, the other horse. The clean one that can't fly."

~

Carlos lay inside his mosquito netting in the afternoon, like a germ in the helix of a human cell. He tore the hind legs off a beetle and watched it struggle on his pant leg, then set his propane burner to heat a coffee pot, as if the three eight balls of snoot he was carrying wasn't enough to keep him right.

Twenty minutes later, he walked half a mile through the palmettos to O'gram and crawled the last few yards to the edge of the field. His binoculars couldn't see anyone, but Christaine's blue van was parked out front. He put his head down and thought about warriors and a line from a book he remembered. This would carry him, give him the strength those warriors had for this noble deed of his, instead of that dope-slinging sniper life around Miami. It would be face-to-face combat with that redneck of hers. He would outsmart him, as those Trojans did. And what was the line the guy wrote in that thick dirty book his friend brought to school when they were kids—the one that clung to his head junk all these years? "And yes, I said. Yes, I will, yes." He was sure Christaine would say that to him.

A car was coming…no, a truck. It was him, the interloper, the hick *cabrone* wife thief. He'd wait until dark to clock the grange better, take a snoop-the-varmint look around, and come back tomorrow.

Aubrey got out of his truck and walked into the house, but immediately came out again and headed to the music shrine.

"What the hell's that building? Maybe it's where he keeps his swamp buggy or something?" Carlos said to a bull ant crawling on the ground. He wanted to get the timetables down, the comings and goings, and yes, be sharp! He pulled the little bottle from his shirt pocket to fix his face again.

Aubrey returned to the main house in a half hour and reappeared in a bathrobe, on his way to an outdoor shower by the pool. When Carlos saw him reach up to turn on the water, it occurred to him this would be the perfect place to kill him before moving into the house to woo Christaine. The hick would be shampooing his hair with his eyes shut, and he would pop his head with a cap through the long silencer coupled to his Glock.

He watched the whole family leave twenty minutes later in Aubrey's truck. It was still light. "What now, creeping Tom?" he asked another bull ant.

Into the compound he went, and gaped at the buildings, caving his nose in and out to pull anything off the unusual residence he could. It looked even more weird up close, not that he hadn't seen eccentric places in Miami, but this place seemed held together by something foreign—just glue on glass and gravity. It made him uncomfortable.

His eyes swept the porch after he did the wood steps. "Ooh!" he said to his reflection in the sliding doors when he found a key under a potted plant and checked the screens, confident there was no security system.

His first study was the living room slide, then he jerked his head from one display window to the next until he got to Little Alex, and cocked his face at him before he turned the corner. The headless Johnny Yuma was there and startled his drug-soaked eyes, but he was not impressed. Wasn't going to allow it. This redneck of hers is not more interesting than him. This guy probably hired a crazy architect or decorator to do all this so he could attract women. It was just too weird.

Upstairs, Carlos cried at the foot of Aubrey and Christaine's bed. Behind his forehead, a hundred thousand years of homo emotions stewed the jealousy designed for his gender. A second wave came, and he pulled his hunting knife to stab the sheets, but decided to wait to shoot Aubrey more than once in the shower. One shot would be for that fucker's genitals. He pulled out his dick and darted around the bed with his gun, pointing both at the pillows.

"Pop, pop, pop!" he shouted. Then he did another bump of coke and shuddered from the burn.

His eyes swept over the farm and surrounding fields from the balcony. "How did this son of a bitch get his hands on this?" He turned back to a laundry hamper and dug out her thong panties and one of her T-shirts to take back to the woods. He spit on Aubrey's Jockey shorts before he closed the lid.

The key was returned under the plant, and he walked by the pool to piss in the outdoor shower so that goober would stand in it before his blood from a real head wound spun through the hair in the drain.

That night, his campsite was a scene of anxiety: manic, confused, illuminated, more confused, ecstatic, sobbing. He kept his nose full and the edge off with vodka and bootleg Quaaludes, dragging his sleeping bag in circles through the dirt like a caddis worm, and sniffing Christ's stolen T-shirt.

When he woke at nine in the morning, he could hear them, by god—those cicadas, "those freaky fucking locusts," torturing like twenty-thousand radios.

Cotton mouthed, he cranked the cooker for powdered eggs and coffee, then leaned against an oak to fix his face with two bumps of the stimulant to level him.

This just could be the day.

~

Aubrey left his love sleeping with Drayton that morning at six and parked on the shell-rock road to zoom over the knee-high Serengeti. He pretended he was a local pilot talking to the tower, then touched down, and drove to the café for more fuel.

"Hey, Janet."

"Mornin, Aubrey. Same thing?"

"No."

Her sneakers skidded.

"I want the Luftwaffle instead."

"Hey, Bernie, Aubrey's gonna have the flyin German."

A couple of regulars looked up.

He fidgeted in the booth and looked for Catholic icons in the marble Formica tabletop. In fact, he couldn't remember sitting in this booth—different patterns than his other tables.

"Hey, Trip, could be an apostolic face here, but which one?"

"Yes, cloud man. See if this jukebox has different songs."

"Chanticleer, here's an Orbison, 'Leah.' Can you still hit the high note on her name?"

"You have to ask?" Trip's tiny voice took off to the top with ease when the reach came.

~

The day was like ooze in the woods. Carlos recited the palindromes he had been infatuated with since he was young.

"I say, Bob, Bob, Bob, Bob. Do geese see god? Do geese see Bob? No, that's not right. God a red nugget, a fat egg under a dog."

He carefully spelled them backward to make sure they were right. Out of patience, he attacked trees with his machete and spewed more palindromes, stomping on small things he thought were moving and walking in infected coon circles. He needed to make it to dark somehow and keep his nose out of the shit. Conserve his energy for battle.

~

Aubrey grabbed a paper on the way out of the café after his waffles and opened it in his truck. The front page was national rerun, so he flipped to the local, and there was one of those headlines he'd never forget: RIVER MAN FOUND DEAD IN HIS HOME. A picture showed Coker Barnes and Reve as young marrieds next to the banana-mango tree.

The paper said a neighbor discovered his body after he missed him on the front porch, where Coker learned the toughest thing about aging: how to just sit with it.

"It's the longest last lap in the world," he had told Aubrey. Not easy for a man who once was a Tarzan.

On his way to Coker's, he passed a highway roadkill marker. The Mr. McKinley song he'd heard when The Junior lay dying that night started singing its assassination rag in his head again, and he saw his cowboy friend with the wind and stars around his poisoned blue face in the Taxman's truck's running lights.

"Aubrey," Trip said. "Don't you find it strange you've never told Christaine about me?"

"Yes, considering the reverence you and I have for veritas." He shook off his vision of The Junior.

"Well, maybe in time, then."

"Yeah, maybe when Drayton has kids we'll be rocking on the porch like Coker, and I'll say, 'Christaine, I'd like to introduce you to this netherworld friend of mine,' as if I just met you in a recent moment of the slip away."

Two cars were parked at Coker's house. On his walk to the porch, Aubrey looked at the spot where Coker had spit blood, and of course, it was gone.

A sister and friend came out and said Coker had lung cancer, but never told anyone or saw a doctor. The sister said it took him days to die there alone, and he had told her once he wasn't going to take that pain stuff in honor of all the people in the world who suffer every day with no medicine. He said he'd just go out like Jesus or some other tribal man who never heard of Jesus. "No dope, dammit."

Aubrey walked out to the banana-mango tree and listened for what he thought he heard at times but never was sure. Maybe it was the foreign Luftwaffles moving through his body instead of Adam and Eve on their familiar raft.

"What's that?" he asked the tree. "You talkin to me, mango?"

His toadstone ring had turned an austere gray, but in the middle was the red speck he always saw, beating like a pinhead heart.

He got in his truck and drove to Asante's to do more work in his new church, the twenty-by-sixty-meter dressage ring of equitation's haute *école*, where he practiced the new religion that would keep him from chewing through the inside of his cheek when he had to bury someone again.

Chapter 17

THE COUNTRY VISIT

Carlos couldn't stand it. He had peppered his septum liberally with the white during the morning to lose the heebie-jeebies and wait for sunset, but just couldn't—it was barely noon. He walked out of camp and turned off the armadillo trail in an overcooked state, then crawled through the burn grass the last ten yards to the edge of the field. Her van was gone. He scanned the grange with binoculars, but could see no one, so he walked up to the key under the potted plant and went straight to the refrigerator for a cold beer and drank that one and two more, fixed his nose again and then looked from one taxidermy display to the other. If he saw the van coming, he planned to jump inside the Johnny Yuma set up and perch his head on the neck stump of the decapitated dummy.

"How funny when she sees that," he said, high as Gideroy's kite to the mannequin, Little Alex.

Christaine was in town shopping for groceries and pushed Drayton in the cart while he talked to everyone with such occasional clarity that some thought she was talking to them. She would point, embarrassed, at Drayton. They stopped at RadioShack to buy a toy dump truck with batteries so he'd wear out quicker for the daily naps. She wanted to be home by one o'clock over coffee, writing the brain hum that never failed to show and was, thank God, louder than the cicadas.

When she turned her key, it was open; she had a habit of forgetting to lock it. Drayton held her hand, and she saw some dirt she thought Aubrey must have tracked in. She released his hand, and he stayed in the big room with his new toy while she rounded the corner past Johnny Yuma for the kitchen.

On her way back to the living room, she noticed the display door wasn't closed and glanced up to that horrible assembly. Carlos's mouth and eyes were wide open on Yuma's neck like something from the guillotine. She opened her own mouth for a scream that never came, blocked by adrenalin closing down her throat. She flew for her son, but Carlos grabbed her wrist, snatched her arm behind her back, and clamped his hand around her chin. Her features and body deflated some when she recognized him.

"Don't do anything stupid to mess up the safety of your kid, Christaine." She shook her head that she wouldn't. He took his hand off her chin and leaned in to smell her. She turned away.

"Carlos, what is this? Home invasion, assault, and five other things that would send you back to jail," she hissed.

"Of course, I know that." He leered at her. "I was a lieutenant detective. There's more charges, but I don't care." He searched her eyes with a hated confidence.

"But why jeopardize your parole status?"

"Oh, I see. You saying I haven't done anything yet, so if I just left now it would be okay. I'm not going, so don't try."

"But I am saying that." Her tone was plangent, trying not to anger him, though she was very scared.

"No, no, I have a busy day. There's lots to do, *senora*, so I'm not leaving. In fact, I'm having a little meeting with that redneck of yours, just to let you both know I call the shots in my life, and a lot of other people's, too. I do what I want, like always, and today this is what I want to do."

She hoped he couldn't see her sweating.

"Do geese see God, Christaine?"

She was silent a moment. She knew this show of his—palindromes, the ones he used to chant from memory when he was feeling cute or drinking.

"I don't know," she said. "But did you know, you can cage a swallow, can't you, but you can't swallow a cage, can you?"

A grin spread across his face. "You remembered, didn't you, baby? I taught you that one a long time ago. You say the words backward in that one."

Now she saw a way to cloy him. "Yes, I remember the night we sat on the end of a dock in Coconut Grove, and the water was full of phosphorus. We kept kicking our feet in it to make it light up."

"I know, *chica*. It was our dock, even though it belonged to the city. I kept telling you that it was ours because I worked for the city, remember?"

"Yes, I remember." The pistol Aubrey used to shoot at the rattlesnake was hidden in the kitchen wall behind her. She began to work the soft part.

"Carlos?"

"*Qué?*"

"Let me get my son and bring him in here so I can give him some lunch, then we can talk."

He squinted. "I'll go with you. So what is all this stuffed stuff this man of yours puts behind the glass? Is he some kind of wacko biologist or something? I mean, what is all this? Is he a prop collector or a big-man hunter? What?"

She thought for a moment and stupidly said, "All the above."

"Well, doesn't that make you proud that a little farm girl like you could be the woman of such a big shot?"

"It's not that," she lied. "He's always been into this, and it freaks me out a little, to tell you the truth."

"What's the boy's name?"

"Drayton."

Carlos squatted next to him. "Hello, Drayton. I'm your Uncle Carlos."

Christ shuddered, picked up the boy, and walked back to the kitchen.

"I'll just put him in his chair and feed him, then we can talk." She wore a convivial face for the trespasser, who, as the good mother, she was planning to kill for the sake of the baby Serengeti man she carried in her arms. God's teeth, she would.

"Your husband is not coming home for lunch, is he?" he asked her back in the kitchen.

181

"No, but any time after that."

"What does he do?"

She slipped again. "Whatever he wants to."

Carlos stood quickly from the table and approached her. He pushed her back into the sharp counter edge and blew his fetid air in her face. "Well, that's good, because that means he is just like me, and I know you like men like that."

Drayton started to talk to himself, and Christaine looked at Carlos. "Yes, you're right. I do like men like that."

He let her go, and she went to her son.

"Doesn't he take a nap or something, like our daughter used to?"

"Yes, when he's not too excited. He will eat and get sleepy. You didn't have to jump up like that and startle him. Don't be so hostile, Carlos. We can talk."

"Okay, but don't say anything that messes with my manhood."

"Sorry. I didn't think anyone could do that." She laughed and was relieved to see him laugh, too. Maybe now she could find a way to work him.

After lunch, she put Drayton down on the living room sofa. Carlos watched from the passageway until she returned to the kitchen and offered him a sandwich. While she sliced the bread, she mentally rehearsed her moves to the pistol in the wall.

"So, why are you here, Carlos? Are you angry with me for not seeing you?"

He broke down. Tears dripped on his hands.

She moved as if to comfort him and get a better look at what she was up against, even though it took her away from the gun in the kitchen wall. A Glock was strapped to his leg, and she knew his backpack on the floor was a grab bag for any number of brickbats or ligature he might be carrying.

"It's you, Christaine, and our poor daughter, my beautiful Marlaine, my beautiful girl, why was that thing? And now where are you both? Tragedy put on me by Deus. And it is my fault, my fault, and my *cornada* bleeds." He sobbed.

His mention of their past made her feel mean again.

"I am destroyed by all of it, too, Carlos, and I felt like a victim after that happened to Marlaine, but then I stood up to Deus."

"You could have waited for me a little longer, baby," he whimpered. "I was going to come out of it, eventually, and I'm coming out of it now. I've made a lot of money for you and me. I want to try us again. We can make Marlaine come back. I know how. I have studied the science and religion with the Santeria people who know about these things in Miami, I have. But now, if you don't see things my way, I don't know what I'm going to do here."

She chose her words. "We just need to talk about it, Carlos, and see if we can make it better for both of us. We have a little time before Aubrey gets home. Why don't you let me make you a cup of coffee instead of a sandwich? I'll heat some milk—only takes a minute. Now tell me what you are thinking, because all of this is scaring me with my little boy in the next room and that gun strapped to your leg."

"I want to apologize to you for everything. God, do I want these palindromes out of my head. Lewd I did live, evil did I dwell. It was Miami, Christaine, and that scene and the streets I grew up on, and everything else I can blame it on that doesn't hold water. And that didn't even sound like a palindrome. There's an error in that one— lewd did I live, evil did I dwell. That's not right, is it?" His eyes went to the ceiling. His head rolled back in searchlight sweeps, his face in curious and distraught alternates. Christaine picked her way down the wall to the stove. It would take five moves: hit the latch, grab the revolver, cock the hammer, turn again, and shoot him. Buck fever? A non sequitur.

She watched him while he tried to figure out the palindrome. Then he came with two more: "Do geese see God? Wo! Nemo, toss a lasso to me now."

Christaine knew her moment, blocked through the moves, spun to her target, but was off to the right by half the width of his lolling head. The bullet blew a hole through the middle of his left ear.

He stiffened and hurled the kitchen table into her. She dropped the pistol and fell to the floor on her back next to the counter as he jumped the distance like a tree frog, pissing down his leg while he grabbed her hair and banged her head against the cabinet doors until she was only semiconscious and unable to move. Blood ran down his neck, and he pushed his little finger through the hole in his ear. He spit on her and called her a *puta chupacabra* bitch. She could hear and see him, but could not move, and her child in the next room never woke for some reason, gunshot and all.

"She put a hole in me!" he spit and fingered his ear again. "She put a hole in me, tried to kill me, a hole in me, a hole in me…and now I'm going to put a hole in her!"

Carlos pushed the table away and pulled her by one leg while he grabbed a kitchen towel with his free hand to wipe his ear and neck. He dropped his pants and wiped the bloody towel on his genitals until they were light rose, then kicked off his shoes to squat on her face and rub his blood-smeared shop over the lips Aubrey held so sacred.

Stunned and cataleptic, she still couldn't move. She had read about sleep paralysis during nightmares and thought this must be what it is like.

Carlos canted his head to the side so he could drip blood from his ear onto her forehead, and she felt him make a cross mark in it with his thumb like a priest on Ash Wednesday. *Only this is Bloody Thursday, isn't it?*

He slid her pistol across the floor and hiked her skirt over her hips, then cut her underwear with his sheath knife, exposing her to the house and the light. He kicked aside one of her legs, spread open.

"You put a hole in me. You bloodied my person." He pouted as he dripped more blood over the lips everyone came through to get their money's worth.

She watched him pull the small coke vial from his pocket and could see its sepia color. Sepia from the Greek word, se˘pien, which means to make putrid. He lifted a heaping load to his face holes and sucked it in like a reef fish.

Carlos stood and searched the cabinets until he found some olive oil. "Virgin, it says on this bottle, how funny for you, you sow of a *puta*," he said to her half-opened eyes.

He massaged his cock with it, but the organ wouldn't stand. Drayton appeared in the doorway.

"What are you and her doing?" she heard her child say. She couldn't see him, because the table was hiding most of her.

Carlos stood straight, half-naked, brakes locked. "I'm helping your mommy clean the kitchen." She saw him smile at her boy and recite his favorite palindrome: "No, son! Onanism's a gross orgasm sin—a no-no, son," as if he was trying to explain his masturbation to her innocent son. It made her sick.

"Oh," Drayton said. Then his clumsy steps shuffled back to the living room, and she heard him scrabbling with the dump truck.

She started to move. He looked down at her and his coked-out limp stem, then pressed a foot on her chest. "Come on, get up, and see what I've done to you, you *puta*."

She looked right into the red-haired fork of his straddle, his mushroom-like testicles rouge, a bulbous nose between them stacked with Christian foreskin.

All of her strength returned. "Drayton!" she half screamed. Carlos knelt to cover her mouth. "You shot and bloodied me, so I bloodied you, and now I'm going to shoot you." He drew the automatic to her temple.

"Carlos, if you want to fuck me, we can go somewhere else in the house so my son can't see, but please, God, don't shoot me here for him to see. Please, Carlos, I will make love to you. I will do anything you want. Let's go upstairs. I was just a mother trying to protect her child. Please don't do this here, I beg you."

"Okay," he said, as if nothing had happened. "Let's go!"

He pulled up his pants and grabbed her pistol off the floor. She could feel her whole body now and saw the blood on her pubic hair and abdomen.

Carlos adjusted his belt and leg holster, his eyes fixed on her without blinking. She smoothed down her loose skirt and adjusted its leather belt, not dreading what was going to happen, only worried for her son, who was singing and rolling his toy on the pine floor while the sand hill cranes and Little Alex stared at him from the diorama displays along the walls of the living room.

She might be able to assuage Carlos if she could get him upstairs—soften him again, even if it took sex. Another handgun was in the closet. A second chance?

"Carlos, let's go upstairs and talk because—"

He cut her off. "No, Señora Shallcross, we'll go to the living room, where you can watch your boy and I can watch the driveway."

"But Carlos, please, in the name of God, we cannot do anything in front of that boy!"

"Who are you to call out for God, you murdering bitch?"

"No, I won't. I won't. I'm calling out to you. Let me take care of your ear."

"No, don't touch it!"

"Okay, can we go to the living room, please?"

"All right," he said nonchalantly and fired off another palindrome. "Won't lovers revolt now?"

Drayton looked up when he saw them. "Face red, Queese [Christ], bang bang, Daddy, bang bang," he said in high-strung baby vocals.

"What's he mean 'bang, bang, Daddy'?"

"His father shoots targets outside. I should wipe this blood off my face, Carlos. It could scare him."

"No, I want it to stay there for your husband to see. Let it scare him."

"Why, Carlos? What are you going to do?"

"I just want to talk, and he'll know I am no one to fool with by the way you look."

"I'm begging you again to leave. I promise you, I'll—"

"Shut up, Christaine! You know, maybe it wasn't me who was crazy all those years. Maybe it was you. Here you are, trying to get me to fuck you to get on my good side right after you tried to take me out. You know I only lived with the underbelly to make us a lot of money, and you left me for it."

"I left you because you never came home, you were with other women, and you had a shitty drug habit."

"It was a thing I was going through to make money, I'm telling you, and now I know it was a mistake. I want to start a new life, and the boy can come, too." He looked at her, proffering.

"Yes, maybe you're right about some of that, but how could I just pick up and leave?" Again, she tried to play him.

"I'll show you. Just wait, baby, and see. We would do it easy and not too fast, you'll see. Jesus, Christ, you tried to shoot me in the head." He laughed. "You're still a passionate woman. I know you were trying to protect your child. God, I love your fire. I always did."

She smiled. The cross on her forehead crinkled and split in the dried blood.

Carlos told her to sit in a chair with Drayton. "If you handle this right, Christaine, it will just be a friendly meeting to let him know that I am a man, too, and I am in the house now, not something you discarded like one of your cigarettes, you understand?"

She nodded.

"And I want you to know I have no qualms about hurting someone, no matter how tall they are, to make my point here, understood? We will all talk, but it's my meeting, and I will only hold the gun to show him, got it?"

He pulled the Glock from his leg holster and laid it next to him on the side table to the right of the front door, then took a Taser out of his backpack and rested it on his thigh. One more reach for the white stuff to fix his face. Christaine watched him throw his head back from the burn and thought she saw his throat flare out red like one of those chameleons on the front porch of the house, when they see another Lizard King walking up the walk.

Carlos looked at her with shorter eyes and repeated the palindrome, "Won't lovers revolt now?"

"No, Carlos, I won't. I promise. Just don't hurt anyone, and we'll talk about a few things."

"Good. Done by am. I maybe nod," he palindromed again.

Chapter 18

FLAME VINE!

Aubrey stopped on his shell-rock road in the middle of the knee-high Serengeti, the wetland he loved. It was four in the afternoon, and he wanted to fly the meridian shadows pointed the opposite way from the mornings.

"You know, Trip, I read something a famous shrink wrote once in *Harper's*. He said, 'People come to see me when the story they've been telling themselves about their life has stopped or become too painful.' I guess the next question is would you rather be able to see that kind of truth and get depressed, or be a blind Tater your whole life and skip it?"

"Believe me, Aubrey, I'd rather know. I'd pick sight Tater any day. I have to know everything about everything, like you. It's essential to my fulfillment."

"Hey, let's fly. Circle the almighty swamp. Ready?"

The blue truck shot up to the treetops. They banked left in a yaw to get a look down and screamed like two kids in a theme park. After three times 'round, they banked the other way and shot through the air in the great pickup royale by Chrysler Motors.

"Sheeit, will that ever get old? I don't think so," Aubrey said. "Swollen. Fuckin varicose. It's all rapture, lately. I mean, me and Christaine and that boy of ours, this thing I've found with these dressage horses, Asante and Solana being such good people."

"Yep, count them all, Your Huge. You're one lucky, lowland gorilla, Aubrey. Now let's go home."

He still was smiling when he got out of the truck and walked across the porch to the open sliding glass door. That's when he saw her sitting with their son, her face horribilis, smeared with dried blood. The line went off in his head, "Red's wrong! Flame vine!" Reve's apex predator had come, as she said it would.

"God, a red nugget, a fat egg under a dog," a man's voice said before the Taser hit Aubrey in the stomach and knocked him down like Caesar in his own house, the electric fit upon him.

He heard Christaine scream and glimpsed the man as he fell. Carlos rose from the couch and told her to shut up, that it only would incapacitate him.

"You said we would talk. You promised, you liar, you said *talk*, and now look what you've done!" she yelled.

"I *will* talk to him! But after I tie him up so he doesn't try some hero number."

He reached into his backpack and pulled out duct tape, rope, and a black rubber handball used to carom off walls all over Hispanic Miami.

Like Christaine on the kitchen floor an hour before, Aubrey watched, numb through his Tasered eyes, as Carlos tied his hands to his waist in front of him.

"Do anything stupid, Christ, I'll kill him. As you can see, he is only stunned, like the gun says, so don't get crazy on me, or I'll turn both of you into geese that get to see God today, *comprendo, señora?*"

"Yes." She covered Drayton's eyes with a hand.

Carlos forced the handball between Aubrey's teeth and wound tape around his head to hold it in place as a zero gag. He smiled at Aubrey with pursed lips, speed-blinked, and waved his hand in his face like a pansy.

Feeling began to return to Aubrey's limbs as he strained to look up from his chest to see Christaine and Drayton.

"It's okay. We are okay, honey," Christaine said. "Do what he says. He promised he just wants to talk."

"So, my friend, you probably are saying to yourself, 'Wo! Nemo, toss a lasso to me now,' eh?" Carlos said.

Aubrey wrinkled his brow.

"I see, Mr. Shallcross. That must be your puzzled look, so let me introduce myself. I'm pleased to meet you and hope you guessed my name, hah! Oh, me, I tell you, I always loved that one, 'cause that was me and that big-lipped dude back then. Yes, I rode a Sherman tank through the streets of Miami in the low Eighties, when the buildings burned and the bodies stank, or something like that. Anyway, my name, as you might have guessed, is Carlos, as in Carlos, her husband. I have come to visit, yeah, you know, like your mannequin friend there behind the glass from the movie, *Heartburn Oranges* or something. You remember, he goes to this guy's house and ties him up, then starts dancing around singing that rain song…jumps his wife's bones right in front of him. Oh, it was an awful mess."

Aubrey shook his head and tried words that sounded like pigs.

"Carlos!" Christaine screamed. "You said we would talk civilized. You said it! You said it! Why are you torturing him? That's not what you promised."

"Oh, yeah, *señora*, and so did you promise, but then you shot a hole in my ear."

Aubrey struggled with the rope on his hands and strained more sounds between his breathing.

Carlos walked over to Christ. "Oh, he sounds like a little girl now, doesn't he?" He kissed her bloody cheek.

"Whose little girl, *chico*?" she said, insinuating their dead child. "Put the kid down, will you, woman, just for a second?"

She shook her head, so he hammered her, child and all, and they fell to the floor. Blood dripped out of her nose, and Drayton screamed like a night heron.

Aubrey kicked harder. He didn't have time to form a rational thought.

"Get up, Christaine, right now!" Carlos yelled. She crawled forward, holding onto Drayton's trousers, and stood with the crying toddler, humming to him and telling him everything was fine. "And you, redneck, I'll help you up. But if you do anything I don't tell you to do, you'll see things that will make you wish your father never climbed your mother, understood?

"So, that is a very interesting bed you have upstairs, huh? That must be the Plaza de Toros for you, redneck. Where you imagine you are the matador, and you drop your pants like a *muleta* to shove your sword into, uh, what? Certainly not a bull. That would scare the shit out of you. No, you only can pierce a willing woman, you big, rich man, you."

Aubrey stared at the wall as if he wasn't there. Carlos kicked him in the stomach.

"No! Please, Carlos, I told you I would do anything," Christaine pleaded. "Take me with you right now. We'll go…just you and me. I'll leave Drayton, so that won't be a problem. Just let me make a call when we are down the road so someone can take care of my baby, and I won't be any trouble, I promise."

Aubrey struggled to breathe.

"Listen to you. Won't lovers revolt now? Won't they revolt? No! I want everyone upstairs to the Plaza de Toros under the big neon sign. What does that say? Florist? Maybe our matador is a Ferdinand. So everyone, let's go, or I start on him again."

Carlos pulled Aubrey to his feet and shoved him after Christaine. Aubrey turned to glance at the *Clockwork Orange* display before he took the first stair and locked eyes with little Alex behind the glass.

Carlos tied him by the waist to one of the pine poles in the bedroom.

"Put the child in there." He pointed at the walk-in closet. "I'm tired of looking at him."

"Carlos, you can't! He's fine here. It will scare him in there."

"You put him in there, or I'll shoot a hole in that Ferdinand's ear like you did mine."

She knelt next to Drayton. "Mommy wants you to stay in here like hide and seek, then Mommy will come get you in a minute."

"Queese come, too."

"No, Queese will stay out here for a minute, then I'll come get you." She closed the door.

Drayton was quiet at first, but started to cry the sound that sits on a mother's heart like the ass end of another body. Carlos pushed her over to another pine pole and tied her hands in front of her, then her waist to the pole.

"Queese, Queese, come!" Drayton called out and sobbed.

"I'm here!" she called back. "I'll come in a minute!"

Carlos propped two pillows against the headboard and leaned back so he could look from Christ to Aubrey.

"What a moment this is for me. I've had this scene in my head many times, and here it is before me now that the hard work is done. I think I'll take a nap." He shut his eyes.

Aubrey and Christaine exchanged a courtroom glance.

"Honey," she whispered.

"Shut up, woman," Carlos said, his eyes still closed. "And don't look at him, or I'll blindfold you both."

Christaine dropped her head and leaned against the rope. Aubrey started the hard part now. He put it all in the jar without a pull on the stone to take it easy and summoned Triple Suiter.

"I'm here, Aubrey."

"What has happened...my family?"

"This Carlos, the ex-husband, has come to do something not good, I think."

"Fuck...oh, you think? Or is this the wrong film I picked tonight?"

"No, it's real, Aubrey, objective-world real. The only irrational thing is this tetanus dressed like a man over there. Look in the jar and see if you can take it apart, find a hole."

Carlos sat up and smiled at Christaine. He canted his head, frowned at Aubrey, and walked over. "Do geese see God?" he asked Aubrey in a little voice.

That sounded familiar to him, but he couldn't seem to light it. He tried to roll it in the jar until Carlos reached around and tore the duct tape off his head—hair, rubber ball, and all.

"Now don't say anything, man, until I say. Understand?" Carlos returned to the bed.

"Trip, what's he mean, 'Do geese see God?'"

"Put it in the jar."

He looked at it literally, then figuratively, disassembling and rearranging the words inside his glass carburetor.

"I got it, Trip, I think, or some of it!"

"What is it?"

"A palindrome, and it's not his. Not original. Chrome likes them. I went over a bunch of them with him in a book once, and I think I recognize that one."

"So it says the same thing spelled backward, right? Where does that leave us?"

A mockingbird began to sing his imitation opus on a guttered corner of the house as sunset darkened the farm and the woods. Night was coming.

Carlos paced the room in crisscrosses. He bobbed his top part and did histrionic lip formations around harder syllables, as if rehearsing, then walked into the bathroom.

Aubrey went inside his head, pressed his back against his tower, and wound the rope around himself and the structure. Each time he lost his concentration, he did another tight turn. After a minute, he took a pull on the toadstone, unwrapped the rope, and flew the crisis lefty loose over the cane field, trying to find a way out.

Money, the strain of the stretch said. Maybe he should offer Carlos money. No, it would not do, but it might. He increased the orbit size, and the jar suggested money again, as if just as lost over what to do as they were.

No, not money. Too par, too stock. You see that in every movie, and it's not what this piece of dirt wants, anyway. He wants her and to shame me.

Carlos was still pacing like a jackanapes mime, mouthing words to some air party, overdoing hand gestures. Aubrey stiffened as he came at him. The animal tilted his head from side to side four inches from his face.

"You can cage a swallow, can't you, but you can't swallow a cage, can you? Well, can you? I'm talking to you, redneck!"

"Uh, no, you can't swallow a cage, no."

"But you can cage a swallow, can't you?"

"Yes, yes, you can cage a swallow."

"And all of you are my caged swallows, this I know for sure. But I'm *not* sure if you can swallow your cages. Maybe I can make you." He continued pacing and mouthing words like something with rat fever.

"Trip," Aubrey said with the inner voice.

"What?"

"That last one's a word palindrome. You have to say it backward, not spell it backward, but I'm having trouble with the cage and swallowing, and I feel like it's coming and I, I think I'm going to crater. The Blind Spot Cathedral thing, Trip, goddamnit."

"No, you're not. Now listen to me. The truth is you could slim it enough to swallow the cage if you're the cane-field flier I think you are. I've seen you swallow whole planets when you slimmed them enough, Aubrey. This palindrome is a message for us. Work it until you find a way to disimagine this cage we're in like the swallow can when he's perfected peace inside his prison. There's a way out of this."

"Shit, right! And I want you to know, all the quantum doolangers out there, the Nineteen Ghost, your God, and anyone else selling salvation through truck radios or scriptures can kiss my Anglo ass if this is how you send the *perfected peace* message."

Carlos walked out of the bathroom for the twentieth time and over to Christaine. Her head was bowed. "You can cage a swallow, can't you, but you can't swallow a cage, can you?" he said again.

When she raised her head, she had a defamatory, cheeky look. "You know something, Carlos? You never have come up with an original one of those as long as I've known you. Those palindromes all came from other people."

"My, my, what do you ever mean, Miss *Puta*?"

"I mean, you've never been able to make up a palindrome of your own, not one."

His face reddened.

"So you know what that makes you? A cyranoid."

He darted his eyes around her feet. "A what?" he asked in a dry whisper.

"A cyranoid...like Christian in *Cyrano de Bergerac* who never had an original thought but conveyed Cyrano's poems to Roxanne, the woman Cyrano loved. That's you. You're Christian. You need a good writer to make you interesting because you don't have any original thoughts."

She looked at Aubrey with goodbye eyes, as if to tell him she wanted to do something, even if it was wrong, instead of just sucking air on these poles while their child cried in the closet.

Carlos threw up his hands, opened his mouth, and clenched his fists until the knuckles turned the color of the bones that formed them. He walked to the bathroom, and they heard the commode seat slam down.

"It will all be okay," Christ whispered. "Let me do it. I'm going to get him one way or another."

Aubrey shook his head and murmured, "Don't provoke him. Let me."

She whispered back, "I can do this better than you, and no matter what I do, it's to save us all. You should close your eyes. I love you," she mouthed.

Carlos returned wearing only his T-shirt and twirling the rosary he asked women to push into his rectum before he tried to impregnate them.

"I did have an original thought while I was in there, as I have had many times before. The toilet has such power for that. Now, I can prove this woman is wrong, and I am not that person she called me. So, Carlos is ready to present a play to you with the help of the lady. It's a drama, something you've never seen in your bedroom. An original I've written, and that is for another man to split you, señora, in front of your husband, or whatever he is, and for you, Sir Redneck, to watch how a great matador like me, Carlos O'Meara, uses his sword, the cock. El *Cordobés* is here, my friends!"

Christaine assumed a tough, head-up, chin-out look. Aubrey felt a dog rage rise inside him. He lost all fear of emotions or psychological storms and started to swap himself out for crazy.

Carlos walked over to Christ and squeezed her crotch until she groaned and bit her lip.

"You coward piece of dirt!" Aubrey screamed at him.

Where was Johnny Yuma? Where was that nerd Holden Caulfield, the great catcher? Where was The Junior, the man who used to watch his back? He knew where Trip was, because even Trip had lost it, and they both strained at the ropes and screamed, snapping their teeth like chained dogs.

Christ's eyes watered as the redheaded man unbuttoned her blouse.

"I'll find a way to kill you or haunt you from the outer regions if you kill me," Aubrey yelled at him. "I'll get you in hell's own machine shop, you piece of shit!"

195

Carlos smiled at Christaine. "This man of yours has some school mouth on him. I think I'll turn it down just a little to make things more romantic." He slugged Aubrey in the teeth and the stomach; blood streamed down his chin. Carlos cavorted in high steps around the room, twirling the rosary, his genitalia flopping as the night double-dyed itself into the farm.

~

Asante and Solana were driving south on U.S. 1 after spending the day in Fort Pierce.

"I can't understand. They don't answer the phone. I think I ask the operator to see if it is not working?" Solana said.

"Aw, come on, they probably busy every time we call. We go by another time. They not expecting us anyway," Asante said.

"But we are going right by their road. I call the operator."

"What do you mean, 'It is out of order'?" Asante heard her say.

"Yes, yes, thank you."

"I don't like it. *Eu estore te a dizerque eu mao gusto.* They said they would be home if we wanted to come by. Maybe they are out for their walk and someone is robbing their house."

"Listen to you, Solana, you sound like you do in hurricane season. We'll be to the road in twenty minutes, probably scare the hell out of them."

~

Carlos leered at Christaine and did another snort of dope, then pulled her blouse open and unsnapped her bra. Aubrey screamed more obscenities at him.

"No, son! Onanism's a gross orgasm sin—a no-no, son," Carlos said and jumped away to pronk around the room again.

Aubrey's ears rang from the blow to his face a moment ago. He was seeing the vicious for once without the Plexiglas he employed for his blacker drifties. The divide that kept him from getting knocked up by a story. Now he was the story, its injuries, its battery, and fluids. He was The Junior, exiting a chopper for the first time in an open rice field as the Plexiglas slid away over the scaffold of his balls. He was in 'Nam, in Normandy, in jail, insane, in Havana with Warren Zevon. His jockstrap wish to fight in a war had come true, and he was tied to a pillar in his house and being beaten with the wishbone.

The *Mimus polyglottos*, the mockingbird on the gutter outside, continued singing the songs of other birds, as Cyrano's Christian did. Aubrey bled from his mouth. He looked out through the glass doors and thought he could see the night critters in his field stop what they were doing and look up at the well-lit room, a chance to see the ruling class tear each other apart. The rattlesnake quit swallowing. Coons quit frog bones. Armadillos stood still on grubs. Owls froze their bloody breath, and a bobcat dropped a dripping liver. All to watch these people, especially the crazy one who pranced around naked from the waist down and occasionally looked off-stage right at them.

That mockingbird sang. While a woman burned in Salem, while blacks were being lynched, while Catholics butchered Protestants on Saint Bartholomew's Day, and while people cut off arms in the Congo, that bird sang. While gut-shot soldiers lay dying, while Congress did deals, while lawyers lied to juries, while doctors made unnecessary incisions, and while Aubrey stared at the redheaded germ in the room preparing to do the second-story act on the love of his life.

Carlos untied Christ from the pole and led her around by the rope that bound her hands. "So now, little lady, my loving little wife and *puta* who will not even acknowledge I exist, I must make you believe I exist. Like when you ask some wise guy if they know where someone is, and they answer, 'If they were up your ass, you'd know where they were.' Ha! Remember that one? Well, I plan to be somewhere in a minute that will let you and your hick there know exactly where I am.

"And you see this rosary, redneck? I was going to have her pull it out of my ass after she pushed it up there, but I think it's a bit too risky tonight with this pistol around, don't you?"

"I'll kill you, Carlos, I swear!" Aubrey shouted.

"Not from there you won't, goober."

The crazy man pulled Christ in front of the bed, ran his fingers through her hair, and whispered something in her ear. He unscrewed the silencer on his Glock to make it more compact and cocked it, then threw the rosary on the floor.

"It's okay, Johnny Cash. I just reminded her of some of the old sex things we used to do to each other, and I promised to do them tonight because the night is so long, and you know what? Then, 'Done by a.m., I maybe nod.'"

Christ didn't look at Aubrey, who was saying *toro feces* and *veritas* at a feverish pitch inside until he blurted it aloud. Carlos dog-cocked his head again and looked at him.

"Shut up, or I'll put a bullet through the closet door!" he yelled at Aubrey.

He pushed Christ down onto the bed and hovered over her with the pistol, warning he would shoot their legs if they tried anything. He ordered her to lie back and pull up the skirt to her waist. Her tied hands gripped the dress and tugged it to mid-abdomen, where it revealed her blood-smeared pubis, inner thighs, and stomach Carlos had painted with his blood in the kitchen earlier.

Aubrey screamed inside and then outside, "What have you done to her? Yuma, I'll kill you! Johnny fucking Yuma, you were here. Reve, Reve, where? Help us, help us! Triple Suiter! Trip, for God's sake, no, no, no!" He shook his body from side to side, violently.

Carlos watched him. "Yuma? Triple what? He's going crazy, I think." Carlos smiled.

Christaine was half-naked, as he had commanded. He ran his thumb and index finger slowly down her divide. She turned her head and stared at the wall as Carlos sucked his finger and smiled at Aubrey. He wrote with his spit, *C.C.* and *Ride Her*, in the dried blood on her abdomen, then looked over for Aubrey's reaction and howled his laughter.

"I'll kill you," Aubrey mouthed.

Carlos reached down to arouse himself while he touched her. Aubrey closed his eyes. When he opened them, thirty seconds later, Carlos was still doing the mano a mano, but nothing had happened with his cue.

"Trip."

"What?" Trip was in the armpit hideout because he didn't want to watch.

"He's having trouble over there. Should I provoke him?"

"You could try if he unties her hands. She might get a chance to shoot him if he comes at you with his fists and forgets the gun. But not unless he unties her."

Carlos kept trying to get hard.

"I'm going to untie your hands, but you better behave or I'll shoot everybody," Carlos said to her. He guided her left hand to his dangling cock and told her to fondle him. She did so in a cursory manner and stared back at the wall.

"Spread your legs, *señora*, because the matador, your *torero*, is about to bring his sword," he said, even though the sword was still in the sheath.

Aubrey tore his skin on the pole and the ropes. "See you in the spirit world, where I will be waiting for you with a talking snake, Carlos."

"Oh, listen to him. How do you know I'm going to kill you? All I'm going to do is show you how a real man makes love, and then she is going with me, and you and that little shit in the closet can stay here until you both rot. Meanwhile, I mustn't keep the lady waiting."

"Trip," Aubrey cried out inside his head. "You gotta be a man and get here and help me hold up, or I'll never forgive you."

"All right, I'm coming. It's the worst day of my life." Trip turned to his armpit apartment mirror. Amper Sand had typed the second verse of the "Battle Hymn of the Republic" on his chest in an appropriate grumble font:

I have read a fiery gospel writ
In burnished rows of steel:
"As YE deal with My contemners
So with you my grace SHALL deal.
Let the hero born of woman
Crush the serpent with his heel,
Since God is marching on."
Drayton began to cry again in the closet.

"What kind of life are you?" Aubrey screamed. "What kind of man?"

"I'll show you, cunt face." He kneeled on the bed between her legs and lay on top of her. But he seemed to just rub around.

"Too much dope," he said. "But any second now, the great *sabre*, the great *ayudado* of the hero will rise." Carlos kept undulating, and nausea piled up inside Aubrey and Trip.

"Put your hands on my beautiful ass," Carlos told Christaine as he moved his gun away from their pancaked bodies so she couldn't snatch it.

Christaine shifted her head to the right of Carlos's head in her hair and looked at a quasi-apoplectic Aubrey. She grinned and curled her bloodstained upper lip into a snarl, then moved her hands down his back to the slope of his butt and softly kneaded the flesh. Carlos, surprised, stopped grinding, and Aubrey gave a start in the ropes.

Christaine purred low, and Carlos raised his head to smile at her. "That's right, baby, now I know you missed your Carlito, didn't you?" He turned his head and licked his lips at Aubrey.

"Yes," she said. "Carlos, let me help you inside me. I know you will swell to a man then."

His eyes went wide at the suggestion. "*Si*, baby."

Aubrey stopped breathing when he heard her and saw her wedge her right hand between them, as if reaching for Carlos's cock. That's when her belt caught his attention.

"Carlos," Christaine said.

"Yes, baby."

"I need to pull out my hand and spit on it, *comprendo?*"

"Oh, yeah, baby. Do that."

He raised his hips, and she withdrew her hand along with the long hatpin hidden in her belt to her mouth as if to lick her fingers for the sex. Carlos's head was turned the other way.

"Carlos?"

"*Que, chica?*"

"Push against me harder while I lick my fingers because it feels so good."

"Oh, I like that," he said to get to Aubrey again and dry-humped her slowly.

Aubrey and Trip froze. They watched and waited, not breathing.

A matador holds his sword a certain way so he doesn't break his wrist. He puts his fist against the guard to drive the blade deep enough to hit the aortic artery by the bull's heart and bring the quick internal bleed as the bull sits down, wags his head, and falls over dying.

Aubrey could see how Christaine positioned her sword when she rested her hand back on the pillow. The round end of the hatpin was in the palm's heel where the lifeline starts, the shaft slightly protruding from the tips of her four fingers and thumb like a spring load.

"Carlos?"

"Um."

"Could you move your head to the other side of mine? You're hurting my shoulder."

He paused as he passed over her face and proudly spoke his rehearsed line from the day before: Yes, I said yes, I will, yes. A slipper named Juan, a good man who had been waiting a lifetime for this moment to escape, moved in a swift gossamer from Carlos's nose into Christaine's as her right hand plunged every inch of the hatpin through Carlos's pupil so true, it followed the optic nerve into his brain and brought on a major seizure.

Carlos convulsed and shook, but Christaine couldn't wriggle free of him. His pistol arm slapped up and down on the bed, and a spastic finger fired the automatic into the cathedral ceiling and the sliding-glass doors. The fourth shot hit a steel plate across a butt joint of beams before ricocheting through Aubrey's skull and out the other side, blowing a piece off the top like a skylight.

The impact jolted Aubrey's head to the left toward the glass doors, but it didn't knock him out, nor did he feel much pain. He saw truck headlights coming down his road and knew it was Asante's from the pattern. Carlos fired two more shots into the ceiling as the truck closed in, and Aubrey saw it speed up, fishtail, and slam to a stop in front of the house.

Asante was at the top of the stairs.

"Papa!" Christaine screamed. "It's Carlos. Get him off me...off me!"

Asante kneeled on the bed and put his left hand on the gun, his right hand around Carlos's throat. The blood rose in the aging father's face. Aubrey, struggling to stay conscious, watched the threaded rod in the old horseman's forearm turn Asante's hand tighter on the redhead's neck. Carlos's body stiffened, and Aubrey heard a crackling sound like someone eating pork rind before the body went still. Asante shook from the effort, but did not let up for five more seconds before prying the gun from Carlos's hand and rolling him off his daughter.

Christaine jumped to her feet and rushed to Aubrey, then ran to the closet to pick up her crying boy. Asante stretched out his arms and looked up through the glass gable at the night sky. "*Mater de Deus,*" he said, his voice shaking.

From the top of the stairs, Solana screamed, "Oh, no! Oh, no!" Christaine handed Drayton to her, and Aubrey watched her hurry back to him hanging there in the ropes. He was half-conscious and talking like Robert Kennedy that day as he lay on the floor of the California hotel after Sirhan.

"Let's untie him, Papa. Aubrey, what's wrong? Look at me."

"Is it bad? Does it look bad?" Aubrey asked softly.

When she saw the skull pieces on the floor and the dribbles of blood, she frantically traced her fingers to the top of his head, where they slipped into the hole.

"He's been shot in the head! My God, there's no skull on top!" She held him and sobbed. "Aubrey, oh, no, no. We'll fix it, baby! That thing is dead over there. He's dead!"

"We go now! The hospital, now!" Asante yelled.

They half-carried him downstairs and pushed him into the backseat of the truck—Solana and Christ holding up him up. Asante drove fast with Drayton beside him down the shell-rock road.

Aubrey was becoming more narcoleptic. He talked some while Christ urged him to stay awake. He saw the knee-high Serengeti go by.

"Hey, Trip, you know where we are?" he said aloud, for everyone to hear. "Want to go for a ride? It's the Serengeti," he said.

Christaine looked at her mother—the look that someone you know is someone else.

Triple did not answer because of the bullet.

"Triple Suiter!" he blurted. "Where are you? Trip! The Serengeti, should we? Let's fly it, Tripper!"

"Aubrey, it's okay," Christ said. "Keep talking, but don't yell. You'll hurt yourself more. We'll be at the hospital soon. Who's Triple Suiter? Talk about that." He didn't answer her.

On U.S. 1, he squinted through the windshield. The headlights lit up the pavement and grass shoulder of the road. He saw them again: the white roadkill crosses, the same ones he saw that night The Junior lay dying in the Tax Man's truck. They looked farmed in rows, like Georgia pine trees—hundreds of them—and he heard a CB radio somewhere and the Nineteen Ghost talking about a murder. The truck's headlights showed less of the road as the highway came closer and closer to the truck until the last of it disappeared into the darkness under the bumper.

"Feenished," the Nineteen Ghost whispered as Aubrey slipped into a coma.

Chapter 19

THE SHALLCROSSES

The doctor came out of the emergency room and spoke to the family: Aubrey had a severe head wound, like his man Ambrose Bierce suffered in the Civil War, and was comatose for the time being. Now he really was like Peyton Farquhar, stuck in the trochal lag time between the top of Owl Creek Bridge and the end of the Yankee's hang rope. They were planning to helicopter him to Jackson Memorial for surgery, and Christaine said she was going, even though she dreaded walking through those doors where her daughter had died. The place was bad luck.

John Chrome was called, and he asked his neurosurgeon friend, Henry Brown, to take the case.

The second Aubrey became unconscious in the objective world, he became conscious in the unconscious world, and Trip showed up. The Tater king lay in the cane field inside his head and stared up at the tower he had invented years ago. Trip was on his forearm, and their memory of what had just happened at O'gram was sealed off in another place.

Trip finally had made it to the big room—the one with its own universe he could never find in their conscious state because the brain is so vast, like the universe. The rope was coiled next to them, but the jar was not there.

Above them was the top of the skull—the dome of the Blind Spot Cathedral, the place described to Trip many times, with the new hole made by Carlos's bullet. The same hole a man called Horse saw when they hauled him to the top of the Sioux lodge so he could speak to *Wakan Tanka*. But now the turning scar, the closed door, was gone because Carlos had blown out an egress with his gun. Aubrey thought for years he would see his old God or Van Gogh's starry night if the hole ever opened like this. Instead, he saw the shell-rock road running through his own Serengeti toward O'gram. He stood. He was not uncomfortable; in fact, he felt damn good.

"My, my, but I do believe I know where I am, the big room, and it's just like you described it," Trip said.

"Yeah, but I have no jar."

"I think we are the jar, Aubrey."

"So does this mean we've finally gone insane and climbed in there with Nell Kitching?"

"You're never insane when you can ask yourself a question like that. My God, look at the size of the tower! It's…it's mastodonic."

Aubrey kept staring up at the opening. "That goes to my road. Get ready for a wild ride, Trip. But first we're gonna have some fun."

"You mean it? I finally get to fly the monster? Can we do some transformation stuff?"

"My man, my Triple man, sidecar Suiter doo lang." Aubrey smiled at him. "Of course, we can. We just need a pure train of thought, and it will externalize from our minds and bodies so we'll become whatever we conjure."

"I've been waiting thirty years for this, A.C."

The sugarcane slapped Aubrey's skin as he sprinted through the field, then rose in the air and looked to his left. He finally would get to show his Trip the best left pearls. "We're in the magic now. What would you like to do?"

"It's staggering! I always wanted to accomplish an instrument, but I never did."

"So pick one, and pick an artist."

"Okay, guitar. Leo Kottke or maybe Django Reinhardt. No, I wanna play guitar like Leo."

Aubrey turned up the orbit speed, round and round the steel sequoia.

"C'mon, Trip, imagine you've got that twelve-string axe in your arms. Think hard and it will happen! Do that song of his, 'Pamela

Brown.'"

Trip closed his eyes, and a beautiful Martin popped into his hands. "Look, it works!" he shrieked.

"I told ya!" Aubrey said as he let out the rope even more. The holy sprite began to play and sing a perfect Leo, the man from Minnesota. The guitar shot fire from its neck at the end of the song, and they turned into a pair of laughing gulls out over the cane doing rolls, loops, and fast drops. This gorgeous salon of improbably marvelous life and transformations seemed like the place to be forever, while Aubrey's unconscious body lay still in quiet breaths in the outer world.

Some people remember dreams or events when they wake from a coma, but others remember nothing while they were there, or nothing ever again. Aubrey and Trip's dream seemed real and conscious, but they knew something was different; they just weren't sure what it was.

The flying schizos circled the field below like kids on a tetherball, and Trip tried other morphologies so he could experience everything. He impersonated his favorite actors and jocks, slam dunking basketballs like the NBA's smallest player, Spud Webb, and acting out capers of Dustin Hoffman as Ratso in *Midnight Cowboy*. Aubrey played the part of Joe Buck and said it seemed even better without the jar because it was so bare ass—no distractions, disinclinations, or Plexiglas covers to lessen the feel. The solemn tower representing the objective world and the rope line out to its hatchery of subjective shapes and ideas brought an uncanny competence to their psycho-generated souvenirs—J.ourneys A.lways R.emembered.

Worn out, they pulled hand over hand on the rope toward the tower and landed in the cane field. Aubrey collapsed and looked up at the hole again. He could see the sun shining on a small hank of his shell-rock road and knew, if he could reach the opening, he could go home and bring Christ and Drayton back here to do this outrageous flying—have a chance to explain the rest of who he was. They would finally meet Trip. Who in the outside world would believe all this unless they saw it for themselves? He and his arch slipper weren't even hungry or thirsty in this place.

"Hey, I gotta get to the hole in the top, Trip. If I turn the orbit on a slant, maybe..."

Aubrey ran the field again. Once in the air, he let out the line, tipped the plane, and just missed the cane as they shot back up toward the hole like the rings around Saturn. At the apogee of this bias the second time, he let the rope go and banged down hard on the edge of the hole. He did it—got his wind back, tied the rope to a pine tree, and unconsciously made the sign of the cross like a natural.

"Ooh-wee, Tarzan, eat your heart out, you all!" Trip yelled.

Aubrey began to walk the familiar surface, and the white glare of the shell rock made him feel like he really was going home. Trip pounded on his skin. Aubrey looked to his left at a shocking sight: bodies hanging on life-size, biblical crosses as far as he could see out into the wetland of his knee-high Serengeti. Not the little roadkill crosses on highways and in hallucinations, but crosses with real people, as in regulation crucified. The figures just floated there, smiling with outstretched arms that seemed to beckon him.

"*Quo vadis*, boyeh?" asked the first man, his feet nailed to the cross block.

Aubrey's mouth dropped. "Exactly. *Quo vadis*. Where am I going, and isn't this my road?"

"This is your road, son, but only as a tenant, like everyone else on the big round candy roller."

"But I own this road."

"If you say so, but after taxes, insurance, probate, I'd say you pay rent, like John Chrome."

"Am I dead? You know John Chrome?"

"No, not dead yet, but one day…and if you die for this land and the road because someone wrongly tried to take it from you, you will be here with us because you died for what you believed in, even if you only *are* renting from the Transcendent Land and Air Company."

"Who are you?"

"Spartacus."

"Like Spartacus?"

"Yes. Did you think I would look like Kirk Douglas?"

Aubrey darted his eyes around. "I guess so."

"Look behind me. Those are my loyal men and women, ex-slaves like me, three thousand out there in that wetland you call the knee-high Serengeti. Each cross has replaced one of your spider webs with a human soul hanging in it. We were slaves who rebelled and died for the belief in our freedom."

Aubrey scanned the marsh scattered with bodies and Roman kill trees. They seemed paradoxical among the acres of Hypericum, or Saint John's wort, an antidepressant growing in the wetland.

"Who else is here?"

"Oh, you'd be surprised. Take a look around and talk to people not with my group. The other stations of the cross run along this road. They will tell you their stories."

"Well, then, if they are dead, I'm looking for a couple of old friends. One was called The Junior, and the other a woman named Reve. Have you heard of them?"

"A poisonous snake bit The Junior, I believe. Was it an accident?" Spartacus asked.

"Yes. Well, I think."

"Then he would not be here. But Reve, that's different. You should ask around about her. Everyone here is a hero-martyr type. The pure accident, suicide, and disease people are elsewhere, but if they died true to what they believed in, then I'm sure it's someplace like here, a paradise of the mind and heart that was with them at the time of death."

"That's unbelievable, I mean, interesting. I'm kinda dazed by all this. Can't even talk straight. I'm walking on down then, and well, I consider it an honor to have met you, sir. I know your story from the film and documentaries."

"Thank you, Aubrey. Now you should see the rest of the gallery."

The great Tater and his sidecar headed toward O'gram and the next cross.

"Hey, Trip?"

"Present!"

"Do you think we or me isn't dead now that we've seen that? That was Spartacus, extra-large and swollen...and large! Did I say large?"

"We are not dead. I would have been contacted, so quit asking me. We're just adrift for a while, I think, like the film you pick at night in the Trazodone Lounge, so enjoy it."

When they reached the next cross, just an old 45-rpm record player was resting on the foot block. The record fell from the thick capstan to the turntable, and familiar lyrics poured out of the speaker's plastic housing. The song was "Tell Laura I Love Her," and it had made Aubrey cry his eyes out years ago. The ballad told the story of Tommy, who died on the racetrack trying to win enough money to buy his Laura a wedding ring. Aubrey was reverent and nostalgic when the song was over.

"Trip, Tommy died for what he believed in, his love for Laura, so the song is here where it should be, in the hero gallery. Shit, Tommy's probably here somewhere, too. I'd die for Christ and my son."

"There's no doubt in my mind you would, Aubrey."

They kept walking until there—his lantern jaw and dimpled chin so obvious—stood the Lizard King himself in his Miami courtroom white suit. Jim. Staring at the horizon as if he was waiting for the...

"Uh...uh...Jim Morrison, sir."

"What's a-matter?" he roared his famous echo chambereeze.

"Exactly!" Aubrey jumped. "With all due respect, didn't you die of a drug overdose or alcohol poisoning in a bathtub?"

"Yeah, that was the end, beautiful friend. But that was what I believed in, so they gave me a pass and let me come here...umm, not that easy. I did have to win it on appeal—something about the crippled message I was sending the youth because of that bungled drunk over in Paris. But that was really me. Kind of like Punky, don't you think, Aubrey. Carburet it?"

"I guess so, sir." *Shit, he knows Punky, Trip.* "I knew your work well, sir, memorized most of it," Aubrey said. "It was that time in my life when you can do that and still be protected by Plexiglas. You know, let's you fantasize about everything as if you could handle it without having to really step into the room with what's on the other side."

"Oh, yeah, I know about the other side, Aubrey. I saw your experience with *The Deer Hunter*, you sitting there in the theater behind your Plexiglas."

"Yeah, like that. And how does everybody know my name up here and what I think about and do?"

Morrison smiled. "I'll tell you how I really got into the Crucified Club. I was carrying the unknown soldier, you know, the one nestled in my hollow shoulder." He took off his white suit jacket and opened his shirt to reveal the large pock in his deltoid. "In fact, he's over there, and I guess I owe it all to him, like Leo owed it all to 'Pamela Brown,' right, Trip? I mean, they weren't gonna let me in, but they needed an unknown soldier for the garden, a patriot, you know, someone from the *True* magazine. I had to give them my revered slipper to get in, goddamnit, and I wasn't happy about it. I mean, how many people get to have a slipper as cool as an unknown soldier? Feenished." He winked.

"I wanted to ask you one more thing: Where is Pam, your wife?"

Tears welled in Morrison's eyes. "You know, I pleaded with them to let her come here after her death because she believed in what she did to be with me. But they frown on that drug and suicide stuff. They let me visit her in the Overdose Park not that far from here and told me I have to wait until they get a cleaner rock star to replace me before I can transfer over. I tell her I love her every time I go, and that I believe in the fire, and the heart is the part that gets higher, just like you tell your Christaine in that song you wrote for her, Aubrey."

"Yes, I do. I'm sorry, Jim."

"Now go on and say hello to the unknown soldier. I hope you always believe in the fire, Aubrey, because that's where the news is read."

"Yeah, it is."

"Hey, Aubrey," Morrison said. Aubrey turned around. "Remember, you are the Tater King. You can do anything."

They paused at the unknown soldier's cross and thanked him for his service in all the armies of the world, whatever his motives, enlisted or conscripted.

"I don't see Elvis or Frankie Lymon up here, Aubrey," Trip said. "Could be over in Overdose Park. You don't think they'd let Elvis in, do you? His death was not that dissimilar to Jim's, even though it was on a toilet instead of a bathtub."

"No, the man simply Od'd. It was not a real die-for-what-you-believe-in thing. Hey, do that Elvis verse you do, c'mon, Aubrey," Trip begged him.

They sat by the ditch laughing, and Aubrey obliged his angel.

ELVIS SAT ON A PORCELAIN THRONE,

FLUSHED THE BOWL AND NOW HE'S GONE.

DOCTOR THEO'S AT THE GATE

WITH THE MEDICATION, BUT IT'S TOO LATE.

I WANNA SING IN A BLAZE OF GLORY,

LIKE THE KING SO SOFT AND SWEET,

DON'T WANNA DIE LIKE HE DID THAT MORNING

IN A LONELY ROOM ON A TOILET SEAT.

Trip applauded and could not stop his laughing. They walked to the next cross. It was Ambrose Bierce.

"Mr. Bierce, I can't believe it's you!"

"Good to see you, Aubrey."

"What happened to you? Did you really die in Mexico in the Battle of Ojinaga?"

"Well, yes, but one must reflect on the motive in my case. I was considered a cynical person with a penchant for the macabre. I did serve my country, but my curse was not so patriotic as it was my belief in the permanence of disturbing paradoxical forces at work in this life…war, pain, existential nausea, euphoria, faux peace that never resolves itself. I was interested in how to move amongst these things and survive, so that's why I fought in the Civil War as a young man— just to see it, so I would know how it breathed. It's not so dissimilar to your and Mr. Suiter's interest in the ampersand symbol, this never-ending thing, the word *and*. This interminable paradox that's really quite horrible sometimes, yet the discovery of its truth can be magnificent in a way.

"I wrote about it so other people could get a sense and wouldn't end up like the blind Taters of the world, as you like to say, Aubrey. You might remember one of the definitions from my work, *The Devil's Lexicographer*: 'Man: An animal [whose]... chief occupation is extermination of other animals and his own species, which, however, multiplies with such insistent rapidity as to infest the whole habitable earth and Canada.' And that is what I lived for, to cover and expose this truth because I believed in what I was doing. And that is what I died for, going to Mexico at seventy-two years old to see the thing man finds irresistible just one more time...this forever war and *merde* of people bombing themselves over and over. It cost me the little bit of time I had left, but it was better than the rubber sheets. I wanted to be in the *True* magazine, Aubrey, and I actually hoped things in the world might change. Alas, it was flawed hope, wasn't it? So human of me because of our little friend, that lone, tiny emperor of truth, your Mr. Amper Sand."

"Yes, sir," Aubrey said. "I read all your stuff. And what about your head wound from the Civil War? Did that affect your mind later?"

"Oh, you'll find out about that."

"What do you mean?"

"Well, we're not allowed to divulge the future up here, and you have a lot more life to live. Let's just say I meant it as a metaphor. Head and heart wounds are part of one's life, and each one has a different sidecar. Oh, and by the way, I was flattered when you made up that character impersonation of me and named him Head Wound. A fine and appropriate use of the sobriquet in my particular case, wouldn't you say?"

"I love your work, Mr. Bierce."

"Ambrose will do, Aubrey, and thank you. And now I have to be somewhere. It was an honor meeting you in person. Titillating. Goodbye."

A hundred feet up the road lay a man crying on a steel gurney under the pine trees, his arms spread to the sides, like the crucified

Jesus.

"I am the innocent man representative, executed by lethal injection via the justice system," the man said. "I stuck to my story till the end. They begged me to confess, but I would not because I was innocent. Strange how these gurneys lay you out like Christ on the cross. I thought about that before I was taken to that room with the audience to be killed for something I didn't do, like he was."

"I'm sorry that happened to you, sir, but it might save others in that cause when your innocence is discovered," Aubrey said.

They moved on.

"Talk about paying so other people could get their money's worth, Trip. Hey, look at this. Who are you?"

"I'm the Wild Man of Borneo," the man said from his cross, in full tribal dress. "I'm here to represent all the native people who would not convert to another religion shoved at them by missionaries and who stayed with the beliefs they were raised on and died for."

"Good man," Aubrey said. "And who is this woman over here?"

"I represent every woman who was persecuted because of gender and blamed for everything, from casting spells and insubordination to causing birth defects. We died by the millions for these things. That misogynist Bierce over there is right to some extent: The dark forces of power and ignorance cartwheel through the hearts and egos of man interminably, like it's just the okay of things."

"Carbureted fully, and well said, ma'am, and it's a privilege to meet you."

"And to meet you, Aubrey. I know you respect women. We see everything down there from up here."

They walked on until they felt they had arrived at that place that doesn't exist, where there is no O'gram or even the ampersand symbol. Where the universe began: The End of the Road.

"But what's this, Aubrey?" Trip said and grinned. "Do you recognize this configuration?" A man on a cross, crucified upside down. He righted himself as they approached.

"Aubrey, Triple Suiter!" He bowed his head reverently at Trip. "Forgive me, but I didn't think you would recognize me without the upside-down look. You know I requested it at the time. So nice to see you and, uh, oh yeah, *quo vadis,* y'all? Ah-ha, ha, ha! I love to say that like Spartacus does, because I remember when that was the toughest question ever posed to me."

Trip stepped up and stood at attention on the forearm. "How fortunate to see you again, Saint Peter. Aubrey and I were walking the road to see the gallery and hoped we were heading home."

"This, this is really Saint Peter, Trip! And he knows you?"

"Of course, I do," Saint Peter said, "and you do, too, Aubrey, in a way, from your catechism. I've been overhearing your conversations, and I want to support the true light who loves and is always with you, the grandiloquent slipper, T. Suiter, the Trip in thrice on your arm. His explanations about following your conscience and the *True* magazine are correct. All this, 'My way or my faith is the only true faith,' really can be a lot of *toro feces,* as you like to say, Aubrey." He bowed his head to Trip. "And, oh yeah, how about the guy who said, 'God is so powerful he doesn't even have to exist to save us.' Good one, don't you think, Trip?" He laughed again and moved his arms in strange semaphores. "Just ask the man next to me, the one who asked me where I was going that day on the Appian Way with Rome burning behind me. Aubrey, meet the legend himself, Jesus Harold Christ, like you, a giant slimerating man, doo lang doo lang."

Aubrey went cataleptic. His throat latched. He didn't know whether to fall on his knees or say *Christe eleison* over and over from fanatical years of conditioned response.

"Ah, it's okay, Aubrey," Jesus said from his cross, and he, too, bowed low to Trip, who smiled and teared up. "I know this is a shocker, but I *am* like the next guy who died for what he believed in. Although those writers of mine, a couple of whom are up here on some of these same crosses, did a turbo job on my biography. Of course, it gave them jobs, too, not to mention audience after audience of adulators. That kind of fame certainly could turn one into a full-blown Tater, right, Aubrey?

"But, I guess it's like Peter just said: That story about me is so powerful that I don't have to exist to save people, because it has saved millions. Still on the bookshelves, and it was not exactly what I had in mind, but it has served a lot of souls with its wide-open metaphors and guidelines based on a faith that inherent goodness and compassion are inside all of us, even the crut! Oh! Don't tell Ambrose.

"I'm proud of those people who believed in me, either as a religion or just a hero story, the one that brings strength and comfort to get them through all those shitty days around the castle. I mean, some aren't going to make it on the pure secular stuff, bless their hearts and carburet it. You know, Aubrey, the foyer folks. They need me so they can pick programs like those disciples of mine wrote, if it helps."

"Are you really just like every other man who died for what he believed in?"

"Essentially, yes, just another hard-working Jew-boy trucker like you and The Junior used to talk about. Even I was agnostic at times back then. I went through those ups and downs and sometimes followed the *Old Testament* and sometimes my conscience."

"Forgive me for asking this, sir. I mean, hate to sound like I'm repeating myself, but did you die so everyone could get their money's worth?"

"Oh, you mean that bumper sticker you guys thought was a cryptic riddle or had a double meaning? Well, it didn't."

"What did it mean?"

"Not only did I die so you could get your money's worth, Aubrey, but everyone up here died and paid for what that bumper sticker says. They're all heroes, so naturally we expect you and everyone else downstairs to be."

"Even Morrison?"

"Even Jim, but, boy, he used to break some blood-level records, huh?"

Saint Peter and Jesus started a big Homeric laugh like The Junior and Aubrey used to do over Punky's antics and stomped their feet on their cross blocks. Aubrey and Trip laughed with them and stomped, too. A strange sight—two men on a crucifix and two on the ground cracking up over the most heavyweight palindrome the standing apes ever asked each other, "Do geese see God?"

"But I must say," Jesus said, "I don't think Morrison would have gotten in here if he hadn't been hiding that little shot-up soldier in his shoulder, that little slipper, right, Pete?" And he burst out again.

"That's right, Jesus, boyeh, and I'm glad he did because he keeps us plenty entertained with his backflip-Ferlinghetti-Rimbaud rants. So you better cherish your own unknown soldier and five star slipper, Aubrey, the amazing and gifted Triple Goddamn Suiter."

"I do! Yes, I do, sirs!" Aubrey yelled.

"So, that's the story from me, the ole fisher-of-men, Jesus Harold Chrysler. I paid the price, just like that soldier in Morrison's shoulder, and I was glad to do it."

Aubrey stood as still as a twitched horse. "Is this heaven? Do your geese see what I'm seeing?"

"Hell, no!" Jesus said, tongue in cheek. "The universe is heaven. The geese know that. This is just a cross garden in a coma's dimension—the backyard of this old Gypsy lady who whipped up these crosses like bird boxes, and eventually us martyr birds filled them up."

"Is her name Reve? She's an old friend."

"Yes, she's out fishing with Coker today, but I'll tell her you asked about her."

"Aubrey!" Trip yelled. "We gotta go! Don't you hear that noise where we came through the hole? I think they're closing it."

"Oh, but one more time, I must. Is it possible you are who those apostles say you are?"

"You mean the one in the *True* magazine?" Jesus winked at Peter. "Like I said, maybe if I am or I'm not, it's still good enough."

Aubrey shook his head, waved at the historical men, and ran down the road toward the opening. He stopped to look back in the direction of O'gram. A storm line was building up a black wind. He noticed all the crosses were empty as they ran by, as if the crucified had taken shelter from its approach. A giant-bladed Sawzall worked the edges around the skull hole. He untied the rope from the tree, then dived through and held tight as he drifted out over the cane field, his eye on the tower.

"Should we spin all that?" Trip asked.

"No, we're going back to the ground and wrap up clockwise. I need a dose of objective world. I think I've had enough of this! Where's my other Christ and my boy, my own lamb that taketh away the sins of the world?"

Chapter 20

THE BROKEN GLASS

Aubrey lay outstretched on an operating table at Miami Jackson. Dr. Brown worked an electric tool on the edge of a ragged crater left by Carlos's bullet. Swelling had triggered the coma, and Brown wanted a porous cover over the hole so the pressure on the bulging brain could find a way out. They would wait to see how long the coma lasted, days or possibly more.

Inside his head, Aubrey stood next to the tower in the field as the light in the skull's huge cavern started to fade from layer after layer of Brown's sterile curtain. Aubrey sat, pulled his legs to his chest, and thought about the crucifixion garden Jesus said was constructed by an old Gypsy woman named Reve. Although he didn't see Reve, it must be true if Jesus said it, even if he did claim to be just another lay figure who died for what he believed in, like the others real and fictional on the shell-rock road.

Aubrey bet Reve put that "Tell Laura I Love Her" song there for him. She had told him once, *roma,* in the word romantic came from the Gypsies, and she knew he would grow up to be a romantic.

Hours passed, and he and Trip talked in the dark and waited. This was the first time he had seen darkness in the psycho-generated church of his big room. He locked his fingers together like his grandmother taught him and said, "This is the church, this is the steeple, open the doors, and see all the people."

Twenty minutes later, he fell asleep. No voices from his foyer came to say, "Pick a film, Aubrey, any film." He was the film now, he guessed.

In an hour, the crackle of flames woke him, and he propped himself on an elbow. The cane was burning, as it did around Lake Okeechobee at harvest time. But who was harvesting it? It's the tower's farm, right? No, he's the one who built the farm and tower. Could he be self-combusting, like those people on the cover of tabloids in the grocery checkout line? The ones in trailer parks who leave only their ashes and bathroom slippers behind for the front page. Or maybe it was the Slim Hand's new plan— burning him to death instead of choking.

The flames lit the skull room like a meat-eater cave. He wished he were a mammoth hunter, his life not so complicated by paradoxes of regular Joe Jesuses on shell-rock roads and infinite ampersands over the number seven on every typewriter. Jakartan shadow puppets worked spidery moves he tried to interpret on the bone palisades around him. The light and heat increased as the fire spread to within fifty feet of the tower. He stood to die, and there it was floating in front of him—the jar, flushed out of the burning cane like a feral animal. He pushed it inside his chest and started climbing the tower; the field was too hot to run.

"Hey, Trip."

"Holy Lord…what?"

"I got the jar back right from the air. When I get higher up, I'll see if I can get us out of here."

Aubrey jumped at the top and circled the Eiffel, then looked in his jar to conjure an exit.

Two more revolutions, and the Jakartan puppets on the bone walls blurred into white cotton suits. He tried to fly it one more time, but it made him cough and lurch into a bed; the cotton-suit people held him down. Christ's face appeared, and she threw her arms around his neck.

"Kyrie, eleison, Aubrey, Christe, eleison!" she cried.

~

He was sedated—soporose—in and out of sleep for two days. They made him sit in a chair for an hour on the third day. Christaine slept on a cot in the room while Asante and Solana stayed with Drayton at the hotel next door. The doctor said the more family around, the better.

On the fourth day, he was assigned a therapist. He kept asking Christaine and Chrome if he had been in a fight or car accident. They told him he had fallen, because the doctor didn't want his cranial blood pressure to spike.

"Well, you have a slight deficiency in your math skill, slight spatial deficit, and one motor skill...some dysphasia, meaning problems with your speech," Dr. Brown said. "But it is small, so we'll take that as good fortune."

Aubrey nodded.

"I want you to try something a little experimental. I think John here told you about this device called a transcranial magnetic stimulator. We can bump up the area of the brain that controls those deficient skills I mentioned. It could give you some peace of mind knowing they're still there. I wish it could help you recover them all today, but it's only able to show you haven't really lost them and that they should come back eventually."

"Ma ga zine?" Aubrey said in his impaired speech. Dr. Brown looked at Chrome.

"He means *for real?*" Chrome said. "Oh, it's for real, Aubrey."

"It'll get you too loose again, Latrec. I promise," Chrome said.

The staff tugged a bathing cap thing onto his head with wires attached. Dr. Brown asked him to draw geometric figures—boxes and triangles—while he adjusted the dials. The figures were as good as they could be for the freehand work of a non-artist, and his speech almost was normal. Brown reminded him he'd still be slightly impaired for a while.

Aubrey asked if he could try to relax alone with the brain hat, and Brown agreed, probably because the Thorazine was nearby and the swelling had pulled back considerably. He said he'd give Aubrey ten minutes to meditate on pleasant thoughts, then set the machine to a safe level and told him not to touch it.

"Okay, we'll be right outside the door." They left.

"Trip."

"Yep."

"I'm going to bump up these dials. Let's go talk in the big room."

"Big room? Good idea. Bumping the dials?"

"I don't care. I really don't."

Trip shrugged because he didn't care, either, as long as he got to go back to the big room. Aubrey conjured the jar, and the machine sent them fast to the base of the tower. He sat on the black ash of the burnt cane field and watched the jar.

"You want to fly it?" Trip asked.

"No, I wanna talk. I feel gigantically lucid, doors of perception and all that shit, with this thing on my head."

"So talk."

He cleared his throat and looked up. "I hope this place I've built in here comes as close to bridging the objective-subjective worlds as I can get. I mean taking an analog of the real world, then separating and convolving its shapes and stacking the colors the way I do around this steel pole to make use of the mind evolution has given me."

"Yes, Aubrey, even though blind Taters and salt-of-the-earth people don't want for what you do, it's okay. The world needs them, too. Needs them to keep too many brainstormers like us from hitting the wall or trying out for emperor."

"Sometimes I wish I was just salt, just infantry."

"But you're not. You bossed that four-way downtown like a general. You turned left for the left pearls as you said you would and missed the cracks that tore down the runway of your hometown heart. Then you drove right out of town with James Taylor in *Two-Lane Blacktop* that night and snubbed the trickster...pulled him up by the roots. Now, my god and your god we met up on the shell-rock road would be proud of you. I mean us. Even newborn seculars like you can call that salvation."

"I think you've been trying to tell me that for years, Trip."

"I have. You are not deluded or crazy, like some people say, and you get to live your books, films, music, and life. You really love being an American Medi Tater. You had to build this thing, this model in here, like a broken bone builds *more* bone, so you could revel in your creations and handle the whittle monster your mind makes. And as far as you and this god thing goes, 'You have to have just as much faith *not* to believe as you do to believe,' somebody once said. It's that time-old struggle with good, evil, the stars, and mental health that man has danced with since he uttered the first metaphor—'a blanket of snow,' or something, then scratched his ass and became a puzzled self-conscious creature forever after that.

"How do you know those things, Trip?"

"Because I'm a polished, balanced, bored and stroked, solid lifter slipper, Chrysler man. A left pearl auguring angel. I know more about that Socratic fried stuff than you think."

"Hey, we've had some great rants, you and me, huh?"

"Yes, monstrous, head-case stuff, Aubrey, like the ancients said we should, because you could not talk to a lot of people with that air puck of yours."

"Well, then, I'm ready to do it, Trip."

"Do what?"

"Ask this thing on my head to take me back to that night. You see, I had a feeling something bad happened before I put on this hat, and I need to get past my old Plexiglas to see what it was. In fact, I need to break all the glass in my life. I wanna know what happened naked, and I mean lunch naked, not a story from someone who'd leave things out to protect me. This gizmo on my head will get me there. I know it will."

"You sure? I got knocked out, too, and I think something bad happened like you before we ended up in this big room."

"Yeah, as much as I've loved this conversation, I can see the squall line coming across the St. Lucie River, like it did when I was a kid. I'm already getting pieces of that night we came in here. I think it's time to close the windows as I used to do with my mother and go to the middle of the house. It's coming."

"All right, but I'm going to give you some final advice as your flying-angel contraption who will go with you to the middle of the house." The wind started to blow in the cane field. "I'm gonna ask you to do that Ulysses thing and tie us tighter than ever to this RKO tower because I have a bad feeling about this. We are going to need all the objective-world guts we can summon in a few minutes. So wrap the rope, my brave argonaut, and don't be afraid to cry out louder than Homer's typewriter when it gets tough in here. And when it's over, it's over, and we'll live with it, you and me. No regrets, you hear?"

"Yes. I love you, Trip."

Six ghouls shoved him through the front door of O'gram and screamed in his ear what he heard when he saw Christ's blood smeared face that day, "Red's wrong! Flame vine! The sand skink man has come."

"Who is he?" Aubrey screamed back at them.

"The psycho samaritan, Mr. Shallcross. He stopped to help you with your car, but is beating you with the tire iron beside the road!"

The monsters ripped the jar away from him, unwrapped the rope from the tower, tore him off the base, and snatched him up O'gram's stairs to watch the assault in the bedroom all over again. Aubrey and Trip howled and wailed. The fiends chanted Carlos's palindromes to mordant music and forced them to fly it so far out on the rope they had to swallow it—helpless as *The Pawnbroker* when he watched the SS man mount his wife; helpless as the young woman when the Straw Dogs trashed her on the couch; helpless as the Indians when they walked the Trail of Tears.

"Swallow it!" the ghouls screamed at them, as if it was nickel-dime, no great shakes, everyday dross—just another afternoon storm turned by the left wheel horse of the galaxy, while the mocking bird sang on the gutter and the red force tore the curtain in the temple to make a hole for a skull filled with claws and saliva to come in and say Mass.

The ghouls dropped him in the cane. He crawled back to the base of the tower and somehow tied himself to it again, then collapsed.

Chrome and Dr. Brown were restraining him when he came out of the big room moaning and in tears. The doctor stopped the machine and gave him a sedative.

"It's all braided now. The model worked," Aubrey said in his broken language. "I have my tower back."

Dr. Brown motioned Chrome to a corner of the room. Aubrey closed his eyes, exhausted, but could hear what they said.

"What's he mean, *the model worked?*" Dr. Brown asked Chrome. "And do you know that idiot—he fooled with the dials on the machine?"

"Look, Henry, he's got a picture of how things are. Don't you? So we best let it be and call Christaine, because that's who he needs right now."

"I bet, and considering what she went through, she needs him. She really killed that guy with a hatpin through his eye?"

"Well, partly. I heard the old man crushed his trachea with a bare hand, so the cops are going to leave it at that, considering."

~

They all left Miami three days later, after a metal plate had been screwed into Aubrey's skull. Christaine thought of the altar boy's sinking figure as they passed the water-filled shell pits on the turnpike home. She jerked in the seat when Aubrey's face appeared on the submerged mannequin, but felt no flutters in her belly or erotic urges this time, only gratitude to the holy families, hers and the other one, because they had escaped all this alive. She considered returning to Sunday Mass to explain why she had helped kill a man, but she had enough sense of dog-eat-dog to pass.

They set up life in O'gram's guesthouse, not wanting to spend another second in the main house. It sat abandoned.

Aubrey and Christ often talked about healing and recharging their lives. He mentioned selling the property, and Christaine hoped he would, yet told him he didn't have to—she knew what the house meant to him but, *God, she never could lie down there again.*

One night, a slipper came to her in a dream in the form of the armadillo called Strike from the story she wrote a while back. Strike struck his toenails together to make a spark and burned down O'gram for her.

~

Aubrey worked in cognitive therapy every day, and it gave him confidence he would get better. He ate breakfasts at the café, as usual, and Janet occasionally sat with him to talk. He still had a slight speech defect, but she was patient.

When he stopped on the shell-rock road in the mornings, the righteous people he had seen on the crosses waved to him from their stands in the wetland. One day, he passed a spot on his road where someone had dumped brush clippings and limbs from a yard in town, and he saw a flame vine had sprung up, climbing and hiding in the branches of two cabbage palms. Its red-orange flowers were in raging bloom, what they call fire on the roof. *How deadly beautiful.*

Even though the hospital had closed his skull with a titanium plate, he had seen through the hole and the blind spot. He'd ridden Carlos's bullet out to the stars and to the gallery of heroes. The dark side of the moon really was just the other side of the moon in the dark, with an honest Jesus on his woodwork admitting his own bouts of agnosticism when he would ask the sky why he was there the way others do, the ones who choose a trail, then leave a trail much smaller than he did, like Punky.

When the bullet opened the door at the top of his skull, Aubrey thought the air would rush in from the stars as he died so he could shoot out on the blowback and orbit the spent spaceship with Keir Dullea's *Two Thousand and None* uterine fetus, joyfully sucking his thumb and circling in the forever of the great slip away. But he didn't die. Like the song Frank Clark sang in the Blue Goose that night, "Another Time."

Aubrey and Christaine did not sell O'Gram, but moved to an old cracker house built by a farmer eighty years ago on the corner of Aubrey's hundred-acre property. O'Gram wasn't visible through the woods, and it sat shuttered in the sun and the dark through South Florida's famous rainstorms and sudden clearings. Aubrey rode every day with Asante and grew better and better at his newfound passion of dressage that had rekindled his love of the horse and brought him his other Christ, the woman with the solar-size eyes and gorgeous split lip.

Out over High Beach, the heat lightning danced through big cumulus in the dark, as it once did over the Paleolithic sea. Aubrey watched it one night, as he wept in Christaine's arms before falling asleep and going down to his Trazadone Lounge.

"Pick a film, Aubrey, any film," the voices said in his dream.

"One of my own films this time, *Blow Hole in the Sun*."

"Yes, Aubrey," the voices said.

In the opening scene, something was circling that circling fetus of Keir Dullea's.

~

One evening, I sat in Aubrey's brain around a campfire with six of my friends—slippers from the minds of Carlos, The Junior, Marla, John Chrome, his beloved Christaine, and one named Earl from Punky, who had made it back to the group. We laughed and talked about people who think those who hear another voice are crazy, yet talk daily to Yahweh, Krishna, and Wakan Tanka.

These friends of mine, all of whom I've spoken to over the years, told me more about their lives with their hosts before they went back to them, and because I have been with Aubrey since he was a small child, I know how his life began and how it will one day end, to be told, as the song said, "Another Time."

All that I have written in this book is in the *True* magazine. I'm Triple Suiter.

Finished.

A Conversation With Ken Braddick
And Charles Porter

Kenneth J. Braddick, the creator of Horse Sport USA, a magazine focused on high-performance dressage and jumping all over the world, is also a veteran news correspondent and has covered major events and several wars around the globe. Braddick is the owner of Dressage-News.com based in Wellington, Florida, one of the epicenters for high-performance sport horses. Dressage-News.com is a highly respected source of news and information in the world of competitive dressage.

KB: So, this is your first novel?

CP: Yes, I'm sort of a backyard word slinger.

KB: I carburet that.

CP: Very funny.

KB: I like that you wrote it over a light frame of the dressage training, too.

CP: Yes, as you know, I have a passion for the animal and the sport, as you do.

KB: Who are your favorite writers today?

CP: Annie Proulx, Colum McCann, Francine Prose, and a woman in Westport, Massachusetts, named Dawn Clifton Tripp, who wrote a book called *Moon Tide*.

KB: Why now, the book, at your age?

CP: The standard answer is I like stories. The not-so-standard is what Colum McCann said: "Stories are the only true human currency." I was also an incredible liar as a child.

KB: You mention the Hearing Voices Network in your dedication. Have you ever been to one of their meetings?

CP: I have not, but it's good they have a place like that to go—kind of an AA for them—free and no proselytizing.

KB: Do you hear another voice?

CP: (Quiet)

KB: Okay, well, you seem to go after religion in this story. Are you an atheist?

CP: I keep going to Bed Bath & Beyond and asking for the Beyond section, but they don't seem to have one. That can piss you off. False advertising like the church.

KB: Do you have a personal beef with religion?

CP: I think we need to write a few stories for the secular side and their struggle to make the transition to something more like the truth for them. I'm tired of books about talking to God in a shack somewhere or seeing Jesus in the operating room when you croak and come back. I'd rather be a Seminole Indian myself and tell people I'm just runnin with the rabbit, as Woody Harrelson said in *Natural Born Killers*.

KB: You believe in these slippers that are inside of us, you said in your introduction to the book.

CP: Slippers, spirits, confounding sounds, and sights…I have that tendency. You tell *me* what those voices are that people hear.

KB: So you think these slippers exist?

CP: Or, we invented them and that might be good enough, as Jesus told Aubrey on the shell-rock road.

KB: I liked how your main character has an obsession with the picture of the picture in the jar Johnny Yuma was holding, getting smaller and smaller as it headed toward infinity until Johnny and the picture disappeared.

CP: Yes, Aubrey is preoccupied and terrified of self-erasure.

KB: The bumper sticker, "Jesus Paid for Our Sins, Now Let's Get Our Money's Worth," where did that come from?

CP: I saw it in a head shop years ago. It was right next to one that said, "Gay Nazis for Christ," but I thought I'd leave that one alone.

KB: Good idea. A friend of mine told me there is a hidden message in the order of drawings in the book. Is that true?

CP: They reflect the events of the story. I like pictures because that's what we see before we can read or talk. These pre-linguistic image things as a child we never forget. *Shallcross* is like a film because I think a lot of people who grew up in the middle and the last part of the twentieth century and write, write film, even if they don't realize it. Up until a hundred years ago, the brain never had seen a movie. It's the closest thing to our subconscious minds we've ever invented. The effects are significantly wonderful and dangerous.

KB: So it's not like that film, *The Ninth Gate*, where the engravings or the pictures in the book take you through nine steps to summon the devil?

CP: What devil? Maybe the Slim Hand. I summon Triple Suiter, and he summons Amper Sand. The illustrations also make the book seem more like another one of my favorite objects and yours, too, I bet—the great American magazine.

KB: Yes. Do you, Triple Suiter, and Amper Sand represent the Trinity in your story, and would you say the three of you wrote this book?

CP: You mean like the Trinity wrote the *Bible* through an earthman's hand?

KB: Yes.

CP: Don't forget that fetus of Keir Dullea's in *2001: A Space Odyssey*. He's a writer, too.

KB: So is the answer yes?

CP: The answer is, I don't know what Triple Suiter is doing when I'm asleep. Finished.

QUESTIONS AND TOPICS FOR DISCUSSION

1) Do you think Charles Porter is suggesting there is another world inside the human head like heaven, Hades, a parallel universe, or Plato's shadow land by introducing us to the bicameral mind of the schizophrenic? Do you think Porter is saying the brain itself is the land of spirits, and that voices like Triple Suiter's are souls who live in that world in the form of what he calls slippers? Is this world, in fact, a yet unknown segment of existence?

2) On the book's cover, we see a pair of slim hands holding a pin to prick the bubble causing the egg to fall from the horse—does Aubrey Shallcross look at life as being that fragile? That scary? Do you? Do you think there is a connection between the pin on the cover to the hat pin in the story carried by Sugarcane Valdez, Marla, and Christaine for defensive reasons?

3) Do the slim hand's actions in the story represent religion being crammed down our throats like the large objects Aubrey thinks are in *his* throat when he blacks out and goes to the Blind Spot Cathedral? Does Porter's use of the word palindrome, *"you can cage a swallow, can't you, but you can't swallow a cage, can you,"* say it all when it comes to certain types of indoctrination?

4) Is this book, its dialogue, more like a kaleidoscopic film instead of a book? Or both?

5) Have you ever seen the movie, *Two-Lane Black Top,* with James Taylor mentioned at the end of chapter one? Aubrey is falling asleep, and the voices ask him to, "Pick a film, Aubrey, any film." Do you think the reference to this movie is an appropriate simile for someone who is searching, racing toward something or nothing as James Taylor was in that film?

6) Have you ever seen the movie mentioned in chapter 11 on the cattle drive, *Lonely Are the Brave* with Kirk Douglas? There is a man driving a truck in the film that shows up intermittently. At the

end, the truck hits Kirk Douglas on his horse. Do you think the same intermittent appearance of Christaine's ex-husband, Carlos, during this story is like that truck—always coming—some bad thing we see every night on the news? Or do you think that would just be a paranoid preoccupation?

7) Do you think, in the age of Google and Netflix, that referencing things like these two films is too much for some readers?

8) After reading *Shallcross,* if you were standing in an old Catholic cathedral and looked up at the high domed ceiling from the basilica area, would you see a blind spot? God? Just the ceiling?

9) Aubrey was in a coma after being shot; do you think Aubrey and Triple Suiter's experience on the shell rock road among the stations of the cross was something that gave him solace about the meaning of the bumper sticker: *Jesus paid for our sins, now let's get our money's worth*? Do you think what Jesus and St. Peter said to Aubrey concerning the bumper sticker, religion, and dying for what you believe in was true?

10) Who do you think was the real narrator of *Shallcross*: Charles Porter or Triple Suiter?

11) Do you buy the suggestion in the end that Triple Suiter wrote this book? The last three paragraphs of the book suddenly go from the third person to the first person narrative, and Trip says, "I sat in Aubrey's brain around a campfire with six of my friends— slippers from the minds of . . . ." These slippers told Triple Suiter everything about their hosts—the other characters in the book. Does that tell us how Trip could know them well enough to take their points of view? Write their thoughts?

12) What does the reader learn over the course of this novel about a person who hears voices, yet can function well in society? Would you be interested in finding out more about the organization called the Hearing Voices Network to which this book is dedicated?

21664885R00139

Made in the USA
Middletown, DE
07 July 2015